MOST VALUABLE PLAYBOY

LAUREN BLAKELY

Copyright © 2017, 2022, 2025 by Lauren Blakely
Cover and internal design © 2025 by Sourcebooks
Cover art and design by Elizabeth Turner Stokes
Emoji art © streptococcus/Adobe Stock
"A Most Irresistible Guy" © 2018 by Lauren Blakely

Sourcebooks and the colophon are registered trademarks of Sourcebooks.

All rights reserved. No part of this book may be reproduced in any form or by any electronic or mechanical means including information storage and retrieval systems—except in the case of brief quotations embodied in critical articles or reviews—without permission in writing from its publisher, Sourcebooks.

No part of this book may be used or reproduced in any manner for the purpose of training artificial intelligence technologies or systems.

The characters and events portrayed in this book are fictitious or are used fictitiously. Any similarity to real persons, living or dead, is purely coincidental and not intended by the author.

All brand names and product names used in this book are trademarks, registered trademarks, or trade names of their respective holders. Sourcebooks is not associated with any product or vendor in this book.

Published by Sourcebooks Casablanca, an imprint of Sourcebooks
P.O. Box 4410, Naperville, Illinois 60567-4410
(630) 961-3900
sourcebooks.com

Most Valuable Playboy was originally self-published in 2017 and updated in 2022 by Lauren Blakely.

"A Most Irresistible Guy" was originally self-published in 2018 by Lauren Blakely.

Cataloging-in-Publication Data is on file with the Library of Congress.

The authorized representative in the EEA is Dorling Kindersley
Verlag GmbH. Arnulfstr. 124, 80636 Munich, Germany
Manufactured in the UK by Clays and distributed by
Dorling Kindersley Limited, London
002-349101-Feb/25
10 9 8 7 6 5 4 3 2

Thank you to Gale for letting me use the name of your hair salon in this book! You're a goddess, Gale!

PROLOGUE

Always a bridesmaid.

No Action Armstrong.

Ball Cap Boy.

Mr. Clean.

The Unused Insurance Plan.

Oh wait. Here's one more, a personal fave.

Best Butt in the NFL.

Those are just some of the nicknames I've been given in the last few years. They don't bug me. Not one bit. They've all been true, especially the last one. You should see my ass. You can bounce a quarter off my cheeks.

Here's the thing—when you spend the first three years of your career warming the bench for the best player in the league, you can't get a chip on your shoulder. You have to stay sharp and be ready for that moment when you swap out a ball cap for a helmet and get your pants dirty.

My time has finally come this season, and so far, we're winning.

But tonight isn't about what happens between the opening kickoff and the end of the fourth quarter.

Tonight is about the one game I've always dominated.

For the last few years, I've been the highest-ticket item in the players' annual charity auction, and I can't help enjoying that. Because the guy I've backed up has been called a lot of things—a legend, the greatest ever, a titan of the game—but the one I most enjoy is "second-best-looking quarterback on the Renegades."

Hey, I didn't give him that name. The media did, deciding the dude who played second-string—me—had a prettier face. Before this season, I'd seen a grand total of 120 minutes of playing time in my first three years, but I've taken home the top honors in the charity auction, where some of the loveliest ladies come to bid on the players they want to take out for a night on the town.

Ah, the memories of those dates have warmed my heart, and other parts, on the sidelines when the games were dull. Evenings in limos, testing the strength of the leather back seat, nights in hotels that lasted way past dawn, mutually and blissfully ignoring the *no physical contact between the winner and the player* rule.

Yeah, I've enjoyed the fuck out of being paraded onstage in front of hundreds of women, raising their bids higher on me than all the other guys. It's been my one chance to shine, even to stand out.

Those days are behind me, though, now that I'm finally

leading the team down the field every single Sunday. I still expect to rake in top dollar for the charity I gladly support, but this time, I won't be living it up and letting loose after hours. I have a reputation to protect, and a season on the line.

Guess that means it's time to call an audible on the line of scrimmage.

CHAPTER 1

My hair is sticking up.

In my defense, it's always sticking up.

I have what's known as permanent bed head. Which can be awesome, if I want to look like I just strolled out of a most excellent roll in the hay, complete with a sexy stranger running her hands through my dark-brown strands.

It's less awesome for pulling off the part of a classy athlete dressed to the nines. I'm decked out in a tailored charcoal-gray suit and parked in a leather chair in a suite at the Whitney Hotel in the heart of San Francisco, along with a bunch of other guys from the team.

Violet's trying to curb my bed head. Her long fingers thread through my hair, aiming for a reverse roll-in-the-hay effect. "I swear, Cooper, you've had the most stubborn hair your entire life."

I wiggle my eyebrows. "It takes after me. I can't be tamed either."

She rolls her amber eyes, her long chestnut hair spilling over her chest. "That's right. You're a wild mustang. Impossible to domesticate."

I neigh.

She stops, sets her hands on my shoulders, and gives me a sharp stare. "Can you count with your hooves too?"

I drag a wing-tipped foot along the carpeted floor one, two, three times. "I can go all the way to ten."

"You let me know when you make it to twenty, Mister Ed. That's when I'll truly be impressed," she says, with the smile I've seen for the last twenty years. I've been friends with Violet since we were kids and I moved to her hometown, a few blocks away from her house.

I rub my palms together. "Excellent. I have a goal to shoot for. You know I love goals."

She laughs. "I do know that."

Give me a task, and I'm nose-to-the-grindstone focused. I've been that way my whole life. Run a mile in under six minutes? Sure thing. Throw a ball downfield twenty-five yards? Let's do it. Win a scholarship to a top-tier school? Consider it done, and done with a smile.

Violet stretches her arm behind her, silver bracelets jingling as she grabs some hair gel in a black tube from the chrome coffee table. "We need to domesticate your lovely locks, Cooper. I don't have a riding crop with me, but I think this gel will do."

I give the tube a skeptical stare. "You're not going to put a ton of goop in my hair, are you?"

She adopts a serious expression. "Absolutely. It's a brand-new product I've been testing at my salon. It's called Goop for Guys. It's so perfect for you." She lowers her voice to a whisper. "But I won't tell anyone you have to use…*product* to look so pretty."

"More like pretty ugly." A deep voice booms the insult across the suite. Jones is the king of put-downs, and one of my closest friends on the team. At the moment, he's lounging in a chair, scrolling through his phone, and wearing a custom-fitted dark-navy suit.

The team publicist, Jillian, organized the event and chose the tailored suit theme for this year's auction, our annual holiday fundraiser for the San Francisco Children's Hospital. Her exact words were, "Suits are like catnip to women, and to men, too, and I want my team of pretty kitties to raise even more money this year."

That's a tall order, but most of the dough comes from the entrance fee—a donation to simply walk in the door. We've already circulated among the crowd, chatting with fans in the ballroom, finishing the mingling session while the speakers played "It's Raining Men." That song presaged the final event of the night—the auction itself, when the single men on the team strut their stuff.

I glance over at Jones, picking up the insult volley. I eye his midsection suspiciously. "How's your girdle fitting you tonight? Is that why you look so nice and trim?"

He pretends to adjust it. "Yeah, I borrowed yours."

"It's a comfort fit. I can see why you'd need it."

"You can wear it next. A *blushing bride* always needs one."

That's what the guys call me now. *Bride*. But hey, I'll take it over *bridesmaid* since it comes with the starting job after three long years on the sidelines.

Violet shakes her head as she flips open the tube. "The two of you—"

"Are clever, brilliant, and handsome devils? Why thank you," I say, straightening my vest. I went three-piece, all the way. If Jillian wants us to wear suits to rake it in, I'll damn well do my best to bring home a four-peat. I've been the recipient of the highest bid the last three years, and since I love streaks, I want to keep it up this year too.

For the kids.

I want to win for the kids. The hospital does amazing work, and I gladly support it.

Plus, bragging rights do rock.

That's all that will be rocking this year. I need all my focus on the field, which means no full-benefits package with this date, even if the opportunity should present itself. I spent the last three years idle on the bench but busy after hours. This season is a whole different beast now that I have a record and reputation to think about. We're closing in on a wild-card spot in the playoffs, and these days the only scoring I plan to do is on the field.

Violet tips her chin at my attire. "I like the vest. You rarely see anyone wearing a vest here."

We live in casual country, home of the hoodie, and land of the jeans. "Is that your way of telling me you're a vest woman?"

She laughs, then lowers her voice. "I'm an *everything* woman." She lets that comment hang between us, and for a moment, my head is in a fog. *Everything*. What sort of everything does Violet Pierson like? Everything in bed? And why the hell am I thinking these thoughts about her? Violet's not only *my* friend, she's also my best friend's sister. "And you're going to clean up, my friend, since there are few things hotter than an athlete dressed in a suit."

"Yeah?" I ask, meeting her eyes as she squeezes the goop onto her hands, and my mind continues to wander down the *everything* yellow-brick road. Every position, every night—is that her sort of everything?

"Of course. You have a great face, a nice body, and that top-notch suit fits like a glove," she says, listing these attributes like they're hardwood floors, a quiet dishwasher, and a front-loading washing machine. Violet meets my eyes, and her tone is cheery. "Don't worry. I'm only saying *nice body* in an empirical sense."

I put on the brakes, since it's not very sexy to be described like an appliance.

"Right. Of course." I nod, wiping the *everything* thoughts from my brain too. "It's a completely objective compliment."

"Totally clinical."

I adjust the vest anyway. Just in case it *empirically* looks better this way. Or clinically, for that matter.

She runs her gel-covered hands through my hair. "Let's at least try to tame you for the cameras."

The auction is being carried live on local TV, and that's why Violet is here—to give us a little touch-up before we go on air. She's a hairstylist, which happens to be one of my favorite professions in the world.

One afternoon during my sophomore year of high school, the grizzled old dude who'd cut my hair forever was out, and his twenty-two-year-old granddaughter filled in for him at the barbershop. I glimpsed the angels in heaven when she leaned in to cut the front of my hair, and I've been a big fan of haircuts ever since.

But I'm not checking out Violet like that, even though her breasts are precariously close to my face as she styles the mop on my head.

I'm absolutely not thinking of the angels I'm seeing.

I can't think of her that way.

She's Trent's sister, and he's been my best friend for twenty years, all the way back in elementary school. That places her firmly in the not-allowed-to-even-consider-whether-she-might-be-hot category. I've never thought of her as a babe, not once in all the years I've known her. Which is all the more impressive considering she has a rocking body, lush chestnut-brown hair, and big amber eyes. Oh, and she has a wicked sense of humor. But I don't think of her as smoking hot, even tonight when she's wearing those black jeans, the kind that look as if they've been painted on, and that silvery tunic thing that clings to her chest.

Nope.

That's why I talk to her like a friend. Or an appliance, for that matter.

"Just don't make me look like a douche," I say.

Jones chimes in from his post on the couch. "Yeah, he can do that just fine on his own."

Violet glances over at him, then back at me as she finishes. "Yes. *Fine* being the operative word. I'd say Cooper looks quite *fine* indeed." She gives me a wink.

Ha, take that, Jones.

She shifts her gaze to the couch and our kicker, Rick. I'd like to say he's our secret weapon, but everyone knows the broody-eyed Stanford grad has the best foot in the league. That right toe of his has hurled the pigskin more than forty yards when he's needed to, and he's only missed one field goal so far this season. Harlan's here, too, his suit jacket hanging over the back of his chair. He's our star running back, and even though I prefer to throw the ball, I'll hand off to him too. He's escaped hordes of humongous linemen with his quicksilver feet.

These guys have seen a hell of a lot more action than I have, since they surrounded the Renegades' superstar Jeff Grant, who retired last year. Despite the ribbing, they've welcomed me as the new quarterback, due in part to the fact that it's December, we're sporting a 9–4 record, and we have a real chance to clinch a wild-card spot in my first season as the starter.

After she wipes her hands on a nearby towel, Violet parks them on her hips, surveying the guys in the room. "Look at you boys. Such pretty Renegades." She waves a hand dismissively. "Don't mind me. I'm just getting into the spirit of objectification for tonight."

"You want to bid on me, don't you, Vi?" Rick calls out, flashing her a gleaming white smile that contrasts with his dark skin.

"It's all I can think about," she says with an over-the-top purr. She leans close to the chrome table, rooting around in her purse. She finds her wallet, flips it open, and shows him a few tens. "Will that be enough for you?"

"We're running a discount on Einstein," Harlan says, scratching his stubbled jaw. "You can have him for a ten and a six-pack."

When we found out Rick had earned a perfect score on the Wonderlic, the cognitive test we have to take before the draft, we naturally had no other option than to nickname our resident brainiac kicker after the world's most famous genius.

"Hell, I'll throw in your favorite bottle of wine if you take him off our hands now," Jones adds.

Rick rolls his eyes and flips us the bird. "Watch me clean up tonight, just like I have to clean up all your messes on the field when you guys can't get it in."

"I *always* get it in," I say, because I can't resist. He went there first. I turn to Harlan. "Think you'll find a new gal to bid on you this year?"

He scowls and taps the side of his nose. Two years ago, an ex-girlfriend of his placed the winning bid on our running back.

Harlan, being a charitable dude, went on a platonic date with her. The next year, Harlan's bids came from nearly all exes, so during his time onstage he tapped the side of his nose, and his agent got the message to place the winning bid. He was saved from the parade of past lovers.

"Violet, why don't you save those bills and bid for me?" Harlan asks. "I don't care if I go for less than the others."

She laughs and glances at me, raising her hands, like scales. "Hmm. I can't decide. Cooper, should I bid for Harlan or you? You or Harlan? Are you as cheap as the others?"

I scoff, lifting my chin. "I'm a premium kind of guy. But if you wanted to bid on me, I'd foot the bill for it."

What the hell just came out of my mouth? I'm not angling for Violet to bid on me or anyone else. I like the come-what-may thrill of the auction. It's worked out pretty well for me in the mutual attraction department three years running, including last year when local news anchor Lourdes Mariano won me, and that black-haired vixen was as unbuttoned in the limo as she was buttoned-up on air.

I can absolutely live with my decision to stay laser-focused on the game. But I'm a competitive bastard, and I want to emerge victorious.

"If you're paying, I'll be sure to bid sky-high," Violet says, then she points at Harlan. "You're next in the hot seat."

Harlan taps the arm of the chair. "It is indeed hot." He doesn't take his eyes off her when he says that, and my shoulders tense as she moves in front of him.

I try to ignore his flirty comments as she works on his long hair, but out of the corner of my eye, I notice him inch closer to Violet. Closer than he needs to be. A strange burst of annoyance spreads in my chest as she combs his hair, smoothing and neatening it.

"Can you cut my hair sometime?" His eyes lock on hers. "What's the name of your salon?"

"You are welcome anytime at Heroes and Hairoines," she says.

I snap my gaze to the running back. "You know your speed comes from your hair." I couldn't give two fucks about the length of his hair, but I don't want him pulling up a chair in her salon.

"Dude. You haven't cut it all season, and we're winning," Jones adds, his blue eyes intense, since he's the keeper of our superstitions, and the four of us have plenty.

"No shit. I'd wait till the end of the season," Harlan says, raising his hand to his hair. "Can't fuck with our luck when we're so damn close to a playoff slot."

"Don't jinx us." Jones crosses his fingers. "And don't cut your hair, man."

Harlan makes the sign of the cross on his chest.

Jones points at Rick. "Einstein chews that pink bubblegum his little sister gave him before every quarter now to make sure we kick ass."

Rick raises his chin and nods, agreeing. "And I brush my teeth on the sidelines, too, once I'm done with the gum."

"Do you use bubblegum toothpaste too?" Jones asks.

"Hell yeah. I added that in once Coop started kicking ass in game three. I amped up the whole ritual then, and it's working."

Jones tips his chin at me. "Plus, Cooper has kept the snake in its cage."

I point to my crotch. "That's why we're winning, I'm sure." I'm not actually as superstitious as he is, but Jones is my go-to guy on the field, so I respect his feelings.

The look in his eyes is intensely serious. "You gotta honor the power of the rituals. Don't mess with them. Don't fuck with them. Just fucking trust them. Michael Jordan wore his college shorts under his uniform during the whole six years when the Bulls were epic in the nineties. Look at me," he says, tapping his ankle. "I haven't changed my game socks all season."

Violet crinkles her nose. "How is it you're still single, Jones?"

He flashes her a dimpled smile. "Talk about miracles, all right. But it mostly comes from an iron-clad commitment to the cause."

A few minutes later, Jillian strides in, looking polished in a dark-gray dress, her sleek black hair twisted on her head.

"You all look gorgeous, as always," she says, with the crisp and businesslike smile that comes with her role as team publicist. "The media is ready and waiting. The crowd is enthusiastic." She waves her jazz hands to demonstrate. "It's showtime. Everyone ready?"

"Yes, we are," Jones says, and as he chats with her, Harlan pulls me aside, lowering his voice.

"Listen, I know Violet is your friend and all, but would you be cool with me—?"

The cloud of annoyance swells, but before he can finish asking my permission to ask her out, Jillian interrupts. "Gentleman, we have a crowded ballroom. More than three hundred attendees are ready and waiting. We have lots of eager ladies who want to bid on you. A few men, too, and some mighty handsome ones, I might add. I must say, the choices look excellent. Let's head backstage to the ballroom. We start in ten minutes."

CHAPTER 2

As the guys file out, Violet calls to me.

I stop and turn and find her right behind me. She's a tall woman, and even taller in a pair of black, high-heeled boots that jack her up on those trimmed, toned legs. But I'm six-four, and I easily have six inches on her in those shoes.

I look down. She reaches a hand up and smooths a strand of hair out of place on my forehead.

"This is your first year out there as the starting quarterback," she says with a soft smile.

I smile. "Wild, huh?"

"You've killed it every year as the backup. You're going to kill it harder as the starter. Plus, you've played great the first three months."

I reach above her head and knock on the wall. "Knock on wood. We need to keep playing great."

"You will, because my ritual is intact too."

I arch a brow, curious. "You don't say. You've come to the superstitious side, Vi?"

Her eyes glint. "I wear my Cooper Armstrong jersey to bed every night and have since your week-three win."

"Excellent." I wag a finger at her. "And it pains me to say this, but no matter how tempted you are, don't switch to lingerie."

She play-punches my shoulder. "Don't you switch to lingerie either."

I gesture to my chest and down to my thighs. "One hundred percent birthday suit at bedtime."

"All right. Get out there. They'll bid even more this season for a date with the new quarterback." She takes a beat. "But not if this piece of hair keeps sticking up." She runs her finger over a strand. "Sheesh, Coop. If this is sticking up backstage, you'll have to peek out and give me a secret signal, so I can rush over and fix it."

"I'll just tug on it."

She swats my shoulder. "You'll do nothing of the sort."

"I have faith you can fix it for me. Because you're a miracle worker."

"Of course I am, and I can." She smooths it out over my ear, and it feels better than it should when she touches me. She steps back and observes her handiwork. "*Empirically.*"

I smile. "*Clinically.*"

She moves her hands to my tie, straightening it. I already did that, but I see no reason to stop her.

"Hey," she says, as the corners of her lips turn up. "What do you call an alligator wearing a vest?"

"I don't know. What do you call an alligator wearing a vest?" I ask, since Violet likes to tell silly jokes.

Her eyebrows rise. "An investigator."

I laugh. "Good one."

She shoos me off. "I need to pack up my supplies, and you need to get your butt to the stage."

A husky voice floats down the hall, a smoky alto, belting out the chorus to "It's Raining Men," and it makes the hair on the back of my neck stand on end.

"What's wrong?"

"It's Maxine," I hiss.

I know that husky voice.

Maxine Randall.

My friend Trent played it for me. A local radio host who's hot for me. She's called me *her boyfriend* on recent episodes. Like, in a jokey way, but also saying she's planning our wedding.

Now, she's ad-libbing the chorus to the tune, crooning *It's raining Cooper.*

That doesn't even fit the rhythm. But whatever. I'm not a poet. I also don't want to be rude to a local media personality, so I brace myself for a run-in as I walk down the hall. Maybe I'll duck into the stairwell to avoid Maxine.

But she hasn't come around the corner yet, so I just turn the other way.

And I come face-to-face with Vera Scott—the team owner's

wife. "Come with me. *Now,*" she says, giving an order in a whisper that says *ignore me at your peril.*

I've been transported to an action flick, where the elegant, erudite, classy-as-hell woman in the Chanel suit tugs me into the stairwell.

Okay.

Once the door shuts, the polished, plum-lipsticked, Louboutin-wearing billionaire flashes me a practiced smile. "Cooper, darling. I'm afraid I have bad news. Maxine has been bragging to everyone about bidding on you tonight. She says *she's gonna get her husband once and for all.*"

I cringe. From head to toe. "Really? She said *that*?"

Vera nods crisply. "She arrived shortly after the cocktail hour, and I wanted to warn you. So you can devise a plan."

I tense. *Plan.* What fucking plan is there for this? Where's the plan for a quarterback sack? But wait. Hold on. Sometimes you see the defensive end barreling at you and you can slip away. That's what I need right now. To avoid the sack.

"Are you going to bid on me?"

She laughs, shaking her head. "Of course not. I can't do that. I'm happily married. That would be so odd." She shrugs, a little too I-told-you so. "But if you joined my matchmaking agency, I could guarantee you will never have to deal with sneak attacks like this ever again. I specialize in pairing high-profile men and high-profile women with just the right partner."

I groan inside but smile outside. Right. I turned her down a few months ago at a golf charity event. She mentioned she ran a matchmaking agency and wanted me to join her stables. Her agency is one of the sponsors of tonight's auction.

I've no interest in being paired off. But right now? Sign me up and save me. I can only imagine what Maxine might say on air if she wins me. Actually, I don't want to imagine. "Okay, so what should I do?" I ask Vera since this is her battlefield. She knows romance and machination.

"You'll need a strategy when you're onstage," she says, then her phone beeps. "Ah, this is one of my clients. A lovely woman who wants to bid on Rick." She smiles, then adds, "A classy client. I only have classy clients."

Ah, hell. I'll offer myself as tribute. "Any other clients here who can bid on me?"

She sighs, giving a sad smile. "No, darling. I run an elite agency. For select clients. Best of luck." She answers the phone. "I'm on my way!" Then she turns to me, covers the phone as she opens the door, then scans the hall. "Coast is clear. Good luck."

I get the hell out of the line of fire. "Thank you." I trot down the hall in my three-piece suit and find the door to the back of the ballroom, then dart inside.

What the hell am I going to do?

Jones is here, leaning against the wall. He narrows his eyes and looks me over. "You okay?"

I shake my head and catch my breath. Then I grab my phone from my pocket. I'll call Trent, ask him to bid on me. Hell, I'll ask him to have one of his wife's girlfriends bid on me. And I'll text Violet, ask her to find someone. I could pull

Jillian aside and ask her to handle it, but I'm not sure what I'd say. *Don't let Maxine bid on me*? I mean, she can't really kick her out just because I don't want her to bid on me.

That's ridiculous. I'm overreacting. I can handle whatever happens.

Besides, I don't have time to issue a mayday text to anyone since Jillian strides backstage and asks me to put my phone away. "The show's about to start."

I square my shoulders. Just deal with it. That's what I've always done. Face life's challenges with a smile and don't fucking complain.

CHAPTER 3

"Sold! To the woman in the pink dress for thirty-four hundred dollars. Enjoy your night with the kicker."

Rick waves to the crowd and heads backstage, holding out a palm. "Pay up, fuckers. I went for more than a six-pack." He taps his head. "Brains and beauty for the win."

Jones smacks his palm, laughing, as Harlan heads to the stage. Meanwhile, I'm *formulating* a plan. If Maxine wins me, I'll just be a gentleman on our date. Of course I'll be a gentleman. That's all I can do. And if I'm all debonair and professional, surely the only things she can say about me on the radio the next day will be of the high-class variety. Nothing about marriage.

I don't need to freak out. Don't need a backup plan.

I've got this.

Onstage, the auburn-haired sports reporter Sierra brings the mic to her mouth and gestures grandly to Harlan as the rest of us watch from the wings.

"Let's give it up for the Renegades' running back. He's one of the leaders in the league in running touchdowns the last two years, but he also is known for his *foosball* skills," she says to the ballroom full of women decked out in little black dresses, or in tight jeans and sky-high heels with sexy tops sloping off shoulders. A few wear Santa hats and wave sprigs of mistletoe above their heads. A couple of men can be spotted in the crowd too. "When Harlan's not busy tearing it up on the turf, you can find him flicking the poles at a local foosball league. Plus, just look at all that hair."

Harlan shakes out his long, golden-blond hair.

Sierra claws at the air. "He's like a beautiful lion."

Someone from a table in the front cheers, and another woman roars like a lioness, then shouts, "I want the king of the jungle to be mine."

I nudge Jones and whisper. "*King of the Jungle.* Damn, that's good. We need to use that, stat."

He holds up a fist for bumping. "You know it. And he does have a lovely mane, Coop."

I laugh to cover my nerves. "So lush and pretty."

"I must get his shampoo recommendation." Jones runs a hand over his own short, dark hair.

From our spot backstage, we watch as Sierra opens the bidding on Harlan and his golden mane. The cheering woman from the front lifts her paddle to offer three hundred dollars, while the gal who imitated the queen of the pride weighs in with four hundred. Quickly, the bidding escalates.

Jillian paces near us in the wings. She's a ball of tension, mouthing the numbers to herself, adding up the take for charity. Jones crosses the few feet over to her. "You're doing good," he whispers.

She flashes a smile and lets out a breath. "Thank you. But I'm still counting on you for a big haul." She taps his chest.

"Don't worry. It'll be unreal," he says.

"The team management is matching the bids for the players. We can bring in so much tonight for the hospital. It would be an amazing thing to do for them, and it helps the team's image."

The Renegades already have a pristine image, since management and the coach run a tight ship, and Jillian wants to keep it that way.

"We will do everything we can to keep up the pace," Jones says.

Sure enough, when Jones heads to the stage after Harlan scores a winning bid of thirty-three hundred dollars, the man eats it up. Jones removes his jacket, letting it hang on his shoulder so everyone can see his broad frame. That's fair play. I used that move last year. The pose just works.

"Jones Beckett is known as *The Hands*, and with good reason. Look at those hands," Sierra says with a whistle of admiration.

From my vantage point, I see Jones hold up his massive paws. The dude was born to catch. His hands are ginormous, and they can wrap around a football.

"And the fingers. My God, those fingers," Sierra adds, fanning herself as the crowd goes apeshit.

Someone leans close to my ear, and I tense instantly, worried it's Maxine. Then I relax when Violet says softly, "And he's not even wearing a vest."

I smile, instantly relaxed. "Apparently vests are magic to you."

She scoffs, then murmurs. "Bet they are to lots of women. With your vest and your hair, they won't be able to keep the paddles in their pockets."

"You do know that sounds dirty," I tease.

"I sure do," she says. Then she gestures to the crowd. "Everyone is having a blast. You'll be fighting off the women."

"Yeah, that's the issue," I say with a heavy sigh, more open with her, since she's not programmed to hassle me like my buddies are.

She raises an eyebrow in a silent question and I'm about to tell her about the Maxine tip that Vera shared. But the noise from the front drowns us out when a bidding war for Jones escalates quickly. Numbers fly back and forth at light speed. Finally, the winning woman lands a date with Jones for forty-four fifty. Damn, that's a sweet number, and well above last year. Jillian cheers and gives him a hug when he returns backstage as Sierra chats with the audience, tossing out questions to the crowd.

Violet grabs my elbow. Her eyes are serious. "Is everything okay?"

Sierra calls out to me, and I step toward the stage, my voice going deadpan as I answer Violet quietly, "The owner's wife warned me about Maxine."

Her eyes widen. "The radio host?"

Ah, hell. I hate complaining. I hate being this guy. But I would do just about anything to escape Maxine. "Let's just say I'd rather ride the bench again than have her win." Violet shoots me sympathetic eyes as I stroll onto the stage. It's my turn.

I wave to the crowd. The ballroom is stuffed full of people with happy, shining faces and eager generosity.

I give Sierra a peck on the cheek. Her eyelids flutter, and she clasps her hand to her cheek. "I'll never wash this cheek again," she says to the crowd, and laughter bounces across the big room. "And now, ladies and gentlemen, for the pièce de résistance, this year's starting quarterback at long last, and the winner of the Most Valuable Playboy auction the last three years in a row. After all, who wouldn't want to take this handsome and talented man out for a night on the town? Everyone loves the quarterback."

Someone scoffs. "He wasn't the quarterback the last few years."

With a wink, Sierra expertly pivots to the positive. "And now we're lucky to have him at the helm."

I lean into the mic. "And it's an honor to have stepped into the shoes of a legend. I will keep doing everything I can to make the fans proud."

Sierra smiles approvingly.

A high-pitched voice from the middle of the room shouts, "We love you, Coop! Win this weekend."

"I'll do my best," I say with a smile.

"You always do," Sierra says.

Someone else boos, and I see it's a guy in the crowd wearing a Jeff Grant jersey. "We want Grant the Greatest back."

I give a grin, since this is all par for the course. "I bet he'd be hard to talk off his fifty-foot yacht, where he's enjoying a well-earned retirement."

"He is indeed," Sierra says, smoothly steering the event like she has all evening. "So let's get to know Cooper Armstrong. How does that sound to all of you?"

More cheers than jeers erupt so I take that as my cue to remove the jacket. That earns me some hollers of "nice vest!" I glance to the wings, and Violet gives me a thumbs-up, mouthing *vests are hot.*

"Cooper is six-four, with light-brown eyes and dark-brown hair. And, are his cheekbones to die for, or what?" I flash a smile, enjoying her compliments. "In addition to his sixty-three percent pass completion rate so far this season, Cooper can make a mean chicken stir-fry, a fantastic jambalaya, and he's also been known to wow dinner guests with his penne pasta." Sierra pauses to wiggle her eyebrows. "There's just something sexy about a man who can cook, am I right, or am I right?"

"You can cook for me anytime," a woman shouts.

"I'm quite talented in the kitchen," I add with a wink.

"A man who can throw like that and cook? I think I might need to toss my hat in the ring." Sierra throws an imaginary hat, and I decide it's time to roll up the sleeves. Give 'em forearm to get 'em going. I peel back my cuffs, folding them up, revealing the arms they all like. Why yes, there's a reason I've won the last few years. I play to the crowd. "He also was a superstar in karaoke last year and loves to go on karaoke dates at the local bar." She brings her hand to her heart. "Cooper, can you sing a little Bon Jovi for us?"

"Why, I never thought you'd ask, Sierra." I take the mic and give them the first line of the greatest karaoke song ever, about a guy named Tommy who used to work on the docks.

Sierra points the mic toward the audience, and they enthusiastically sing the next line about the union on strike.

I smile, feeling for the first time like I might escape Maxine's clutches after all. Everything's going well so far, and the crowd is fantastic. Maybe Vera got it wrong. I don't even spot Maxine in the sea of people.

"And now, let the bidding begin," Sierra declares.

Trent blows me an exaggerated kiss from his table. Holly waves too. She was his high school sweetheart, and now she's his wife. She cups her hands over her mouth and shouts, "Ten bucks for The Coop."

Sierra chuckles, then chides them. "Don't we think he's worth more than that?"

Trent lifts his index finger. "Fine, we'll take him home with us for twenty dollars. He can do yard work."

Sierra gives me a serious look. "What do you think, Cooper? Can we get more than twenty dollars for you?"

I scratch my chin and shrug, giving my best self-deprecating smile. "Hard to say. I did mow lawns in high school, though, so I might have to ask for thirty dollars, just on account of my ability to make the green grass in a garden look so very pretty."

Sierra wiggles her eyebrows. "And somehow, a man this handsome makes everything sound like innuendo."

I flash a smile.

"Fifty bucks. But we want a money-back guarantee," Trent says.

Holly thrusts her hands in the air, shouting, "He's coming home with us as the new lawn boy."

Sierra peers at the crowd. "What do you say? Would anyone like to bid on an actual date with this star athlete?"

I shake my head, because hell, I'd love if Trent and Holly won with a fifty-dollar bid. I'd gladly fork over the rest to raise money for the charity.

Then, I hear someone say, "Three thousand dollars."

My blood goes cold at the husky sound. Maxine has powered her way to the front of the crowd, planting herself in the middle of the action. Wearing a tight red dress, she flicks her blond hair off her shoulders, standing tall and proud.

Sierra arches a brow. "That's quite a jump."

"He's worth every penny," Maxine purrs, her voice bursting with determination, her gray eyes aimed my way, like guns.

My insides coil tightly.

But I remind myself—I can do this. I'm chill. I'm cool. I can fend off the radio host. I've done this my whole life—let things roll off me. No father? No problem. No money? Not an issue. No playing time? Slap on a happy face and fucking learn everything until it's your turn.

I can deal with a local media darling who's declared me her...*husband*.

I cringe inside.

But it'll be fine, especially since others are getting into the bidding now. A brunette in a crisp gray business suit raises her paddle and offers three thousand two hundred fifty dollars. A lady with blue hair and pearls trumps her by one hundred.

Maxine matches them dollar for dollar. She raises her arm, bidding more and more.

A guy in jeans and a black turtleneck jumps in. He looks vaguely familiar. Maybe he's a well-known tech entrepreneur. "I'll take him for three thousand five hundred dollars."

I'm not into dudes, but I'd happily go on a platonic date. I could easily enjoy a dinner with this guy, talk about sports and stats and shoot the breeze.

The man keeps vying with Maxine as Sierra plays auctioneer, counting off their bids, while others chime in from time to time like a county fair crowd bidding on my rump roast. The man ups the ante to four thousand, and I bet Jillian is jumping for holiday joy as she adds up the moolah.

The business-suit woman raises a hand, offering forty-one hundred.

Maxine's eyes laser in on me, and she slashes an arm through the air. "Five thousand dollars," she says, jacking the price up by nine hundred and staking her claim. I shudder inside.

The guy's eyes widen, and he holds up his hands. "I'm out."

My stomach plummets when the business-suit woman shakes her head.

"Going once?" Sierra asks, scanning the tables, looking for perhaps one last big spender. My eyes scan the crowd too. Hell, maybe I'll find an escape hatch. A trapdoor to drop into and disappear like in a magic act. Maybe Trent will learn to read my mind. *Trent, I'll cover you for anything you bid. Just raise that hand, name a price, and save me.*

My best friend's expression is merely curious now as he watches Maxine and Sierra, waiting for the verdict. My opportunity to play yard boy slips through my fingers.

The look in Maxine's eyes is pure satisfaction as she waits for the final word.

A flash of chestnut-brown hair in the back catches my attention. A flurry of silver. It's Violet, hands in the air, wildly flapping over her head in the middle of the ballroom. She brings her hand to her hair, tugs on a strand. She's a miracle worker indeed, and she devised the greatest solution in the universe at once.

Her secret signal.

My heart goes wild.

It hammers in my chest. This is like finding an open receiver a second before you're sacked.

"Going twice…" Sierra says, trailing off as she waits.

I raise my arm and tug on a strand of hair too.

"Ten thousand dollars," she shouts, full of bravado.

Holy shit. Violet does not mess around with my money. Her eyes widen, as if she's surprised she bid that high.

My gaze finds Trent. He's staring at his sister, slack-jawed.

Sierra's smile is bright and wide. "Ten thousand dollars. Do we have ten thousand, one hundred?"

The room is hushed. Maxine's expression is blank. She must be shocked. She probably didn't expect anyone to vie with her to this extent.

I tap my foot, willing Sierra to close this quickly. *Just slam the door shut, please, fucking please.*

"Going once. Going twice."

I say a silent prayer. I cross my fingers. I hope.

Maxine blinks, opens her mouth, and I steel myself for a disgustingly high counterbid.

But there's only silence. No words come. Violet has shocked her speechless. This type of bid wasn't in Maxine's playbook.

Sierra raises her arm. "And a night with the quarterback is sold for ten thousand dollars."

Talk about a Hail Mary.

CHAPTER 4

In the movie *Bull Durham*, the veteran catcher Crash Davis taught a newbie pitcher what to say in interviews. Phrases like *play 'em one day at a time. Just happy to help the team. I just want to give it my best shot and the good Lord willing, things will work out.*

Forget that it's a movie about baseball. My point is there's nothing a baller ever needs to say to the press that hasn't been covered by the Crash Davis School of Public Relations.

I channel the fictional legend when Sierra declares she's gobsmacked.

"Simply gobsmacked." Sierra shakes her head like she still can't fathom this turn of events. She places her hand on my arm. "That's the highest amount anyone's ever gone for."

And I'll be paying it all myself. Gladly.

"I'm just happy to be able to help," I say.

"That's more than helpful. That's astonishing. In fact, we have a representative here from the Children's Hospital, Connie Wolfson."

Sierra calls a woman onto the stage who strides out from the audience in a prim royal-blue suit. Connie shakes my hand, then says, "I'm so grateful. Where is the lovely lady who bid so high on you for such a good cause? I must thank her personally."

Yes, me too. She's a savior.

I knew hairstylists were heavenly, but I think Violet might have earned sainthood status today. I'm so jazzed up about this turn of events that I feel buzzed and lightheaded as Violet weaves through the crowd, women and men parting like the Red Sea for her. She looks dazed, like maybe she can't quite believe she pulled this off either. Trent appears about the same, too, rubbing his eyes, shell-shocked. As Violet walks past Maxine, the woman in red narrows her eyes and folds her arms over her chest.

Violet makes it to the front, and since the stage is two feet off the floor, I bend and offer her a hand. Then I think *fuck it*.

I grab her slim hips, lift her onstage, and plant a quick kiss on her cheek. I catch a faint whiff of her shampoo, or maybe it's her perfume, like peach and a soft breeze. It flutters across me and catches me off guard. I wasn't expecting to enjoy her smell so much.

She gasps her surprise, and Sierra emits a small *eek*. The hospital rep beams, as if she's a proud matchmaker. She extends a hand to Violet. "We are so very grateful for your generosity."

"It was truly my pleasure," Violet says, and I can tell from her voice she's still surprised she's onstage. "We're so happy to give our support."

Sierra arches a brow at the word *we're*.

"I mean, *I* am," Violet corrects, bringing her hand to her chest, even though, of course, *I am* so happy to give the support. I tug her in close, my way of letting her know her *we* comment was just fine. She fits nice and snug next to me. Sierra notices, her green eyes sliding over us. "You two are so adorable together. You know each other, don't you?"

Sierra sure knows how to read a situation. Violet and I have always gotten along well. Even though she's Trent's sister, the three of us have been buds, and I consider Violet one of my closest friends too.

"She's from my hometown," I answer quickly. "I've known Violet my whole life."

"Well, he moved to Petaluma when I was five and he was six," Violet interjects. "Not entirely our whole lives. For instance, I never saw him in diapers."

"Thank God for that," I say, wiping my brow in a *whew* gesture.

"Do you remember the day you met Cooper?" Sierra asks.

Violet nods. "I was riding my bike with the purple tassels and pink wicker basket, and I saw him moving in down the street. All I thought was boys were yucky."

Laughter floats from the tables, and Holly shouts, "I used to think that too."

"We're still yucky," I say with a smile.

"You're adorable," someone shouts from the audience.

"And what do you do now, Violet?"

"I'm a hairstylist," she says with a smile. She's humble, too, since she's more than a stylist. She's a business owner.

"She's not just a stylist," I chime in. "She owns a salon."

Sierra flicks her hand through her auburn locks. "I've been looking for a new hairdresser."

Violet laughs. "I'll give you your first cut on the house."

Sierra beams. "I'm there!"

Another person yells, "Violet, I want your boyfriend. Can you share him?"

Violet swallows and blinks at that word. *Boyfriend.*

The hospital rep thanks Violet again, then exits the stage while Sierra continues her questions. "Tell us what made you bid so high for Cooper."

The hostess thrusts her mic at Violet. She looks at Sierra, then me, her eyes saying *you decide, Coop. I was just trying to save your sorry ass.*

"She wanted to make sure no one else got me, of course," I say, as if there can't be any other answer.

"Well, naturally, that's the point of a high bid. But does that mean you've been wanting to bid on him for a long time?" Sierra asks, and as soon as the question comes out of her mouth, I know what's happening. She's constructing the story everyone wants to hear. The hometown girl crushing on the guy who made good. Before either of us can correct her, since that's not the case in the least, Sierra's eyes light up, flashing with the thrill of discovery. "Wait! You two *are* together. You're boyfriend and girlfriend, aren't you?" Sierra asks, then points to Violet. "And that's why you didn't want your man to go home with anyone else tonight. Am I right?"

She's wrong. She's so wrong she'll never be right. Violet shakes her head, but when she sees Maxine in the crowd, still staring at me, Violet's *no* turns into a *maybe* as she looks at me, her eyes asking me if that's the new story.

I glance at the woman who wants me to be her hallelujah and make a split-second decision.

Fuck yeah.

Sierra has handed us the perfect cover. Who cares that Violet and I would never happen? God bless reporters and their hunt for a story.

I smile brightly. "That's right, Sierra. That's exactly it. We might as well admit it now." I drape my arm over Violet's shoulder and tug her closer. "She's my girlfriend, and I couldn't be more thrilled she won me, since she's the one I want to spend every night with, but especially for a good cause."

I hope to hell Trent isn't pissed at me, but when my eyes find him in the audience, he looks more like he's rubbernecking. No surprise—he knows Violet and I would never be together. I'll just make sure he knows the score later, on all counts.

Sierra gives me an expectant look. "Well?"

"Well, what?" I ask, knitting my brow. What else does she want from me? She's got the story, she has a record-high bid, and the auction was a hit. Time for us to strut offstage, toast to our little ruse, and go our separate ways home. Problem solved, game over.

Right?

But Sierra pins me with her journalistic gaze. She gestures pointedly to the lady in my arms. "Don't you want to kiss the woman who just gave ten thousand dollars for a date with her boyfriend?"

That was a play-action fake I wasn't expecting.

I square my shoulders, clear my throat, and sneak a peek at Violet. Her amber eyes are unreadable, and I'm honestly not sure what to do next.

Then, someone starts clapping. Another woman cheers. Hoots and hollers bounce off the walls.

Seems the audience wants a show.

When you play a game on TV in front of millions, and in front of fifty thousand people in the stadium, you aren't uncomfortable with an audience witnessing your failures and your victories. But when I angle to look directly at Violet, nerves spike inside me, and I'm not sure why. I've known her for more than twenty years, since that day she thought I was yucky.

Maybe I'm still yucky to her, and that's why she's frozen.

Hell, the woman saved the day, but I can't imagine Violet wants to amp up the ruse. Maybe she'll want to come clean this second, and admit we aren't really a couple.

I swallow, prepping for the unraveling of our little fable. Instead, her gaze shifts to the audience, as if she's pointing at them. As if she's saying *give them what they want*.

I blink. Holy shit. She's serious?

"Kiss me," she whispers so damn quietly.

She's serious.

"She's open, Coop. Give her a kiss!" someone shouts from the crowd, and I suppose I should ask for Trent's permission. I should check and see if he cares that I'm about to kiss his sister. But she's already signed the permission slip, and she's the one calling the shots.

As I bend closer to her, I don't think of a damn thing but her lips, and her request.

Kiss me.

I tell myself to keep it chaste. Keep it tasteful, because this is being simulcast. But hey, it's local cable access. So maybe a little tongue is fine. TV tongue, not porno tongue. Just a quick kiss to seal this charade. No one will know she's just my best friend's sister.

Her chin is tipped up, her amber eyes are inviting, and there's that scent again. Peaches. It does something to me. Floats into my nostrils. Scrambles my brain. Makes me want to taste her pretty peach lips for real.

Kiss me.

I brush my lips to hers and tell myself to pull away, pull away, pull away. All we need is a kiss for the cameras. For the show. To put a neat little bow on this night. Then, we can dust off our hands and return to what we've always been.

Buddies.

But I don't pull away.

I don't break the contact. Nor does she. Neither one of us makes a move to stop. And that, right there, changes the game.

This isn't a peck anymore. It ratchets up the kiss scale. Violet slides her lips over mine, and I groan from the feel. My head is a haze, and I'm not sure I can move. She moves, though. She kisses me as if she's telling the whole crowd I belong to her. As if she wants everyone to know she's claimed me. That she's taking me home tonight and every night.

Hell, this woman can act.

The problem is my dick is a method actor.

Because this should just be an ordinary staged kiss.

But he's gone rogue.

The idiot between my legs is malfunctioning, pointing at the wrong person in an absolutely inappropriate manner. Violet resides in the not-allowed-to-think-of-as-hot category. I'm friends with her whole family, for Christ's sake. I'm not supposed to be attracted to her, I shouldn't be turned on by her, and I'm not going to let myself get carried away with this performance. But tell that to my body, because I'm immensely turned on as Violet and I kiss more deeply. I'm sinking into this kiss, and I need to wrestle some control back. It's not possible for me to be this goddamn attracted to a woman who's been like a sister to me.

I let that word echo in my head. *Sister*.

Except, there's nothing sisterly about the softness of her lips, or the peach taste of her gloss, or the scent of her fresh and minty breath.

I'm not thinking of sisters. I'm thinking of *this woman*.

I take over, cupping her cheeks with my hands. I hold her

face and seal my mouth to hers with a deeper, more passionate kiss. I forget where I am. I forget the crowd. The attendees. The emcee. My teammates. Jillian. Maxine. Trent. I kiss Violet onstage, savoring her taste, reveling in the sweetness of her lips, delighting in the scent that engulfs me. I kiss her like she is my girlfriend, like she's the only one who should be winning a date with me, because she's the only one I could possibly want.

When our lips slide apart, her lip gloss is smudged. Her amber eyes are glassy and dazed. I wonder how mine look and if they match hers.

The crowd goes wild.

Sierra cheers, then says, "The quarterback and the hometown girl. Now, that is a winning bid."

The collective *awww* tells me this is a story they like.

But when I head backstage, Violet's hand in mine, I see we've slid into a whole new pack of problems.

CHAPTER 5

Jillian marches up to me, her heels clicking on the floor. Her eyes drill holes through me. Her lips approximate a thin line. Her arms go straight in front of her. She pushes my chest. She's tough, but I don't move.

"What's wrong?" I ask, confused, because she should be happy, right? "Your pretty kitties earned so much money."

The smile that spreads quickly tells me she's one happy mama cat. "I know! I'm so thrilled!" She shoves me again.

"Then why are you pushing me?"

Another shove. "Because you didn't tell me." Jillian gestures wildly from Violet to me. "How could you *not* tell me you were dating? We were all in the suite together, and I had no idea."

Jones gives me a satisfied smirk from his post backstage. He knows Violet and I aren't together. He keeps his mouth zipped, though. Harlan, too, is quiet, and so is Rick.

I take a deep breath, and in that span of a few seconds, I consider my choices. Let her believe the fib, or let her in on the ruse. The thing is, Jillian works for the team. Even though she's friendly with us, she's still management. She's not a teammate. She's not taking hits for me on the field.

If I told the guys the truth, they'd have my back, since that's what we do for each other. But I don't know where Jillian's loyalties lie, so it's best not to tip my hand.

"You know how these things go," I say, keeping it vague as I squeeze Violet's hand. I startle when I realize I'm still holding it. How did that happen? I guess I grabbed on when we left the stage and never let go. She squeezes back, giving me a smile. Okay, fine, we're officially still holding hands.

Jillian's eyes widen, and her grin is huge and hungry. "No. I don't know how it goes. Tell me." Her tone is rich with excitement. I suppose these stories can be the fun ones for a publicist. She's eating it up, like Sierra did. "I want details. You know I'm going to get calls from the press asking about the two of you. I already have reporters texting me, wanting to know the story, wanting to know who your lovely stylist-turned-girlfriend is." She brandishes her cell phone.

I scrub a hand across the back of my neck. "Damn, they work fast."

And I need to work faster. I need to figure out what our story is. *Think, Armstrong, think.*

Jones meets my gaze, then steps in. "Here's what you tell them. Tell them it's none of their fucking business." Then he softens and gives the publicist a hug. "Good night, Jillian."

When he breaks the embrace, he tips his head to the exit. "We have an early practice tomorrow."

"But we have paperwork to do from the auction," she calls out as he pushes on the heavy door. "Totals, sign-off from the bidders, et cetera."

Violet grabs a pen from her purse while Jillian thrusts the clipboard at her with the papers indicating she won me with a ten-thousand-dollar bid. My good friend scribbles her signature, yawns, and says, "I'm exhausted. Can we catch up on everything else tomorrow?"

She smiles sweetly at Jillian, charming the minx.

Jillian is powerless before her. "Of course."

Jones ushers us into the hall, down the stairwell, and to the employee parking lot that the hotel let us use tonight. He arches a brow when we reach Violet's car. "I assume you two have shit to get straight. So, I'll let you figure the rest out." He nods decisively. "You just let me know what you need me to say, got it?"

"Thanks, man," I say.

"Don't even think twice about it."

He walks away, and it's just Violet and me at her emerald-green Mini Cooper.

"So..."

She nibbles on the corner of her lip. "So..."

Your lips taste amazing.

You kiss like a dream.

You turned me on more than you should.

Whoa. I don't know where the hell those thoughts came

from, but I'm evidently drunk from that kiss. I lift the corner of the carpet in my mind and sweep those ridiculous ideas under it. There. I'm not thinking about her lips anymore. I clear my throat. "I believe a thank-you is in order. You are a goddess and a saint, and I'm incredibly grateful."

Just focus on the bid, not the kiss.

She punches my arm in an *old buddy, old pal* way. "You should be thanking your bank account. You just bought yourself for a pretty penny."

I laugh. "True, that. I'm quite a generous contributor to charity."

"You are." She fiddles with her bracelets and then looks up at me. Concern flickers across her eyes. "I didn't bid too high, did I? Are you pissed?"

My jaw clangs to the pavement of the parking lot. "Are you kidding me?" My voice echoes loud in the cavernous space. I lower it. "Fuck no. I meant it when I said I'd rather get splinters in my ass. Plus, I've got the money, and it's a great cause."

She wipes the back of her hand dramatically over her forehead. "I knew it was a lot, and I was a touch concerned that you'd freak out. But mostly you looked like you needed rescuing."

"Was it that obvious?"

She tugs on a lock of her hair. "I figured it out pretty damn quickly."

"Thank the Lord." I tilt my head in the direction Jones made his exit. "What should I tell Jillian when she asks again? Do I tell her we split up? That it was a short-lived thing?" I ask, but each of those options feels wrong, and I'm not entirely sure why. "Or do I say we've been together for a while, and leave it at that?"

Violet hums, like she's thinking. "That could work, especially if you play up the whole privacy angle. Like we haven't said anything for that reason and we want to keep it that way?"

I screw up the corner of my lips, hunting for an answer too. "Or, maybe I should see if it all blows over tomorrow? Maybe it won't be that big a deal?"

Violet's eyes light up. "There are so many more interesting things to talk about in this town. We'll be the flavor of the night, and I'm sure by tomorrow no one will care."

"Exactly. No one will care," I echo.

She dips a hand into the side of her pink leather handbag—it's a Coach, and I know this because my mom loves handbags, and I take her shopping for them regularly. Violet finds her keys, then flashes me a friendly smile. "I should go. The salon opens at nine tomorrow, but the landlord is coming by at eight thirty for a meeting."

I groan. "What does he want this time?"

She sighs. "Who knows? Last time, he dropped by to tell me I was generating too much trash, which is kind of ridiculous since most of our trash is...wait for it...*hair*."

"Hair, of course, occupies an inordinate amount of space in the dumpster."

"I know. The time before it was noise. Because hair dryers are soooo *loud*," she says, rolling her eyes.

"Violet, don't be silly," I say in mock seriousness. "It was probably the sound of the aerosol hairspray that's violating eardrums."

She laughs. "But I suspect he wants to lease the space to some friend of his who's keen to sell Sausalito tchotchkes to tourists." Her salon is located in the heart of the tourist town's commercial district. Prime pickings for peddling snow globes of boats and the houses perched on hills the town is known for.

"I feel like the world doesn't need more tchotchkes."

She holds up a finger to make a point. "But they do need better hairstyles."

"Absolutely."

I realize I'm delaying her. I'm standing here volleying with her when the woman has said she needs to cruise. What am I keeping her for, anyway? For her to tell me she wants to bang in her back seat? It's a small car, and ideally, I'd rather spread her out on my bed. But if she wanted to test the strength of—

What the hell?

I slam on the mental brakes, skidding away from the five-car pileup of filth I was headed for. Not only am I taking a sex sabbatical this season, I also distinctly remember ridding my brain of all dirty fantasies about my good friend. But the dirty lobe is working overtime tonight, and I need to shut it down. Better to focus on knickknacks, and dickish landlords, and an early bedtime. "We have practice early, so I should call it a night too."

She points her keys at the car. "Do you want a ride home?"

I cabbed it over here, so I take her up on the offer. I open the door for her, click it shut, then walk around to the passenger seat, reminding myself that Violet and I simply need to segue back to the way we were.

Inside the car, we're silent at first, as she grabs roughly at the seat belt. The belt sticks, and she tugs it hard, yanking it across her, her elbow nearly smacking me.

"Sorry," she mutters.

I hold up my hands. "All good."

She clicks in the buckle, then goes to start the car, but she fumbles the key in the ignition.

Shit. She's nervous. And since she saved me, I need to make sure she's cool with us. I set a hand on her wrist, stilling her moves. "Are you weirded out that we kissed?"

She wrenches back. "What? No. Of course not."

"Okay, then." I take a beat and try to study her face, to figure out where she's at. "I guess we're all good, then?"

"Of course. We're always good." She lifts her keys again as I buckle my belt. "But kisses are weird," she blurts out.

I snap my gaze to her. "They are?"

"Just since I've known you for so long," she says, as if she's trying to explain a faux pas.

"Right, right." I rub my palms on my pants. "Not because you think I'm a weird kisser?"

Her eyes widen into moons. "*No.* You're not a weird kisser. Do you think you're a weird kisser?"

I furrow my brow. She's talking in circles. She has me all

twisted up. "I never thought so before, but I'm beginning to now. Did I kiss you weirdly?"

"Did I kiss you weirdly?" she counters, tapping her chest.

And round and round we go. I shake my head. "No. Not in the least."

"Good," she says with a nervous laugh as she slides the key into the ignition, getting it right this time. She backs up, shifts into drive, and pulls forward. "I'm not into weird kisses," she adds.

Nor am I. But I am into fixing things with Violet and restoring the order of our friendship. "Tell the truth. You're into sloppy, wet kisses. Like a dog kiss." I'm not honestly sure what she *does* want, so humor is the easiest way through this awkward patch. "Admit it."

This time, the sound of her laughter isn't nervous as she rounds the corner of the parking stalls, heading toward the exit ramp. "Oh yes, that's precisely what I want. Your slobbery kiss."

I lean over the console and lick her cheek. A long, wet, slurpy kiss engineered to cut the tension.

She shoots a *what gives* look as she turns the wheel. "Okay, *that* was definitely bizarre, Cooper."

We both laugh, then I straighten my tie. "Fine, you think I'm a bizarre kisser. I can live with that," I say, teasing, since that's the safest route. I can connect the dots. Violet hasn't said she liked the kiss. In fact, she's danced around the topic, sidestepping it in a way that tells me clearly she wasn't *into* it.

There's a part of me, I admit, that wishes she wanted to hump my leg right now, even though I'd have to turn down humping of any part of my anatomy for the sake of maintaining my season-long streak. But I'm man enough to accept when a woman doesn't dig me. Hell, if I expect Maxine to get a clue that I'm not ripe for her plucking, I'd better get the hint from Violet that the kiss extravaganza didn't float her boat. It's a bummer, but that's life.

She slows at the ticket booth, grabbing my arm. "I never said you're a bizarre kisser. I didn't mean it like that."

But I don't get a chance to ask what she did mean, because the bored woman at the gate grunts, "Ticket, please." Violet hands her our validated ticket, and we roll out of the garage.

Once we leave, my phone lights up like the Fourth of July as cell reception returns. My screen bleats with missed calls from reporters, a text from my married friends Chris and McKenna, a slew of messages from Jillian, and even an all-caps text from my mom.

Mom: WHY AM I THE LAST TO KNOW THESE THINGS? I ALWAYS LIKED HER. YOU TWO WERE SO CUTE AT HER PROM TOGETHER. I'M LOOKING AT THE PHOTO NOW.

I fire back a reply.

Cooper: I'll call you tomorrow to explain.
Mom: I explained the birds and bees to you when you were younger. No need to explain. 🙄

Cooper: Seriously, Mom.

As I scroll through the rest of the notifications, I spot a few texts from my agent. Normally, I love talking to Ford, but with the contract overhang, and the anxiety over whether we're extending the deal with the Renegades, I'm not in the mood this second. Plus, Trent is calling me, and even his name looks pissed off as it flashes on the screen.

"Hey, man," I say, keeping it casual when I answer.

"Why, yes, I would love to meet you for a beer right the fuck now and find out what's going on."

"I can explain. It's kind of a funny story."

"I'm chuckling up a storm," he says. But there's no laughter in his voice. Nor in my head.

CHAPTER 6

Life in San Francisco is comprised of two tasks: finding a parking spot, and everything else.

Tonight, the pursuit of a space by a curb occupies fifteen awkward minutes. Or maybe they're not so awkward, since it gives Violet and me something to focus on besides a hot-as-sin, weird-as-hell, I-liked-it-she-didn't kiss.

"Try Jackson Street," I tell her, pointing to the right-hand side of the street. She turns, but our hunt is fruitless since the block is stuffed full of vehicles. She tries Webster, but we're SOL there too.

"Crap," I mutter.

"I hate parking in this city."

"It's the worst thing in the world. Literally. Studies have revealed that searching for a parking spot in San Francisco can result in depression, anxiety, and a really bad day."

She laughs faintly as she turns onto Clay. "By that same token, finding a spot quickly has been known to cause euphoria."

"Better than an orgasm?" I ask, because evidently the word *euphoria* makes me think of only one thing.

Even in the dark, a hint of red splashes across her cheek. "I suppose that depends on the giver."

"And on the parking spot?"

She laughs. "Yes. But if you combine the two, it's like multiples."

I clear my throat, reminding myself to cease the flirting. "Listen, I can just go by myself. You have your meeting tomorrow morning."

She shakes her head. "I'm sure Trent wants to give me a hard time too. Better for me to get it out of the way now. That is, if he can focus his attention long enough."

Trent is notoriously distracted by his own desire to tell amusing tales, often ones that poke fun at himself. As we turn onto another block, an idea pops into my head. "Do you want to park at my place? I'm not far from here, and I have a two-car garage." I'm not sure why I tell her that, when she's parked in it before. The garage was a must-have when I bought my condo a couple years ago. No way was I living in this city without a garage for my Tesla. Even so, I still avoid driving if I can, on account of the utter pain-in-the-ass that is searching for a patch of open asphalt.

"No," Violet answers, swiftly. So swiftly she might have set a new record for the seconds required for the word *no* to fire from her mouth.

The message is loud and clear. She doesn't want to be near my place. "It was just an idea," I say, looking away.

"It's just..." she begins, then she points to a red BMW whipping out of a spot a hundred feet away. She floors the gas, as if she's a goddamn snow leopard snagging her prey and guarding it from other predators. She grabs the spot, executing a parallel-parking slam dunk that honestly kind of turns me on. There's just something about women who are completely independent, confident, and capable that gets my blood going.

But I refuse to be any more turned on by her, no matter how well she can park or smooch.

We head into the bar. A huge TV screen blasts a Warriors game, while another carries ESPN's *SportsCenter*. Waiters in jerseys boasting their favorite teams circulate with drinks and appetizers. A curly-haired guy with a pointy chin stops in his tracks, the beers on his tray nearly sloshing. "Hey, man," he says with a big smile.

I don't know him. I give a quick wave. "Hey there."

"Kick ass on Sunday."

"That's the plan."

As we walk past the booths, a few heads turn, but I stay focused, and we find Trent and Holly at a quiet four-top in the corner. A few years ago, they started a sports bar in Petaluma where we grew up, and it was so successful they opened several more in the Bay Area, including this one off Fillmore Street. Trent raises a glass of beer and takes a long swallow as I walk over. His eyes never leave me. Why do I feel as if I'm in trouble? Oh wait. I kissed his sister in a ballroom on cable TV.

That's why.

When I reach him, I say, "Am I being sent to bed without supper?"

He rolls his eyes as I pull out a barstool for Violet. I grab the one next to her. I try not to look at her, but I swear I can see the remnants of my kiss still on her lips. They look redder, fuller. Or maybe I'm spending more time studying them than I usually do. I really shouldn't, but sometimes once you see something you can't unsee it.

Like when you finish off a sleeve of Pringles, stare at the tube, and realize the cartoon dude looks just like Mr. Monopoly. Or, when Jimmy Fallon points out that the raccoon from *Guardians of the Galaxy* bears a striking resemblance to Paddington Bear. And now I'm thinking Rocket is a bear in a raincoat, a rich board game character once sold snack food, and my best friend's sister kissed me so passionately I don't know how I'll erase the image from my mind when I go to bed tonight.

Or whether I'll want to let that memory slip away at all.

I should *unfeel* it. Only, it felt too damn good to forget.

Trent drums his fingers on the table and stares at me, waiting. "Anything you want to tell me?"

I adopt a serious expression. "Did you know that Mr. Monopoly used to sell chips as the Pringles dude?"

Trent shakes his head. "What?"

He's not the only one flummoxed. Violet furrows her brow, and Holly blinks in surprise. Before I can explain, a blond waitress sporting a San Francisco Giants jersey arrives to take our orders. I opt for a beer, and Violet asks for white wine. When she leaves, Trent asks, "What was that all about?"

"It's called taking an order. It's what employees who wait on tables do in restaurants," I deadpan.

Holly laughs. Trent rolls his eyes. "The Pringles comment, dickhead."

"The Pringles guy and Mr. Monopoly. Doppelgängers. Google them. Once you do, you can't unsee it."

"Dude, are we playing the *unsee* game? Because I'm happy to tell you about the time my mom finally figured out I didn't have a cold when I was fifteen, and she couldn't unsee that in her mind's eye."

Holly gives him a curious look as she grabs her phone and taps on the screen. "What are you talking about?"

"Mom couldn't figure out why I went through so many boxes of tissues. She thought I had a cold that lasted several months."

Violet arches an eyebrow. "Seriously? How do you know Mom figured out the tissues were for your *morning habit*?"

"Because I saw the look on her face when she replaced the box next time. It was sort of like this." Trent crinkles his nose and curls up the corner of his lips. "She couldn't *unsee* the reason why I needed a tissue box on the nightstand."

"I feel so bad for your mom," I say sympathetically. "And for myself, because now I can't unsee it either."

Violet shakes her head. "Like I said earlier, boys are yucky."

The waitress returns with our drinks. "For you," the waitress says to Violet, handing her the wine.

When she gives me the beer, she smiles brightly, pointing to her chest and the Giants shirt she's wearing. "Don't let the jersey worry you. My Armstrong one is in the wash."

"Thank you very much, Liz," I say, reading her name tag.

Liz giggles. "Cooper, you're so very welcome." The way her eyes sparkle, I'm pretty sure her *you're welcome* translates into *you can take me home tonight and do bad things to me.*

Which I have no interest in doing.

Trent turns to the waitress. "Thanks for the drinks, Liz. We're all good."

And that means *I've told you a million times not to hit on Cooper when he comes to my bar.*

Liz leaves, and Violet takes a drink of her wine as I return to the subject of Trent's handy days. "Thanks for ruining my image of Kleenex now too. Also, why didn't you just jack it in the shower?"

He points his thumb at his sister. "Don't you remember? Violet put a clown head in the shower to get back at me for a prank, and I hate clowns."

"Oh shit. That's right," I say as the memory slides into place. "Was that after you put the zombie hand in the toilet bowl to freak her out?"

Violet takes over. "Yes, and it was the only time he ever put the lid down, so I should have suspected something. Clearly, a clown head in the shower was the only acceptable retribution for an undead hand in the toilet."

Holly swats her husband's elbow. "And this is why you can't get it up in the shower."

Trent rolls his eyes at his wife. "Oh, please. I believe this morning proves I've moved on from the clown-head-in-the-shower issue."

Violet raises her hands in frustration, giving her brother a pointed look. "I know you're going to find this hard to believe, but shockingly, I don't want to hear about your shower issues—"

"I got over the shower issue," Trent points out.

"Nor do I want to hear stories about your teenage masturbatory habits. Bad enough I had to live in the same house as you when you were getting it on with your hand."

Trent's tone shifts from strolling down Amused Lane to Seriously Annoyed Town again. "And I don't like finding out you're dating *him* onstage at a beauty pageant."

"Him?" I ask, affronted. "I've been reduced to a nameless *him*?"

"Oh c'mon, hon. That auction was better than a beauty pageant," Holly says to Trent, then she lifts her phone, flipping between the Pringles dude and Mr. Monopoly. "Dead ringers for each other."

"Exactly."

My friend points at me, undistracted by the chips-to-houses revelation. "Fess up. How long have you two been together?"

Violet scoffs. "Seriously? You bought into it?"

Trent looks perplexed. "Of course. It seemed totally legit."

Violet laughs harder and meets Holly's gaze. "You could tell, right?"

Holly shakes her head. But Violet doesn't let go of her stare.

Something shifts in Holly's expression, as if she's picked up on a key data point. Friend code, maybe? "Yes, of course I could tell," Holly says robotically, straightening her shoulders as she nods at Violet.

"You mean that was all a charade?" Trent asks. "The whole boyfriend-girlfriend thing?"

I lower my voice. "Look, what I'm about to say is not for public consumption, okay?"

Trent nods his understanding. Everyone leans in.

"Maxine Randall, the radio host, was bidding on me. I don't need to make waves by being a dick to her and turning her down. So, Violet saved me. That's all. Case closed."

Trent scrubs his hand over his jaw. "You guys really aren't dating? You sure?"

Violet sighs heavily as she lifts her wineglass. "I think I'd know if we were dating."

"I have to say you had me fooled," Holly chimes in, and Violet shoots her another laser-eyed look. Holly quickly amends her comment. "But of course, it makes sense that it was a joke. You love to tell jokes."

"Just a joke to help my friend," Violet says, emphasizing *friend*, as if she's trying to imprint the word on everyone's mind.

Why do I feel as if they're speaking in tongues? Like these women are trying to remind each other of what they're *supposed* to say?

But I can't quite slide one puzzle piece into the other, so I'm left with curved edges that don't align with round holes. This is why men fuck up relationships. Because sometimes, women make no sense.

Violet puts her hand on my shoulder. "Our man needed help. I helped him. That's what we do. We're a pack. Like when he took me to prom after Jamie ditched me. It seemed only fair."

Ding, ding, ding! The bell rings. The buzzer sounds.

The situation is crystal clear. Tonight's save-and-smooch was simply the return of a favor from years ago. I laugh quietly, a relieved sound, because I *get* it. At last, I understand what went down tonight. The kiss was part of the show, and the show was part of the rescue, and the rescue was her long-overdue thank-you.

Even though I wasn't banking on one. I was simply happy to have helped her when she needed it.

Her senior prom fell over Memorial Day weekend seven years ago, and I happened to be home from my freshman year of college, visiting my mom. Violet's date bailed at the last minute, breaking up with her the day before to hook up with another girl.

Total dick move.

"Let me take you," I'd said as soon as I heard.

She'd shaken her head, wiped tears off her face, and slapped on a plastic smile. "I'll be fine. I have a pint of ice cream and a movie to watch."

I scowled. "That's ridiculous. You have me to dance with, cheesy photos to take, and a smoking-hot dress to wear. You're going, and I'm your new date."

"You don't have to do that."

"I know I don't *have* to. I *want* to. Don't you want to wear the dress?" I asked, because I suspected the fashionista in her would have had a hard time resisting getting dolled up as she'd intended. Focusing on the dress was the best way to get her to say yes, and I didn't want her to remember prom as the day she was stood up.

Her smile turned real. "It's a really pretty dress."

"Then you need to wear it."

Her dress was more than pretty. It was stunning. The lavender material hugged her trim waist and covered her breasts enough to be classy, but not so much to be prim. Her long brown hair was twisted up onto her head, held in place with a silver clip as soft strands framed her face.

We danced to fast songs and swayed to a few slow songs, then we hung out downtown, drinking diet sodas from the convenience store and debating the best and worst prom songs, prom couples, and prom outfits. We grabbed a pint of ice cream and watched a movie in the cozy living room at my house. One of those fast and even more furious car movies that was mindless and a perfect popcorn flick for that night.

At the end of the movie, she put her head on my shoulder and murmured, "Thanks for taking me. Someday, if you ever need a date, I'll be your fill-in."

Now, back in the present, the fading memory only affirms what she said to me in her car on the way over. The kiss *was* weird, because we have history, because we've never been real, because we're only friends. She was simply repaying a favor.

Trent leans back in the barstool, stretching his arms behind him. "I'm glad we cleared that up. I just couldn't see you two together."

I furrow my brow. "Because that's the most ridiculous thing in the world?"

He laughs. "It kind of is, Coop." He waves a hand at me. "You're a playboy, and she's, well, she's my sister."

But that's not the real issue. The real issue is she's just not into me.

CHAPTER 7

If games are battles, then practices are duels.

No one goes easy on the opponent in a duel, and the same is true for a practice. Especially after a tough game like last weekend, when we eked out a win by a mere three points, and especially with a coach like Mike Greenhaven. He's the living, breathing manifestation of the word *intensity*. You know how Tommy Lee Jones looks all the time? As if he's doing math every second of every day?

That's Greenhaven. He only cracks a smile when we've won the Super Bowl.

Correction: when Jeff Grant won him the Super Bowl.

Those two were as tight as coach and superstar could be. They were the unbeatable NFL combo. Double G. Grant and Greenhaven. G squared. Sometimes, I wished they had last names starting with D so their nickname in the press could have been Double D. That would have amused the hell out of me. But it probably wouldn't have fazed the man who sets our agenda.

Greenhaven presides over practice from his post on the sidelines, arms crossed, his unflinching eyes missing nothing. He might even have eyes in the back of his head, as well as his knees. Toes too.

Our game this coming Sunday is against Dallas, and he's putting us through our paces. We work harder, and longer, and later. Just like we did earlier in the season after we choked the first two games. Or really, after I lost them for us, when I threw a whopping total of three interceptions between them.

Man, those were two of the worst games of my life. The fans let me have it. The local reporters lamented the retirement of Jeff Grant all over again, calling me the Big Flop, the Multimillion-Dollar Bust, and The Insurance Plan That Didn't Pay Out.

I found my footing after that, adjusted to the speed and intensity of the game, and stopped googling myself. That's when we won nine of the next eleven games, putting us in playoff contention. Our biggest rivals, the Los Angeles Devil Sharks, already secured the division, and that's why we're hunting for a wild-card slot.

This morning at the training facility where we practice, we run through the playbook, and since Greenhaven graduated from the school that favors the passing game, that means my right arm is in motion all morning long. Throwing to one of our wide receivers. Firing long bombs to the tight end. As the fog starts to break, I gun a pass to Jones. He reaches high while on the run and grabs it, as if he's poised to win a leaping competition, but the ball spills from his fingers when out of nowhere, the cornerback slams into him.

I curse, frustration crashing into me. But the offensive coach barks orders for us to do it again. There's no time to be pissed. No space to be annoyed.

"Do it better this time."

I bear down, focusing on the perfect timing, and when I launch the ball, Jones snags it and gets out-of-bounds before the cornerback can hit him. He pumps a fist subtly.

Greenhaven doesn't like self-congratulatory gestures.

We go again, running drills, running routes, ten more times, twenty, thirty. Run it till you can do it from muscle memory, till it feels like taking a breath. That's what the plays should be. So damn natural and easy. By the time the sun shines high overhead, peeking through the fog that's burning away, Greenhaven grabs his megaphone and tells the team to run a few laps. I've jogged twenty feet when he pulls me aside.

"Armstrong," he says gruffly.

"Yes, sir."

"Dallas is tough. Their line is the fiercest in the league."

I nod, knowing that from observing them, and all the other teams, over the last few years. I studied every second of every game I didn't play in. I've been assembling a plan of attack against every defense in the league for years. I know how to read coverage pre-snap and make split-second decisions. With Dallas, that also means moving at the speed of sound.

"You need to get rid of the ball quickly. Think fast. Think on your feet. Nothing less."

"Yes, sir."

He clamps his hand on my shoulder. "One more thing. I already told the Mack Trucks. I don't want to see you sacked."

He means the Renegades' offensive line, the guys whose job it is to make sure I have time in the pocket. Greenhaven convinced Jasper Scott to strengthen the offensive line several years ago, trading for many Mack Truck men. "You're only as good as your quarterback, but the quarterback can only be good if he has a great line," Greenhaven had said.

Jasper had listened to Greenhaven, approving every request to shore up those positions. When Greenhaven wants players, chances are he gets them, since the man knows what it takes to win. There's another reason Greenhaven despises sacks. He wants his legacy to live on not only in the number of rings he wears, but also in the number of concussions his men don't suffer. That works for me. Fewer sacks equals fewer chances for my skull to whack against the inside of the helmet.

"That sounds good to me, sir."

He nods, a sign that I'm dismissed. But he doesn't let go of my shoulder. "By the way, congrats on the nice haul last night," he says drily.

I didn't expect the coach to give a flying rat's ass about the auction, or to know final tallies. But then, I shouldn't be surprised, because this is the man who sees everything. He has a photographic memory of every play in every game. "Thank you, sir."

"Glad to see you men raising money for a good cause," he says in that solid, steady tone that reveals nothing. And yet, his words say everything. He has a zero-bullshit policy. He'd rather his players be upstanding citizens, giving back, representing the city proudly, than driving drunk, smashing cars, and knocking up underage chicks. A few of the teams in the league have racked up some pretty impressive stats in all of those areas. Greenhaven wants the opposite. Cool, calm, stable soldiers of the game.

"We're just doing our part and grateful to be able to," I say, Crash-Davising it all the way.

He lets go of my shoulder, and perhaps now I'm truly excused. I make a move to rejoin the guys, but Greenhaven adds, "And it's always nice to see a woman provide a stabilizing effect on a man."

I stop in my tracks, my muscles tightening.

Holy shit.

He doesn't just see everything. He has an opinion on it too.

"Yes indeed, sir. I couldn't agree more," I say in my best cool and calm tone. I blow out a long stream of air and trot back to the field. As I join the guys, I try to figure out what it means that our coach knows the finer workings not only of every opponent's offense and defense, but also of our fucking love lives. What's next? Is he going to know if I jack off in the shower tomorrow morning?

By the time we finish running, my muscles are sore and my lungs are spent. We watch game film for an hour, and when the practice mercifully ends midafternoon, all I can think about is doing a whole lot of nothing the rest of the day. Maybe take a nap. Cook a good, clean dinner with protein and vegetables, then watch game film to work on a plan of attack for the field, and study the playbook once more.

But when I turn on my phone after I'm showered and dressed, it's clear none of that is on the agenda for this evening. I swear it feels like my phone has been weighed down with calls from my agent. I stare at the screen, scrolling through one message after another from Ford Grayson. The dude is one relentless motherfucker. I'm surprised he doesn't jump out of my mobile device like a goddamn jack-in-the-box. In the midst of his notes, a voicemail notification pops up, but hell if I know how to work that thing. Does anyone even know how to retrieve voicemails anymore? It's probably a credit card spammer anyway. I spot a text from Violet asking me to call her later.

I text back letting her know I'll do just that, then I call Ford as I leave the locker room, hair wet and sticking up from the shower. "What's going on, Ford? You lose your balls and need me to find them?"

"Oh," he says with a hiss. "I am so going to make you pay for that comment."

"You'll make me pay *and* you'll take your three percent."

"Damn fucking straight I will. I might even ask for special dispensation to raise my rates to five percent for you on account of you being so goddamn hard to reach," he says, firing off each word like a bullet. "It's like getting an audience with Ethan Hunt once he's gone rogue."

"Please. Ethan's got nothing on me. Anyway, what's going on?" I ask as I walk down the hall.

"What's going on? What's going on?" I can feel his frustration radiating off him in fumes. His voice climbs an octave. He already speaks at the speed of light.

"Aww, you're still upset with me. That's cute," I say, since I love to yank his chain.

"Don't fuck with me, Coop. Don't fucking fuck with me. Also, speaking of losing shit that matters, did you lose your ever-loving mind?"

I rap my knuckles against the side of my head, so loudly I'm sure he can hear. "Still here. Anyway, you need to relax. Want me to take you to the duck pond to settle you down?" I tease, since I know that's where he goes when he's ready to blow his gasket over whatever dickhead move whatever dickhead GM he's dealing with is trying to pull.

"I've already been. It's duck mating season, and even that didn't make me less pissed at you. I need to see you right the fuck now."

"What is duck mating season like? Are there feathers just flying everywhere?" I ask as I near the heavy doors that lead to the players' lot.

He ignores me. "You didn't return my calls last night."

I stop in my tracks as I reach the end of the hall. "Shoot, man. I'm sorry. Last night was wild. The auction and all," I say, but the truth is, I wasn't in the mood to chat after what went down.

"When the whole town is buzzing with you suddenly being attached, and your contract is coming due, that is shit I need to know."

I laugh. "Everyone seems to know. Greenhaven even mentioned it."

It's like a teapot whistles on the other end of the phone. I hear Ford suck in his breath through his nostrils. He might start to hyperventilate. "I'm a tree. I'm a calmly rustling tree. I'm one with the universe," he says in a deliberately placid voice.

"You okay, Ford?"

"One with the universe...mmm."

"Ford?"

"Oh, sorry. Excuse fucking me. I was practicing my yoga mantras so I don't whack you upside the head when I see you in two minutes."

I glance at my watch. "You're ambitious. Did you have jetpacks installed on your feet?"

"I drove. I'm outside the field."

"You're here?"

"You say that like it's a surprise I tracked you down. Did I or did I not track you down in the first place?"

"You did."

Ford Grayson is a determined bastard. We give each other a hard time because this man has my back completely. He sought me out during my final season of college ball. I swear, the second I walked off the field after our bowl game—we won, thank you very much—he was waiting for me. He made sure I signed with no one but him. I love the man. A few months later, I went in the first round of the draft, and he landed me a sweet deal with the Renegades. That deal is the reason my mom lives in a beautiful three-bedroom home overlooking the water in Sausalito with her dogs and boyfriend.

Oh, and that deal is why I never have to work again if I don't want to.

But I want to.

I love what I do as much as I love breathing. It's life. It's sustenance. It makes my bones hum.

"And I did again. I'm at your car," Ford tells me. "My assistant, Tucker, is here. He'll drive mine home since you and I are going somewhere so we can have a little chitchat right now."

"That sounds ominous."

"Ominous doesn't even begin to cover it."

CHAPTER 8

Ford snaps a photo of a duck at Mallard Lake in Golden Gate Park. The waterfowl swims faster through the pond and dips his green head below the surface. When he raises his beak, almost like he's performing for the phone camera, my agent snaps another pic. Then, he takes more shots of a quartet of ducklings paddling through the water.

I stroke my chin. "Let me guess. You called this meeting to let me know you're officially a wildlife photographer now, Ford."

"You have brains and beauty."

"Speed too," I say.

"Yes. I'm changing professions. Wildlife is much more manageable than athletes," he says, taking one more picture. Truth is, he's a reformed duck feeder. But it's bad for waterfowl, so now he photographs them instead.

"Are you calm now?" I ask, gesturing to the placid water. The small pond is edged by a quiet path and a smattering of flowers.

Ford slaps on a smile, his straight white teeth gleaming. The man looks like a million bucks, from the tailored black pants, to the white shirt with green checks, to the polished shoes. Not a blond hair on his head is out of place. His hair wouldn't permit it.

"Like a Zen beast."

He inhales deeply before he turns to me, tucking his phone into his back pocket. He's a gesticulator of the highest order, so he needs his hands free to talk. "Okay, I'm ready now. Tell me again what went down last night."

I raise one eyebrow. "Everything?"

His blue eyes nearly bug out. "Everything. I'm your priest."

I share a solid SparkNotes version with him, from Vera pulling me aside with the warning, to Maxine's bids, to Violet, finishing with, "That's why everyone thinks Violet is now my girlfriend, since otherwise, Maxine might have kept up her whole *Cooper is my husband and I'm going to take him home and have him, I dunno, make babies* bit?" I ask, and wow. That sounds awful. But what sounded better was what she said on air this morning—*I'll miss my husband. Le sigh.* I hope last night was enough for her on-air crush to be over.

Ford scrubs his hand over his whole face. "I'm not happy about this. She shouldn't talk about you that way, whether you're attached or not. It's just...fucking rude."

"Right, but disaster averted, so can we just move on? I have enough on my mind with the prospect of playoffs and, oh yeah, that other matter of not knowing whether I'm getting an extension."

"In theory, we can move on." He takes a beat, stares at me, then delivers his edict. "But in practice, you're better off pretending with Violet. For now, while I negotiate."

I blink. He can't be serious, can he? How the hell does he think I'm going to pretend to be with a woman who's just a friend? I point out the obvious. "Why? Also, it's not real."

"Wah. Wah. Wah."

I park a hand on my hip. "Did you just mock me like I'm being a baby?"

He grabs his imaginary violin and plays a sad tune. "I did. Is that so hard, to pretend you're with her?"

I give him a *you-can't-be-serious* look. "Pretend we're together for real?"

"You did it onstage last night. I'm presuming you've got some fucking stamina. Keep that shit up."

"I have more stamina in one night than you will ever have in a lifetime."

"Brains, beauty, and humility," he says, smacking my back. "God, I love you. Listen, this is your time. Earlier in the season, the GM would have dropped you like a hot potato. They were going to let you become a free agent with the way you were playing."

I heave a sigh, hating the reminder of those first two games. "I know."

"But I knew you had it in you to turn it around, and you

did. You did it with a workmanlike focus on the game. You did it by doing your goddamn job. Things are different now, and we need to strike just the right balance to get the best possible deal. You keep throwing like this, and no way will they let you go to free agency. You're playing like the field general they want you to be, and if you keep it up through the last two games, they'll want to lock you up. And that's what we want. But it's a dance, Coop."

Ford shakes his hips. "I can't just call them and say *make him an offer now or we'll walk*. We need to go through the steps of the dance."

My chest tightens, and a rare dose of nerves floods through me. I have every faith in the world that Ford knows what he's doing, but I also want the security that comes with a done deal.

"So then, keep on dancing," I say, but I frown, since I'm fuck-all confused. "But why do I need to pretend I'm with Violet?"

He stares dead-eyed at me. "Are you seriously asking me?"

"Yeah. I am."

He huffs. "Sweetheart. You lied last night. No shade from me. I get it. You needed to scramble away from a situation that had 'uncomfortable' written all over it. A situation the owner's wife warned you about, so you can bet she told Jasper what went down and that you've now got a lovely lady on your arm. And see, to do the dance, there's no way we can let on that you lied last night."

I cringe at the word *lie*. "You say that like I didn't disclose I took hush money from a foreign government."

"Did you?"

"No."

"Want me to soften *lie* for you?" He sketches air quotes. "A fast one? A ploy? A white lie? Do those better suit your sensibilities, superstar?"

"Fine, fine. A lie. It was a lie," I admit grudgingly.

"The point being, you need to keep your dick in your pants, like you've done all season because you're a superstitious motherfucker. And you'll let me keep dancing with the GM. We don't need any red flags, any concerns, any issues that make you look like anything but the future of this franchise. That's what Greenhaven wants you to be, and all personnel decisions are vetted by him."

I snap my fingers. "Yeah, speaking of Coach…"

Ford rolls his eyes. "Don't make me need to take an extra yoga class."

I draw a deep breath and tell him what the coach said on the sidelines about a woman being a stabilizing influence on a young man.

Ford cracks up, then beckons for me to come closer, as if he's going to tell me a secret. "Want to know what I call Greenhaven? *Mr. Squeaky Clean.* That's how he operates, and that's what he wants from you. And that's what you're going to be now." He ticks off items on his fingers. "You've got a girlfriend from your hometown, you've known her your whole life, and you're so motherfucking happy. This'll keep the Maxine problem in the rearview mirror, and it'll make the man with the Midas touch happy."

"And what are we supposed to do? Parade down Market Street holding hands? Kiss in the stadium after I throw a game-winning pass?"

Ford's eyes light up at that one. "I do like game-winning passes."

"Yeah, me too. Shocking, isn't it?"

He claps me on the back. "Listen, you don't need to make a reality show about how you and your new woman like to go on picnics and tandem bicycle rides. All we need are a few dates, a few pictures on Instagram, a few comments in the press. Boom." He swipes one palm against the other.

I scowl. "You know I hate all that social media shit, and I don't even have an Instagram account." Life is for living, not for living online. I've no interest in snapping stories or chatting photos or hashtagging my days away when I can keep my head up and enjoy the real world rather than a screen.

"Man, I might need to rescind my comment about brains. You honestly think I'd make you handle a social media account? You send me a few pictures, and Tucker will take care of it. My assistant is aces at social shit, and we reserved your social handles a long time ago. We'll just fire it up."

Damn. Ford covers all his bases. "Fine." I heave a sigh and shift gears. "Violet isn't going to be happy about this."

He cocks his head to the side. "Why won't she be happy? You're friends. You've known her forever."

"Hard as it may be to believe, she's not into me that way."

His reaction is instant. Ford doubles over. He grabs his

stomach, then sets his palms on his thighs and laughs, cries, and guffaws. Nothing has entertained Ford Grayson quite like that admission. "Oh, that's a good one. That's awesome. Tell that to me again. I can't hear that enough."

"By the way, did I mention Maddox LeGrande called me?" I say casually, naming one of his biggest rivals.

He straightens, and his eyes turn into pistols. "And you said, 'No, no, no, never ever. Ford Grayson is my guy.'"

I laugh, taunting him. "Maybe. Maybe not."

Ford breathes deeply and raises his arms heavenward. "I am calm. I am a tree. I am peaceful."

"No, he didn't call," I say. "But thanks for having a laugh at my expense."

"It's karma." He lowers his arms. "Karma is coming back for you."

"How so?"

"Years of you cleaning up with the ladies. Years of women throwing panties, bras, and stockings at you—"

"Stockings? When was that?"

"You can't even remember the riches the good Lord rained down? It was the time Tucker and I went with you to the club in that warehouse in SoMa last year. By my count, you had six free drinks sent your way, and we gladly finished them for you while you danced with the ladies. Then a woman threw her fishnets at you."

I draw a blank.

He shakes his head, bemused with me. "You don't even remember?"

I scratch my jaw and shrug. "I think you might have mistaken me for someone else when it comes to the fishnet story."

"Some other young, cocky rising star I rep who earned a multimillion-dollar contract at age twenty-two to ride the bench and back up a great? It was definitely you, and you took the fishnets home along with the woman who wore them."

"Are you sure it wasn't someone who *started* games at twenty-two?"

He shoots me a look. "No one starts at twenty-two."

I wave behind me. "Look, those days are in the rearview mirror. I'm not a player off the field anymore. I'm all about the game. The team. Leading the guys to victory. My days of catching fishnets are over."

"No fucking shit they are. That's because your number one fan"—he taps his heart—"is going to score a big, fat payday for you. That four-year rookie contract will pale in comparison. You'll be buying your mama a couple mansions." He hands out imaginary dollar bills like he's holding a fat stack of greenbacks.

"Man. You're as cocky as Einstein."

Ford waggles his eyebrows. Rick is his client too. "And his foot is golden. God, I love kickers and quarterbacks and linemen." He knocks his knuckles on my head. "Now, listen, you take that smart head of yours and your multimillion-dollar arm, and you keep up the act with your woman."

"How long?"

"At least through the next two games. Maybe longer. But definitely as long as it takes for me to score you the sweetest deal. And meanwhile, you don't score. You've spent the whole season not scoring with women so you can score on the field, and far be it from me to mess with your superstitions when they involve your two favorite things."

I arch a brow. "What are my two favorite things?"

"Your dick and football."

I smirk. "I plead the fifth."

"Does that all sound reasonable to you?"

"To me? Hell, yeah. But now I have to convince Violet to pretend to be mine."

Ford laughs, an eminently satisfied cackle. "This is beautiful. You're not afraid to run with the ball if you can't find a man open, but you're terrified to ask a woman you've known your whole life to play fake lovers sitting in a tree k-i-s-s-i-n-g?"

I scoff. "I'm not terrified."

He holds up his thumb and forefinger. "A little afraid, though?"

I square my shoulders. "Fuck off."

I make like I'm leaving.

"Wait." He grabs my shoulder. "One favor."

"What is it?"

"Can you record that conversation with her for me? Just so I have something to play back when I need a good laugh?"

"Why do I let you have three percent of my earnings? Remind me."

He waves his arms from the sky to the ground. "Because when I make it rain, you are going to get down on your knees and thank me for making you one of the richest quarterbacks in history. You, Coop, are the real deal, so let's remember to not fuck this up." He sobers and stares at me, his blue eyes darkly serious. "And, also, because I will put my neck on the line for you."

And he would. I know that.

After I say goodbye to Ford, who catches a Lyft, I take a deep breath, pick up my phone, and call Violet. It goes straight to voicemail. I look up the number for her salon and call to try to schedule a haircut. I don't give the receptionist my name, and she tells me Violet is booked for the evening, asking if I would like to schedule something for a week from now.

I say no thanks.

I can't wait a week, so I'll have to make an unscheduled appearance.

CHAPTER 9

I cross the Golden Gate Bridge and round the curve on the hill that leads into downtown Sausalito, singing along to Foreigner. How can I not? It's against the laws of the universe to listen to this song and *not* sing. As the sun dips in the sky, I croon about climbing any mountain and sailing across a stormy sea. The car practically vibrates from the music and the sheer awesomeness of "Feels Like the First Time."

This tune has the added benefit of keeping my brain occupied. The more I think about what to say to Violet, the more it's going to drive me nuts. Executing a play on the field is one thing. Those need to be practiced, memorized, and turned into a habit. But this is a delicate situation—a request—and it needs to come from the heart.

The problem is there's nothing in it for her. I need her to say yes, but she gets zilch out of this deal. That's why I need to appeal to our friendship. My request for her to play along needs to feel natural, not as if I've been plotting the words to say as I drive.

I focus on the breathtaking view of the navy-blue water in Richardson Bay, on the choppy waves that crash against the rocks and the sand, and on the chorus to the second-best karaoke song ever written. Hell, if I weren't any good at football, I'd try to find a way to be a professional karaoke singer. Every man needs at least one great party trick. Mine is killing it at the karaoke machine, and I aced every competition we had in college in my dorm. I still try to go to Gomez Hawks, a chill karaoke bar in the city, with some of my good friends—like Chris and his wife McKenna, and some of my other friends from the non-football side of my life.

The way I see it, I had no choice but to love rock music. I grew up with music blasting from every speaker in the house. My mom worked in customer service for an internet shopping giant, and when she came home from hours dealing with phone complaints, she needed loud music as the antidote to a day full of "I'm sorry to hear your shipment of Nicholas Cage pillowcases arrived late" and "Of course we'll replace the fifty-five-gallon drum of lube with the seventy-five-gallon one you meant to purchase."

As my mom tells it, I was conceived at a Pearl Jam concert with a guy she met in the audience. Apparently, their music did the trick, a detail my mom shared when I was eleven and one of their songs was blasting as I cleared the dinner table. "As soon as Eddie Vedder finished singing, that's when the man in the audience and I sneaked off."

Honestly, I'm still a little pissed at her for ruining Pearl Jam for me.

When my mom found out she was pregnant, she tracked the dude down and told him the news. He said to her, "Don't look at me. That's your problem."

That was the last she ever saw of him.

As a kid, I was angry that he never cared about me. Now, as a man, I'm grateful that the fucker never came looking for her or me with opportunity in his eyes. But we got the last laugh. We didn't need him, and the fact that he doesn't even know my name—because he never knew *her* last name—means he can't get anything from me.

Ever.

But my mom? She gets whatever she wants, and that's been one of my greatest joys in life.

She lives on the way to Violet's salon, and I picked something up in the city for her. As I reach the bottom of the hill and pull into her driveway, a familiar sense of pride surges in my chest. She loves her house—it's a three-bedroom, two-story home on stilts on a small patch of beach in Sausalito, a beautiful seaside town just across the bay from the city. I cut the engine and grab the bag of takeout I picked up from her favorite Chinese restaurant on Chestnut Street. I head around the side of her house, take the steps two at a time to the wraparound deck, and knock on the glass door. But she's not inside. She calls out from the sand.

"Is that my favorite Chinese deliveryman?" She cups her hands over her eyes.

"Yes, ma'am. One order of spicy eggplant, one order of pepper steak, and one order of scallion pancakes."

I head to the sand. The breeze blows Mom's blond hair across her cheek, and she gathers it back. Dyed blond, courtesy of Violet. My mom says she refuses to become a silver fox, especially since she's not even fifty, so she's a religiously regular customer at Heroes and Hairoines, with an appointment every three weeks.

Her dog, Miss Moneypenny, a golden retriever mix, bounds over to me and plops herself down, asking nicely for food. "Hey, girl," I say, scratching her silky chin as my mom walks over in a billowy green sweatshirt, a tennis ball in one hand and two Chihuahua mixes, James and Bond, by her side.

The spy franchise, rock music, and football—that's what my home was filled with growing up.

"I got your favorite and Dan's," I say, holding up the bag.

"Always so thoughtful, even though I know I'm just a pit stop on your way to see your girlfriend."

"Just as I know you'll be happy to watch *The Spy Who Loved Me* with Dan, the dogs, and the Chinese food," I point out.

"Touché." She leans in to give me a kiss on the cheek and ruffles my hair. "Now." Shifting her tone, she parks one hand on her hip and stares sharply at me. "Were you ever going to tell your dear, old mom?"

"Mom, there's hardly anything to tell."

"Seems there's something. Ready to confess?"

I laugh. "It's complicated, but in a nutshell, I had to say all that stuff about us being together to prevent some potential trouble with a radio host."

She arches a brow. "What sort of trouble?"

"Nothing you need to worry about. Just someone who was bidding on me, and it might have been...awkward. Just know I kind of need to pretend Violet and I are a thing for a little while."

"That seems a bit dicey."

"It'll be fine, Mom."

Mom has never stopped worrying about me in the dog-eat-dog world of pro sports. "Be careful, Cooper."

"I'm always careful. You'll keep my secret?"

She ruffles my hair. "Cooper, I'm your mother. Of course I'll keep my mouth shut, even if I don't understand why you need to do this."

"It'll all be worth it, I promise," I say, then hand her the bag.

"Wait. Let me amend that. Keep bribing me with Chinese food, and I won't blab."

"We've got a deal."

She opens the bag and inhales. "My mouth is watering."

"Make sure Miss Moneypenny doesn't eat it all," I tell her, but her big dog is far more interested in the tennis ball.

"She would never steal food. She's too well-trained," Mom says proudly. She flashes me the happiest grin in the world. "Such a shame that training them is all I have to do all day long."

I smile too. "And that's the way it should be."

She's the classic football mom. She worked hard when I was a kid, picking up extra money for uniforms and equipment with babysitting gigs in the evenings. She drove me to every practice, attended every game, and cheered the loudest. Mom had rented her whole life, and what she wanted most was to own a home here in Sausalito and to spend her days with her dogs. I made it happen for her, and I'm glad she lives nearby.

I drop a kiss to her forehead. "Enjoy dinner. I have to go see Violet."

"Good luck getting in. There's a line out the door."

CHAPTER 10

I wouldn't say I'm famous.

I wouldn't even classify myself as terribly well-known yet. I've snagged a pack of condoms at the CVS on Fillmore without the paparazzi reporting on it. I've bought salmon at Whole Foods without any speculation on whether I've started an all-fish diet. (The answer is no, because I like steak too much.)

Once your name is slapped on the back of jerseys, though, you give up full-time anonymity. You take the chance that someone might recognize you anytime you leave the house. But I have this theory. People don't always recognize you when you're walking around town because they don't expect to see you grocery shopping or buying your own prophylactics. You can blend in more easily.

Even so, I do take the necessary precautions. Grabbing a Giants ball cap from my car, I pull it low on my forehead and cover my eyes with shades, even though the sun is slipping behind the water. I walk from my mom's house along the beach and into town, jagged rocks and sand on one side of me, the main drag on the other.

When I reach the shops along the waterfront, I stop at a lamppost and survey the scene on the other side of the street.

Violet's salon hangs out next to a wine shop on one side and a bicycle store on the other. Her block is also home to a dress boutique, an ice cream parlor, and one of those stores that sells horrendous T-shirts with sayings like "Old Guys Rule" and "Gone Fishing." Heroes and Hairoines shuts its doors at six on Wednesdays, and as I stare at the floor-to-ceiling windows of the salon, an hour before closing, I can safely say my mom was exaggerating.

But only by a smidge.

The line doesn't snake out the door, but a parade of tourists—and perhaps locals too—crowds the front, snapping shots of the salon even at dusk.

I grab my phone, steeling myself as I open Google News, searching for my name. I aim to avoid personal searches, since they yield about the same level of satisfaction as eating cardboard for dinner does.

I lean against the lamppost by the water as a seagull lands by my side, squawking for food. "I don't have any. Go find Ford," I tell him. But this bird is one of those seagulls that doesn't speak English, so he doesn't move.

Quickly, I learn that Ford was right. The local online media has picked up on last night's auction news, dubbing us

The Quarterback and the Hometown Girl in one article, *The Renegade and the Stylist* in another. My favorite headline is one from a local gossip rag calling us *The Baller and the Babe*.

That's some honest reporting right there. Violet is a total babe. I read the brief mention.

> Ladies and gents in the Bay Area who'd been hoping for a night with the most valuable playboy will be crying in their cereal. The Renegades' new starting quarterback is off the market since the fox from his hometown claimed him at auction last night. It turns out the baller who leads the team and the babe who snips hair in Sausalito have been locking lips for a while now. Let's all just sigh and moan because it's not fair that hot athletes only date models or hometown girls. How about us regular gals? Do we ever stand a chance with a superstar? At least the receiver is still single. Have you seen Jones Beckett's hands?

Damn. The press jumped all over the event like paratroopers from a plane. I hop over to social to see what fans are saying, and a quick search reveals exactly why Violet's shop is suddenly on the map in a whole new way.

> Darn, I'd been planning on flashing my boobs at him during the next home game.

The universe hates me. Not only is his GF hot, she's also so sweet. But on the plus side, a new salon for me!

If I go to Heroes and Hairoines, maybe the Renegade hottie will show up and realize he wants me instead!

Who cares about dumb athletes? Did you see her hair? I'm so jelly of those locks!

I scoff at the last one, muttering, "Three-point-five GPA in college, thank you very much. And it was *not* inflated. But Violet's hair is pretty."

As I scroll some more, I find cell phone shots of a woman standing outside the salon, pointing her thumb at it, wearing an Armstrong jersey. There's one from last night of us answering questions onstage. Then a photo of us kissing. Then another. Then another. I zoom in on one, like the pervert I am. In this shot, I'm holding her face, my lips are crushed to hers, and her arms circle my neck. Spreading my thumbs on the screen, I enlarge the photo even more, zeroing in on her hands on the back of my head. Her fingers are threaded through my hair, and she's clutching me tight. That does not look like the way a woman holds a man who kisses her weirdly.

That looks like a woman who wants to be kissed. Who wants to be touched. Who wants to be taken.

My blood heats as I remember the kiss. How my head was

a haze and my body was amped full of electricity. How there was nothing else in that moment but the *feel* of her.

And now, as my skin heats, I want another moment like that.

Get yourself together.

I refuse to get turned on from a cell phone shot.

I jump out of the underbelly of the web and return to the keypad. I try to call Violet once more, but her phone goes straight to voicemail again. Time to head into the fray. I slip my phone into the back pocket of my jeans, cross the street, and walk to the entrance.

"Excuse me," I say as I weave around a mom pushing a stroller.

"No problem," she says, then her lips twitch up. "Go Renegades!"

I give a quick fist pump then dart around a few more people crowding the sidewalk. A teenager up the street lifts his phone and takes a picture as I push on the mistletoe-decorated door.

The receptionist looks up and then beams, her bright-green eyes wide and eager. "Hi, Cooper!"

Several faces snap in my direction at once. Customers seated on a white leather couch in the waiting area gawk, while a woman in a salon chair with tinfoil in her hair peers over the top of her glasses. A lady with cherry-red hair stares my way as one of Violet's half dozen or so stylists snips her hair.

There's no point pretending I'm anyone else, so I give a friendly wave, then drum my fingers on the receptionist's desk.

"Hey, Sage," I say to the woman with silvery-purple hair and bangles up to her elbows. "I don't have an appointment, but I was hoping to see—"

"Your girlfriend," she says brightly, her voice matching the jingle of her jewelry.

I don't answer right away. I let the word *girlfriend* bang around in my skull for a little longer. The last time I had a girlfriend was in college. Kelly was a track star, and we were a good fit since we were both more obsessed with sports than schoolwork, partying, or frankly, even the opposite sex. Don't get me wrong—we engaged in plenty of horizontal exercise, but neither one of us was keen on anything that dug much deeper on an emotional level. Hell, maybe that was why we were together for an entire year. We were easy, we were painless, and we were good. We broke up when she transferred to another school that had a better track team.

"Yes, I'm here to see my girlfriend," I say to Sage, and I hear whispers behind me.

A few seconds later, the click of heels across the tile catches my attention. Violet walks toward me, and it takes me a few seconds to process what she's wearing. Black leather pants. Holy hell, she's wearing black leather pants, and she looks like a rock star in them, and I want to know how they'd look wrapped around my hips as I push her against the wall.

Rewind.

The pants are off in this fantasy. But she can leave those black boots on. They hug her calves and stretch all the way to her knees, and I bet she'd look hot as fuck in those boots and nothing else. I'm so damn glad she loves to wear boots. My eyes travel up her body. A flowy pink top clings to her breasts. A long gold chain with a feather on it hangs between those beauties. Her clothes are so fucking lucky.

Her smile is wide and devious. "Hey, baby."

Baby?

"Hey, sweetie pie," I say, trying that on for size, if we're going to toss terms of endearment at each other now.

When she reaches me, I steel myself for a number of possibilities. She might be pissed that everyone is still calling her my girlfriend. She might be annoyed because her landlord is a dick. Or she might be ready to remind me that I shouldn't show up without an appointment.

Instead, she grabs my hand, tugs me over to the nook in the front of the store with shelves of shampoos for sale, then throws her arms around me. She tugs me in close, pressing those sweet breasts against my chest.

Well, hello there, angels. So nice to see you again.

She threads a hand in my hair, and heat sweeps over me. She tilts her face up and nibbles on the corner of her lips. An electric charge surges down my spine. When she curls her fingers around the back of my head, I'm ready to call a two-minute warning because if she moves any closer, she'll know there's nothing fake about the way my body responds to her.

I've gone from zero to fully aroused in less than ten seconds. She presses her cheek to mine, her soft lips brushing near my earlobe. My chest rumbles. What the hell is she doing to me? Forget aroused. I'm ridiculously turned on, and also confused as hell. But I'm a physical man, so I go with it. I wrap my arms around her, holding her close.

"I texted you," she says softly. "Did you get them?"

I can barely think with her lips so close to me, with her soft voice floating in my ear. "No. I mean, yeah. Maybe. I don't know." English is hard with her breasts getting acquainted with my chest, and me wanting to know how they'd feel without all these clothes between us. "Then Ford ambushed me and there were ducks, so…"

Yes, speaking in complete sentences is far too difficult.

"I sent you a couple. I left you a voicemail too."

"Sorry. I missed them," I whisper, and I hope she keeps this conversation up all night long, because her hair smells so good, and her body feels amazing, and I can't even think about text messages or voicemails when her hair tickles my neck like that. My brain short-circuits as I imagine my hands threading through all those soft strands. Yanking it back. Exposing that pretty neck. I'd suck on her jaw, lick a path up the column of her throat, and nibble on her ear. Then I'd kiss the breath out of her. Kiss her so damn hard and good that she loses her mind with pleasure. Like she's doing to me in my head.

"Anyway," she says quietly, "I called because I wanted to ask you something."

"Sure."

Her voice drops lower, goes even softer, and I can barely

make out the words, but they sound a lot like, "Is there any chance you could pretend we're still together for a few more days?"

I break the hug, meet her eyes, and say, "Funny, I was coming to ask you the same thing."

CHAPTER 11

An hour later, Violet says goodbye to the final customer, waving and blowing a kiss. "One more picture?" the brunette with a short blunt cut asks as she stands in the doorway.

"Of course." I drape an arm around my pretend girlfriend.

The woman giggles and points upward. God bless mistletoe.

I drop a kiss to Violet's cheek for the camera. She turns and plants one on my lips, and that's like a shot of lust straight to my groin. To my mind. Through my whole body. This whole pretend-girlfriend ruse is pretty awesome if it involves so much kissing for random cameras. Then I remember, Violet isn't into me. These fake kisses can suck it.

She breaks apart and says goodbye to the brunette. As soon as she's gone, Violet yanks down the blinds, locks the door, then breathes.

"So..."

"So..."

"You want to start?" I ask as I park myself on the leather

couch in the front of the shop. "Because it's a helluva lucky break that we both need a plus-one."

She sits next to me, crossing those lovely legs of hers. "I had the meeting with the landlord. He basically said he has offers left and right for a higher fee on my space. And my lease is up in a few months. Which means he'll be jacking up the rates."

"What an ass."

"But, if I can keep up this kind of business, then I can make the salon more popular, and I can afford the increase. So that's why I was calling you earlier. To see if you'd be amenable to pretending to be mine." She fiddles with her bracelets. "I don't want to put you out, though. I know last night was an exception, and if you have dates or whatnot planned with other women, or if this will cramp your style…"

I laugh loudly, setting a hand on her arm. "It's all good, and I don't have a *style*."

She knits her brow, speaking softly. "You kind of do, though, don't you?"

"Maybe I did, but I'm all about football this year," I say, pointing straight ahead. Eye on the ball.

"And that means you're a monk?"

"Took my vow before the season opener."

She tilts her head. "Jones was serious when he said you kept your…?" She lets her question trail off, not repeating the phrase my friend used last night.

"Snake in a cage?"

"Yes. That."

"I took my vow of chastity at the start of the season. He doesn't come out to play."

She arches a skeptical brow. "For real?"

I nod. "Yeah, for real. I did that for me, to keep my focus on the game. Then it became part of this informal pact between the four of us once we started playing well—Harlan, Jones, Einstein, and me. As soon as we had a winning record, we figured we needed to maintain our superstitions, so we've kept them up."

"And why that one for you?"

"Two reasons. First, my right hand still works. Like, really fucking well."

She laughs loudly.

"Oh wait. I forgot. No monkey-spanking comments in front of you."

"Please. That applied to my brother. It doesn't bother me if *you* mention it."

"Good. Feel free to talk about your solo habits too."

She rolls her eyes. "Keep dreaming."

"I will."

"Is pretend dating me going to be a problem for your monkhood?"

I laugh. "Since it's pretend dating, no."

"What was the second reason for the vow?"

"I just figured focusing on football only would be best for my game, and I need my game to be excellent."

She nods, taking it in. "Hence, the vow of chastity."

I pat the belt loops on my jeans. "Here's my chastity belt."

She slams a hand on her thigh, laughing. "Oh, Coop. I think your chastity belt was broken a long time ago."

I laugh with her because that's the thing about best friends' sisters. They know your dirt. They know who you were when you were six, moving to a new town with next to nothing. They know who you were when your face was covered in zits and your voice seesawed from high to low during the most awful time of life ever—puberty. They overheard you telling your friend about the night you spent with Katrina Smith your junior year of high school, and how quickly you came when you lost your virginity with the head cheerleader. Violet knows who I am. She knows who I've been. But there's something I don't know about her. There are parts of her that have simply been private.

"When was yours broken?" I ask, curiously.

A pink blush spreads across her cheeks. She lets her hair fall over her cheek. I can't resist. I brush it away. "Tell me," I say softly. "Was it Jamie? The guy I filled in for at prom?"

"Actually," she says, taking her time with her words as she folds her hands in her lap, "that's why he broke up with me. Because I wouldn't sleep with him."

My jaw falls open. "Wow. He's a total ass."

She nods. "He said if I wasn't going to put out, he didn't need to shell out for prom."

"Ouch," I say, cringing.

"Needless to say, I wasn't terribly interested in *putting out* for anyone after that." She meets my eyes. The look in hers is shy. "I lost my chastity belt when I was twenty."

I try not to imagine her soft, sensual twenty-year-old body, but it's a futile effort. Just talking about sex and virginity has me undressing her in my head, and that's the shit I need to stop.

Instead, I reassure her that I don't think it's odd she took her time. "Nothing wrong with waiting, Vi."

"Yeah?"

"Absolutely. Better to wait until you're ready. Until it feels right."

"I believe that too," she says, and for a flash, I wonder if it would ever feel right to her with me.

Then I reroute the conversation for real this time. I glance around her shop, gesturing from her to me. "It's kind of ridiculous that something like this—us supposedly being together—makes a shop more popular."

She pats my arm. "Sometimes, I think you don't realize the effect you can have on people."

My brow pinches. "What do you mean?"

"You think just because Jeff was so popular that you can fly under the radar. That doesn't happen anymore. Everyone wants to see you succeed because they love the team. They equate things like this—you and me supposedly being a thing"—she puts a heavy emphasis on *supposedly*, maybe as a reminder that it's all trumped up—"as part of the key to success."

"I suppose that's true. Greenhaven certainly saw it like that, and I don't want to rub him the wrong way. The GM basically does what Greenhaven wants when it comes to keeping players and letting players go." I give her the lowdown on what the coach said, then on my meeting with Ford. "He made it clear he doesn't want me backpedaling during the negotiations. It's all very sensitive. Like a dance."

"How long do you think they'll last?"

I drag a hand through my hair. "I'm not sure. Sometimes it takes a few days. Sometimes it takes weeks."

Her eyebrows inch up, and she stares at me as if I've done something terribly wrong.

"What?"

She leans closer. "Your hair." Her voice is softer, like it was earlier.

I watch her lift her hand. "Sticking up again?"

"You messed it up."

"You're dying to fix it, aren't you?" I ask, teasing.

She runs her teeth over her lip. "It's taking enormous self-restraint not to."

I throw down a challenge. "I'm not sure you can fix it without your lotions and potions."

She lasers me with a sharp-eyed stare. "You doubt me?"

"Yes. I doubt you," I say, loving the twinkle in her light-brown eyes.

She pokes me in the sternum. "You don't see me getting on the field and telling you that you can't get the ball in the end zone. You don't come into my shop and tell me I can't fix your hair with my bare hands."

My smile spreads. Damn, I love this feisty side of her. "It's so sexy when you talk like that about your...*bare hands*."

She lifts them, as if she's Wolverine and these are her weapons. She rises to her knees, inches closer, and smooths a hand over my hair. I tell myself to be cool, to be still, to not get turned on. Like I can enter the mind-over-erection zone.

But the funny thing is, I don't ruminate on how good it feels when her hands slide into my hair.

Instead, I study her. I stare at her neck. I'm mesmerized by the way she swallows—almost harshly as she licks a few fingers to wet them. I'm intrigued by how her shoulders rise and fall in a steady rhythm. My ears home in on the sound of her breath hitching as she slides her fingers back onto my head.

My chest burns, and the space between us falls silent. Her fingers glide through my messy hair, smoothing, straightening, taming. The only sounds are the hum of the heater and the faint sound of traffic from outside.

Her voice breaks the quiet. "I don't think I've told you this before..."

"Told me what?" I ask, my voice raspy, and for the briefest second, I hope that she's about to utter something magnificent like *I've never been this turned on before* or *can I just rub my tits against your face?*

The response to the first is *me, neither*, and the answer to the next one is *for as long as you want to, please*.

But she says something better. "Cooper, your hair is so soft."

The emphasis is on the *so*. As if she's tasting the word. As if it's rolling around on her tongue, lingering in her mouth. And when she moves back, sitting next to me, crossing her legs, I let my eyes drift down to her neck and the exposed skin above her cleavage, flushed pink.

As if she's aroused too.

I raise my gaze, blinking, trying to center myself and reconnect to this moment. To my friend. To my best friend's sister.

My voice comes out gravelly. "We probably need to let Trent know we have to keep this up."

"Yes, Trent," she says, and there's nothing to kill a mood faster than his name.

I'm grateful for the buzzkill. Being this close to Violet is dangerous. Something changed last night. I'm not sure how to name it—the way I feel being near her. But I like it. I like it too much for my own good.

She calls Trent and puts her phone on speaker on her thigh. Quickly, she explains what went down with the landlord, and I tell him about Ford.

"So, we wanted you to know," she says.

"Hey, I get it," Trent says, because even if he doesn't want us together, he's not a dick. He's a good guy. "And I'm glad this game of pretend can help you both. Feel free to tell any of your new clients, Vi, that if they want to go to the best sports bar in the Bay Area they should hit Trent's Brew Company."

I laugh. "I'll always send business to you, too, man."

"All right. Holly and I need to do inventory."

I scratch my chin. "Why do I feel that's code for something?"

"I wish it were. We really do need to do inventory," he says seriously, and I meet Violet's eyes and stick out my tongue.

She laughs quietly. "If you say so."

"Have fun pretending, and Cooper, don't touch my sister," he says in a deliberately stern tone, as if he's giving me a Very Serious Warning. He says it as if it's a ridiculous idea too. As if I'd never want to touch his sister.

But as we end the call and Violet grabs her pink purse, whatever shifted last night has become clear. I know how to name the feeling. I understand what it is.

I want to touch her.

I want to kiss her.

I want to taste her.

Last night, my body wasn't playing tricks on me. It was telling a truth that perhaps has existed for some time now. A truth that was dormant and is now awakened and insistent. It doesn't want to take no for an answer.

I'm wildly attracted to my best friend's sister, but I have to pretend I don't want to kiss her, touch her, fuck her, and take her home with me.

That's where the true faking starts for me.

CHAPTER 12

It's our impromptu first date.

We stroll along the streets of downtown Sausalito as night falls across the sky and the town's Christmas lights sparkle on signs and trees above us. We wander past the ice cream shop, and we drop into a wine store that's having a tasting. The sommelier is oblivious, but a customer drinking a red can't take his eyes off us. That might have to do with the fact that he's wearing a Renegades jersey. It's a Jeff Grant jersey, but hell if I care.

When we leave, he calls out, "Kick some Dallas ass this weekend."

I turn around. "Absolutely. Nothing less."

Out on the street, with the cool December breeze softly blowing, Violet takes my hand, and her touch ignites a spark inside me.

I look at our joined hands for a moment, liking how we fit. Then I remind myself she's just touching me as part of the date.

"Are you ready for this weekend?" she asks.

"Yeah. I think so. We had a tough practice today, but I think we'll take no prisoners on the field. I'm going to spend more time tonight studying the playbook."

"Don't you have it memorized by now?"

I smile. "I do. I'll memorize it even more."

She laughs, then her voice turns serious again. "Do you ever get nervous before a game?"

I look to the night sky, pondering her question. "Honestly, no. Because if I do, then I'll overthink every move. I need to be in the zone both physically and mentally, so I don't give myself time to feel nervous, if that makes sense. Mostly, I'm pumped full of adrenaline. But a focused kind of adrenaline that beats out the nerves and leaves only this intense desire to get out on the field and win."

"Intense desire," she says, like she enjoys the sound of those words. "You make football sound so passionate."

"Of course it's passionate. How else could you play but passionately?"

"I style hair passionately," she says, playful, fluffing out her hair.

"You touch hair passionately."

"I guess your hair just brings out the passionate hairdresser in me," she says as we reach the fountain near the ferry. A string of red and green lights decorates the ceramic fountain. The water gurgles a gentle tune. She snaps her fingers. "The Passionate Hairdresser! Would that be the most ridiculous or one of the most ridiculous names ever for a salon?"

I tilt my head and screw up the corner of my lips, as if I'm considering it. "Second most."

She gives me an intense look. "Because Curl Up and Dye is the most ridiculous, right?" she asks, emphasis on *dye*.

"That would indeed be the worst."

She laughs, then flops down on the edge of the fountain, gazing at the lights of San Francisco in the distance. "I have to say, Cooper, I'm so happy Jeff Grant finally retired. I know this city loves him, but I was rooting for you the whole time."

"Yeah?" I ask, sitting next to her.

"Of course. I never wanted to say it at the time, because I didn't want to put pressure on you, but I'm so glad it's your team now. Ever since high school, since I watched you play on Friday nights, I always wanted to see you in the pros."

"Are you coming to my game this weekend, then?"

She blinks, meeting my eyes. "What?"

"You say that like it's a surprise. You've been to a couple already. I get you, Trent and Holly and your parents and my mom and Dan tickets. You're my people."

"But this time I'd be coming as your *girlfriend*?" she asks, drawing quotes around the last word.

I sketch them back in the cool night air. "Yes, since that's what you are right now. And if you're my girlfriend, I would think you'd want to come to the game in that role. Wear that jersey you sleep in," I say, wiggling my eyebrows.

She lowers her voice. "I won't wear my sleep jersey. But I

will wear one with your number on it. Root for my man and all," she says, nudging me with her shoulder.

I drape an arm around her and pull her close. "You should absolutely root for your man. Besides, I suspect you'd be a good-luck charm."

"What if I'm not? What if you have the worst game of your career?"

I set my finger on her lips, shushing her. "Never say that again."

She smiles beneath my finger. "Sorry."

"You're not allowed to speak. You're in trouble for saying something horrible."

"You'll have the best game of your career," she whispers.

I nod. "Much better."

"And I'll be your good-luck charm."

"Excellent. That's what I thought." I lower my finger, thinking that's one lucky digit to be so close to those pretty lips. "By the way, you really thought I was a weird kisser, didn't you?"

Might as well get it all out in the open now.

She laughs, then arches an eyebrow, challenging me. "I can't seem to remember."

I shake my head. "You're killing me."

She taps her bottom lip. "Just give me a peck and remind me." She grabs her phone. "I'll take a kissing selfie."

"That reminds me. Ford wants me to send him one."

"Ford wants a shot of us kissing? He's the weirdo."

"It's for Instagram or something. He's setting up an account for me."

"Well, let's give him something to post."

She holds up her phone, selfie style, and I suppose it's time to find out how weird she thinks I kiss.

This time I lead. This time I'm in charge. I cup her cheek and look into her eyes. I swear, I fucking swear, I see desire flicker across them. She parts her lips, and I wait, and I wait. Making sure she wants it. Making sure, this time, she feels it everywhere.

I breathe her in, and it feels like I'm holding in so much. Then I kiss her.

I'm only gentle for a few seconds. I kiss her harder and deeper, and if she thinks this kiss is weird, then she's an alien. This kiss rocks the motherfucking world of kisses. Soon, she lowers her phone, and that's my cue to stop. But I don't, since she doesn't. She brushes her lips over mine, sliding, dusting, kissing. She flicks the tip of her tongue over me. I groan as her tongue slides between my lips, and we kiss, hard and greedy, for one, two, three seconds.

Then we stop.

She looks intoxicated. I feel infatuated.

She sets a hand on my shoulder. "Better send you home to memorize that playbook."

But the playbook I want to learn is the one for her body.

CHAPTER 13

When I return to my place a little after eight, with plenty of time for a good night's rest, I can't believe I actually do this, but I send a picture of me kissing Violet to my agent. His reply is swift—Awww. Melting from the cuteness. Xoxo

I write back, instructing him to never reply to a kissing photo again.

When I get into bed, my text notification winks at me. I groan, thinking it's Ford. But it's Violet.

> **Violet:** There's something I have to tell you.
> **Cooper:** Tell me.
> **Violet:** You're not a weird kisser.
> **Cooper:** I'm not? I was pretty sure I was. 😁
> **Violet:** Not at all.
> **Cooper:** A little bizarre? It's okay. I've had a day to process your condemnation.
> **Violet:** Not even a little, I swear. Not even the smallest amount of bizarre.

Cooper: What am I then?

I wait, my skin warm, my heart doing funny things in my chest as I stare at the bubbles that tell me she's tapping out a reply.

Violet: You're the opposite of weird.
Cooper: Ah, so a normal kisser, then. I can live with that.
Violet: No. God, no.
Cooper: An average kisser?
Violet: I'm almost afraid to tell you because I don't want it to go to your head, and it might be big already.
Cooper: It's big. Everything is big, Vi.
Violet: Can you see me roll my eyes from across the bridge?
Cooper: I can see it and I can feel it. But please, let's not digress. I can handle the praise. Heap it on me.
Violet: You're an amazing kisser.
Cooper: Yeah?
Violet: That's what I wanted to say in the car last night. But then your phone rang, and there was craziness, and yada, yada, yada. So, now I can tell you. Your. Kisses. Rock. I mean, for a pretend boyfriend. 😄
Cooper: So do yours. For a pretend girlfriend. 😄
Violet: Good. I didn't want you going to bed thinking your kisses were anything but epic.

Cooper: I'll take epic. But I'm not sure I can sleep now.

Violet: You need your beauty sleep. Good night, Cooper.

Cooper: Good night, Violet.

Violet: See you soon.

Cooper: See you soon.

Violet: Why does a moon rock taste better than an earth rock?

I laugh as I ask why.

Violet: Because it's a little meteor.

I find a laughing seal emoji and text it to her. I don't send Ford a screenshot of that. He'd have a field day with it. Just like I'm having a field night right now because it feels like neither one of us wants to say goodbye. Like I could text her all evening long.

It's only as I start to drift off that I realize I'm supposed to be keeping it in my pants this season. But we only kissed, I remind myself. My dick is safely in my drawers, thank you very much, and no way will it come out to play. I might want her, but at the end of the day, we're only friends who pretend.

A few years ago, the Miami Mavericks drafted a quarterback in the fourth round named Quinn Mahoney. Boasting strong college stats and an impressive bowl record, he was regarded as a solid, steady choice. He turned out to be a steal since the Mavericks went all the way to the Super Bowl with him in his second season.

Mahoney is a thinker. He's quick on his feet, possesses razor-sharp instincts, and is fast in the pocket. I admire the fuck out of him.

Mahoney is also the reason I'm up at the crack of dawn, lacing my sneakers, and pulling on a running T-shirt.

The dirty little secret about quarterbacks is this—you don't have to be fit to play the position. Ironic, isn't it?

Look around, and you'll see the guys in the league who are in the best shape are usually running backs and receivers. But the guys who lead the team downfield? Most won't be posing for the Abs-R-Us calendar. You don't have to be a specimen to know where to throw and launch a ball with on-the-money accuracy. A quarterback's best asset is between his ears and in his chest—brain and instinct.

But hell if I'm going to ever have anyone say about me what was said about Mahoney in his draft report.

Frumpy body with hardly any muscular definition. Mahoney doesn't look the part. His uninspired body type will turn off some teams.

Mahoney has a ring, a wife, a baby, and a fat contract, so his *frumpy body* didn't change his fortune.

Still.

Maybe I'm vain, but I don't want that kind of epithet

thrown at me. But more than that, I like being fit. I like how it feels. I like how it looks. I like the effort it takes to get there. And I don't ever want a woman to say Cooper Armstrong is uninspiring when he removes his shirt. I especially don't want Violet to say that. If the situation ever presents itself, I want her to rip off my shirt, tear off my shorts, and murmur, "Your body is unreal."

Then I'd show her how inspired this unfrumpy body can make her feel.

Crap. Fuck. Dammit.

I did it again.

My brain went there.

Out-of-bounds.

I lift my hand as I run up a steep hill. "This is your fault for being my closest companion," I mutter.

My hand doesn't reply.

"You could at least make a joke."

Still nothing. I lower my hand.

I force myself to remember the rules. Violet's a friend, a fake girlfriend, and my best friend's sister.

On top of that, I have a season on the line and a pact with my guys. Winning is my only job right now. And honestly, that's the real reason I run from Pacific Heights down to the marina and back up Divisadero on Thursday morning as the dark sky hugs the city by the bay. The streets are quiet. My only company is a lone car gliding by now and then and the rare early-morning exercise warrior. The first time I ran this steep stretch of road, years ago, it felt like my lungs were on fire and my thighs would burn to ash. Now, it feels like a good workout.

As I reach the top of the hill, my breath coming fast and hard, I turn around and inhale the view. My reward. The city lies at my feet. From here, I drink in the hills and homes, the curl of the early-morning fog, and the Golden Gate Bridge, a beautiful beast standing proud between the Pacific and the bay.

My gaze drifts farther, imagining what's beyond the bridge on the other side, in a little rental cottage tucked into the hills of Sausalito. Surely the woman who lives there is fast asleep under the covers. I wonder what she looks like sleeping. How her hair looks fanned out across her pillows. If she snores or breathes quietly. If she starfishes or curls up on her side near the edge of the bed.

I blink away the possibilities, shelving them in a drawer of things I will never know, right alongside what causes static electricity, and why the hell do baby carrots taste astronomically better than the regular small ones?

My phone buzzes in my shorts pocket with an incoming text. I grab it as I head the other direction, and it's like a reward for heeding the 5:00 a.m. workout wake-up call.

Violet: Since second grade, anything kid-related, and the time you threw the game-winning 26-yarder to Jones with 1:30 left against the Seattle Stallions.

I furrow my brow, trying to make sense of her message.

With the street unfolding blissfully on the downhill, I jog lightly as I reply.

> **Cooper:** I tried Google Translate with womanspeak as the language, but it came out as gibberish. Also, what are you doing up now?
>
> **Violet:** I open at eight, and there's a morning spin class calling my name. Anyway, the womanspeak translation is this—I'm practicing what to say in case anyone quizzes me about us at the game on Sunday. Those are my answers for what I suspect will be the top three questions.

Interesting. It's hardly 6:00 a.m. and she's already texting me.

Don't read into it, dickhead. She's covering her bases.

As I pick up the pace, zipping past a hipster coffee shop opening its doors, I text her back. Yup, I've become that idiot who's running while staring at his screen in the inky-blue dawn. And I don't care.

> **Cooper:** Is this a game of Jeopardy? Clearly, the last one is what was your favorite play your boyfriend made this season? By the way, excellent choice. One of my favorite plays too.
>
> **Violet:** Yes, and anything kid-related is the answer to what is your favorite charity to support since I figure

> that's a question anyone dating an athlete would need to have an answer to. Plus, it's true.
>
> **Cooper:** That's my answer, too, so we're in sync. But I think you're mixed up on since second grade. I met you when I was in second grade and you were in first, so since second grade can't be your answer to how long we've known each other.

I scratch my head as I slow at a light. A street sweeper trudges along as I jog in place. The light changes, and I run, replying before she can finish hers. And now I'm that idiot who's running, and texting, and grinning like a fool. And I still don't care.

> **Cooper:** Got it! Must be the first time I pulled your pigtails. That'll melt the hearts of anyone asking you.
>
> **Violet:** I never wore pigtails. But it's my answer for anyone who asks when I first had a crush on you. How is that for a totally adorable answer? 😉

As I run, I stare at the winking emoji like I can turn the symbol upside down and find some hidden meaning. I study it, searching for her true intention, until I nearly trip on a cracked section of sidewalk.

I regain my footing, reminding myself that her answer is a joke. Like Sierra at the auction, she's weaving the story everyone wants to hear—the hometown girl crushing on the guy who made good. It's a story that'll go down easily, something the press, the fans, and the players' wives will eat up with a spoon because there's nothing cuter than childhood sweethearts.

> **Cooper:** It's perfect.
> **Violet:** By the way, I don't actually think anyone will ask, but in the movies, when someone has a fake boyfriend or girlfriend, they always need to get their stories straight. Got any other questions for me as I prep?

I choose a true one. Something I absolutely want to know.

> **Cooper:** Yes. Truth. Do you really sleep in my jersey?

As I turn onto the next block, her reply dings. There are no words in it. It's a multimedia image, and it takes a frustratingly long time to load as I blast by a row of Victorian homes.

Then it lands.

I stop running.

I can't do anything but stare. There's a shot of her from the neck down in bed. She wears a long blue shirt with the number sixteen on it, the fabric hitting near the tops of her thighs. Her legs are bare and beautiful, stretched out on rumpled red sheets.

God help me.

I'm dying to know what she's wearing *under* that shirt, but this image will feed me for days.

The phone *dings* with another reply. It's a shot of the empty bed, and the words: And now I'm up. Time to spin.

I text her goodbye, and when I return to my house, my heart pounds harder, but I don't think it's from the run. I head to the kitchen, pour a glass of water, and down it as I click open the photo again. And I stare, and I stare, and I stare.

I might possibly salivate over those legs. So toned and creamy white. My God, even her toes look pretty with bright-green holiday polish on her nails. And those red sheets. I want to run through the city, across the bridge, and down the hills. I want to bang on her door, scoop her up in my arms, and spread her out on those sheets.

Then kiss every square inch of those legs.

And that keeps me occupied quite nicely in my shower. But then, as I run a towel over my wet hair, I ruminate on the questions she prepped for. What will my answer be if someone asks how long I've liked her? Violet has her finger on the trigger of her phony answer. I suppose my fake reply would be the same. *Since second grade.*

But my real answer? The one I keep locked tight in my chest would be this—*since last night*. It's been at least since last night that I've known how very much I like Violet Pierson.

Real like. Real emotion. Real fucking scary.

My heart beats harder, wishing she had a real answer that matched mine.

But my heart pounds in a whole new way when I run into Jillian that morning at our training facility and she shouts, "You're in big trouble."

CHAPTER 14

Her heels click across the concrete floor as I head to the locker room.

I clench my teeth. Jillian must have found out that Violet and I are a sham, and now she's going to lay into me for lying to her.

But am I lying? I flash back to this morning and the texts, to last night and the kisses, and there's nothing made-up about the way my best friend's sister has staked a claim on my mental real estate in the last forty-eight hours.

I turn around. "Why would I be in trouble when I'm so good?"

"*This*," Jillian says, her eyes narrow and accusatory as she brandishes her cell phone at me.

The tension prickles over my shoulders, but I've dealt with linemen who want to kill me. Though, in all fairness, Jillian's eyes right now are as intense as the Dallas defense.

I step closer to see what's on her screen.

It's the selfie from last night at the fountain.

She flicks her thumb to another shot on my new Instagram account. This one is of Einstein and me after he kicked a game-winning field goal earlier in the season. I chuckle to myself. Of course Ford would work another of his clients into the shot. But the dude is brilliant. Ford had his assistant post a picture of me from a few months ago, lacing up in the morning with the running shoes from the sneaker company I endorse, and then a shot of me playing basketball with kids at a local community center.

But Jillian fixates on the kiss, stabbing her finger at the screen.

I scrub a hand over my chin. "Yeah, it seems I might have kissed her last night. Am I in trouble now for kissing?" I ask, batting my eyes innocently.

She taps the toe of her red pumps and wags a finger at me. "You're in trouble for telling me it was none of my business that you and Violet were involved, and then going and posting a kissing selfie." She pokes my chest with a perfectly manicured silver nail. "And that was the cutest kissing photo ever."

She might as well be floating right now.

"Did you mean 'evah'?"

Jillian laughs.

"Also, I'm not the one who said it was none of your business," I say, pointing at myself. "That was Jones who said it the other night."

Like he heard his cue from offstage, the man who defended

my privacy after the auction rounds the corner of the corridor, appearing behind Jillian. When he sees me talking to her, he slows down and pads quietly, like a cartoon mouse sneaking behind a cat.

She huffs. "Then Jones is in trouble too."

Jones narrows his eyes and brings his finger to his mouth. I adopt the stoniest expression ever in the history of stony expressions.

"He should be punished," I say.

"Absolutely," Jillian says, while Jones whips out his imaginary flogger and smacks his own ass. *I've been bad*, he mouths behind Jillian's back.

The corner of my lips twitch. "Anyway, sorry I didn't tell you all the details. But you know how it goes."

Jillian brings a hand to her chest, and I swear I see hearts and flowers fluttering above her head. "I'm dying to know more. *Off the record.* Just for me."

Might as well serve it up. "We've been friends forever, and she's great. She's funny, supportive, smart, kind, and she keeps me on my toes. How could I not be into her?" When the words come out, there's not a false note in them.

Even though Jones wraps his arms around nothing and kisses his air-girlfriend.

A huge smile takes over Jillian's face. "Oh, this is just too perfect. And that's why I'm so excited to share some good news with you." She lowers her voice to whisper, "Since you're my new favorite Renegade."

Jones points to himself, doe-eyed, and pretends to cry.

"You mean Jones isn't your favorite Renegade?" I ask, figuring it's a perfect time to give Mime Jones as much shit as I can.

Her brows knit in confusion. "Jones? No. Why?"

"Oh, just because he's such a swell fella," I say with a too-big smile.

She gives me a look as if that's the craziest idea. "Swell? Jones? Maybe you mean swollen head. But enough about him. I wanted to find you because the hospital from the auction called and invited you to take a short tour of its new facilities, and I thought, wouldn't it be perfect for you and Violet to stop by, show your support, and see the kids? What do you say? Can you go with her?"

I smile. "Of course. I'll have to check her schedule, but Vi and I love helping charities for kids."

And that's not a lie at all either.

Jillian squeals. "You're the best! You're such a good guy. Unlike Jones. Who is right behind me, pretending to be a complete pig."

Busted.

I crack up as Jillian swivels around and points at the man who now holds his big hands in the air like he's being arrested.

"You're a total troublemaker," Jillian says.

"I take that as a profound compliment," he says, intensely serious.

She marches up to him and parks her hands on her hips. "How did you think I didn't know you were here?"

Jones laughs and shrugs. "Maybe because you don't have eyes in the back of your head?"

She taps an earlobe. "I have ears, Jones."

"It was fun regardless," he says in a flirty tone.

She shakes her head, though she's clearly amused with his antics.

"Let me know the details, Jillian, and we'll be there. Meanwhile, I'll get this asshole out to the field, where he can make trouble with some balls."

"You can't resist throwing your balls to me, can you, Coop?"

We head to the field and practice our passing routes, where Jones shows off exactly how much he loves catching balls.

CHAPTER 15

"Looking good, Cooper."

I snap my gaze to Greenhaven after we finish a light practice—no pads for today.

He's only called me by my first name once before. Since I signed, I've always been Armstrong. That's it. Plain and simple. "Thank you, sir," I say, still curious about the change in names.

But he gives no indication as to what it means, only a quick, crisp nod. Then, another first. He cracks a smile. It's barely there, just a hint of a grin, and it disappears quickly on his gruff, weathered features. "Looking forward to Sunday?"

"Absolutely."

He walks the other way, across the grass. For a moment, I watch him, his bulky figure cutting a solitary path up the field, crossing the fifty-yard line. I first talked to him the day I was drafted. As is the custom, the scouting director made the phone call to tell me I'd been picked in the first round, then said he'd put the head coach on the phone.

Talk about nerves. I was flooded with them, knowing I was getting an audience with the man.

When Greenhaven picked up, he said, "Congratulations, Cooper. We couldn't be more pleased to have you as a Renegade."

"I'm thrilled, sir. Absolutely thrilled. This is a dream come true."

It was the culmination of everything I'd ever hoped for, and it was the start of a whole new future.

Only, it was the start of the longest wait of my life. Jeff Grant had been injured the season I was drafted, and the team picked me expecting Father Time was winning the battle with the star. But Grant was legendary for a reason. He recovered faster than anyone expected and returned even stronger, defying the odds for three endless years. During that time, I was Armstrong to the coach, and Grant was Jeff.

That's a small thing, and it didn't bother me. There's a pecking order on a team, and you have to do your time. I hadn't done mine yet.

Greenhaven has used my surname all season long too.

Until now.

Maybe this means nothing. But maybe it means more. Maybe it means I'm *his guy*. Not just for a few games, but for longer. For a couple years, maybe even for several. Perhaps enough to make me the face of the franchise. The prospect makes me a little giddy—not gonna lie. That's the dream among dreams come true. I turn the other way to head inside. I'm nearly tempted to text Ford and tell him what Greenhaven just called me.

But I don't.

Because it feels like something that's between player and coach.

And honestly, if I did, I'd sound like a pathetic ass trying to decipher a text message from a lover.

What does this mean, Jones? Does this mean she likes me, Harlan? Can you tell if she's into me, Einstein?

I roll my eyes at the prospect.

Nope. I won't be that guy. Instead, I'm going to enjoy this moment for what it is. *Mine.*

As I reach the goalposts, I stop and turn to the stands. They're empty, of course, and this isn't even where we play games. But I imagine the stadium on Sunday. It's sold out, packed with cheering crowds. That's who I'm most grateful for. You play for the owner, you play for the team, you play for the coach, but at the end of the day, we're all playing for the fans.

Once inside the locker room, I grab my phone from the top shelf. But before I can text Violet about Jillian's request, Harlan smacks me on the back.

"C'mon, you lazy-ass passer. Time for steps."

"Let's do it."

I follow him back outside, where we're joined by Jones and Rick. We trot to the stands, and section by section, we run up the steps, down the steps, till we cover the stands.

Spent and exhausted, as we should be.

The four of us flop down in the second row. I grab the hem of my T-shirt and wipe the sweat off my forehead. It's fifty-five degrees in December in San Francisco, and I'm sweaty as hell from the workout.

"Are we ready now?" I ask.

Harlan drags a hand through his long hair. "I'm ready."

Jones taps his ankles. "My stinky game socks are *not* in the wash."

"And I've got a brand-new bag of bubblegum. My little sister picked it up for me since she loves pink bubblegum," Rick says, his dark eyes flashing confidence as he imitates kicking a ball.

They stare at me. I roll my eyes as I jerk my fist up and down. "I'm all good." Then, I lean forward, parking my hands on my knees, and stare out at the open field. "You guys don't really think that's why we're playing well, do you?"

Rick laughs. "Who knows? We haven't lost a game since Pittsburgh more than a month ago."

"But Coop has been a monk since the season started," Harlan says. "I haven't cut my hair in months, and we did lose a few games."

"But we've won way more than we've lost, though," Rick says. "So, is it the superstitions, or something else?"

"When you have a ritual you believe in, you do it even if you lose," Jones answers, his deep voice full of certainty. "Wade Boggs ate chicken before every baseball game, win or lose, rain or shine. He's a Hall of Famer now. He didn't alter the routine. Serena Williams bounced the tennis ball five times before every serve, no matter what. And for us, we have a winning record, so we keep doing it."

Rick raises a finger, his voice inquisitive, as if he's in class. "So, does it extend to the postseason? If we make the postseason."

Like we're synchronized swimmers, the four of us lean forward and rap our knuckles on the back of the seats in front of us. "Knock on wood," I murmur, even though it's plastic.

"We need a guru of superstitions and what they mean," Rick continues. "We need to make sure it's all good."

"Guys," Jones says as he wraps his hands tighter over the back of the chair in front of him. "Here's what the superstitions are about for us. The rituals are a pact. It means we have each other's backs." He draws a circle in the air around us. "Whether it's the four of us, or whether it's the eleven guys on the field on Sunday—we do this together. We're a team."

He holds up his fist, and I knock mine to his, then Rick piles on, then Harlan slams his hard against the top. "To the pact," Jones says, and we echo his words.

Soon, the guys stand and file out, and I tell them I'll catch up. I'm alone in the stands.

I grab my phone and tap out a text to Violet. But before I hit send, I dial her number instead. God bless texting, but sometimes a voice is better.

She picks up on the second ring. "I'm in the middle of coloring a blond red and white for Christmas, so make this good."

Her voice is worlds better. "You didn't actually answer the phone while dyeing hair, did you?"

"Of course. I can multitask like nobody's business. Just

kidding. I'm actually in the back office paying bills. I finished a tint early so I have ten minutes before my two p.m."

"I won't keep you long. But Jillian asked if we can visit the Children's Hospital. Would you be able to?"

"Of course. I'd love to," she says, her tone genuine. "I meant it when I said I love helping with kids."

"Does next Tuesday work for you? Pretty please," I ask, making my voice as sweet as pie.

"Well, since you said pretty please, the answer to Tuesday is yes. That's my day off next week anyway."

I smile. "Have I mentioned you're a most excellent pretend girlfriend?"

"Have I mentioned you're a most excellent pretend boyfriend?"

"Why, no. You haven't. Do tell me what an amazing fake boyfriend I make." I kick back, lifting my sneakers onto the seat in front of me and crossing my ankles.

She sighs happily. "My salon is packed again today, and every single stylist is booked solid for the next few weeks. Suddenly, everyone wants a cut from here, or a holiday updo for an event."

I run my palm over the back of my head. "Speaking of, my locks are getting shaggy."

"You are welcome here anytime," she says, then laughs. "My God, if you were in the salon, I'd sell out appointments for the year."

I sit up straighter. "Yeah? And the landlord would be off your back?"

"Probably. But you don't have to do that. I don't want to take advantage of you."

I scoff. "First, you can take advantage of me anytime. Second, you're helping me with this whole boyfriend-girlfriend deal. If cutting my shaggy hair helps you, I'm all yours."

"I like the sound of that," she says softly, and my heart threatens to kick into overdrive.

I rein it in. "One more thing. Do you want to sit somewhere special on Sunday? I can get you tickets with the players' wives and girlfriends in a suite, which is cool but it's kind of cliquey. Or I can get you tickets on the fifty-yard line with Trent and Holly and my mom."

She inhales deeply. "Gee. I don't know. Sit with a bunch of women I don't know, or sit close to the action? I just can't decide. Okay, if I have to, I'll be at the fifty-yard line with pom-poms."

I laugh. "Now that's a sight I eagerly await."

"You have a little quarterback-cheerleader fantasy I need to know about? Because I'll have you know I don't have an ounce of cheerleader blood in me."

"I know that about you. Trust me. I do." Violet was never the ponytail and pom-poms girl. She was into fashion, indie music, jewelry, and her friends. In high school, I'd run into her tangled up in a group of girls, laughing, listening to their iPods, trading tunes, and looking out for each other. She'd wave and say hello. I'd always give her a hug, wrapping my arms around her, inhaling her hair, enjoying her softness against me. The memory is so visceral.

Whoa.

I liked to touch her back then?

Of course you did, dickhead. She was a babe then, still is, and you like babes. Doesn't make you the Sherlock of Romance to put that together.

"Hey, Vi?"

"Yeah?"

"Since high school," I say firmly.

"What do you mean?"

"If anyone asks when I first had a crush on you, that's what I'll say."

"Oh. Is that so?" she asks, and I can hear the smile in her voice. The invitation too. Like she likes this idea.

"We can't very well have the same answer, can we? So, since high school sounds about right."

When I end the call, I don't need anyone to tell me what our conversation means. It means she's coming to my game this weekend, and for a guy like me, there's something a whole lot of awesome about playing in front of the woman you like.

CHAPTER 16

The crowd roars. They slam their feet against the stands, pounding out a cheer that thrums through the stadium and echoes across the field.

It's third and nine. There's no breathing room in this game. Two minutes till halftime, and the score is still tied. We've traded leads every possession, it seems.

I take the snap from shotgun as three receivers race downfield. My heart pounds rocket-fast, but my nerves are cool. My brick wall of linemen buy me time, as they've done all day, holding off Dallas. I scan for an open target, but McCormick is swarmed by the secondary. Another receiver is flanked too. I find Jones, scrambling to break away from the cornerback.

"C'mon, man," I mutter.

I'm waiting.

Fucking waiting, ready to throw the second he's free.

A big-ass lineman busts through, but the center slams into

the guy's barrel body, protecting me as I launch the ball the instant Jones peels away from the coverage.

He doubles back, and those beautiful hands are ready. The ball soars, and he pulls it down pristinely, cradling it, then carrying it for twelve yards before he runs out-of-bounds, avoiding a tackle.

I pump a fist and point downfield. We run, line up for the first down, and we're all business the rest of the way. I hand off to Harlan, who powers his way around the defense, gaining eight yards, and putting us squarely in field-goal range.

But hell if I want to go for three right now. I glance to the sidelines, briefly making eye contact with the coach. He gives a nod, and even though that's his go-to gesture for nearly everything, I know this time it means go for six. A new wide receiver comes in, bringing the play with him.

After the snap, I'm in the pocket, and I throw easily to an open McCormick, who takes off like a cheetah. The rookie hauls ass twenty-five yards into the motherfucking end zone.

The crowd erupts.

My heart jackhammers.

I run to McCormick, clapping him on the back and congratulating him as we trot to the sidelines.

"You rock, man."

"No, you fucking do," the rookie says, with a baby-faced grin.

"Beautiful," Greenhaven grunts as I grab some water and Einstein does his job with the extra point.

That gives us a welcome seven-point lead at halftime. I take off my helmet, turn to the stands, and my eyes find my family. My mom waves a number-one foam finger, and her boyfriend, Dan, plants a kiss on her cheek. Ford shakes his hips back and forth, calling out something unintelligible that's clearly a compliment. Next to them, Trent and Holly are hollering happily, arms raised in the air. I give them all a huge thumbs-up.

My gaze drifts beyond my best friend to his sister, the woman I've known for most of my life, who's smiling up a storm and cheering like this is the best day ever.

And so far, it's pretty fucking good.

I give her a tip of the proverbial cap, then a lopsided grin. The smile that returns my way is priceless, like a shot of pure happiness in my body.

Ford drapes an arm around Violet and says something to her.

I turn away and head to the locker room with the team.

CHAPTER 17

Violet: Oh my God. He's taking me into the lion's den.
Holly: Do you have your retractable claws ready to go?
Violet: No, but he makes it seem like I need them. He says the players' wives are dying to meet me, and I need to be on my toes.
Holly: I have no doubt they want to know who's about to become the new leader of the pack in one fell swoop. That's probably what they think.
Violet: Stahp. Just stahp. I'm nobody.
Holly: Oh, Vi. I love you and all, but if you're the quarterback's woman, you're on track to become everybody.
Violet: This is unreal.
Holly: They all know you might become the new Queen Bee.
Violet: Will they want to dethrone me then? Steal my stinger? Wait, do queen bees have stingers?

Holly: No, they're full of eggs that then become larva, so it's kind of a bad example.
Violet: Here goes nothing.
Holly: Just smile and wave...

Holly: It's been thirty minutes... Are you alive? Celine Dion already sang.
Holly: They've taken you.
Holly: You've left me. You've officially left the little people behind, and now you're eating sushi and canapés and crudités in the players' wives' suite.
Holly: Incidentally, if they have any yellow tail, bring me one. I love yellow tail.
Holly: And mini cupcakes.
Holly: But they probably don't have that. Unless they're made of air, and I don't want an air cupcake. Back to the original plan. Bring me a sushi roll.
Holly: If I ever see you again.
Holly: Okay, halftime is nearly over. Celine is done, Lady Gaga made a special appearance, the marching band for all the high schools in the universe performed, and you're gone.
Holly: It was fun being friends. Sniff, sniff.
Violet: The sushi was to die for! I stuffed my bra full of tuna rolls just for you.

Holly: Bitch.

Violet: But seriously! They were all so nice. The center's wife is so sweet. She invited me over. The guard's wife had her baby with her, and he was totally cute, and I even cuddled and held him. McCormick's girlfriend from high school was there. And the tight end's fiancée was amazing. Admittedly, I was nearly blinded by her ring. It's about the size of my head. No lying.

Holly: I know that's not a lie. Those ladies have ring bling!

Violet: Ford made it seem like the lion's den, but I didn't feel that way at all.

Holly: Did they ask about Cooper? Did they give you the relationship third degree?

Violet: Yes. How long we've been together, when I knew I liked him, how we started dating, what I thought of the game. It was easy to answer everything.

Holly: Because you have the answers ready!

Violet: I sure do.

Holly: You always have...

Violet: Yes, I'm aware. Very well aware. Also, such a shame to miss Celine and Lady Gaga and the marching for all the high schools in the universe. But I'm sure they'll be at the next regular season game 😊

CHAPTER 18

Rick chews the pink gum, spits it out, and brushes his teeth on the sidelines. Then, the defense holds off Dallas in the third quarter, but their line nearly kills me. I manage a few handoffs and a couple of short passes, but we don't push past the fifty-yard line.

Dallas gets possession, and they march downfield with precision. My chest tightens, and I pace along the sidelines, eager to get back in because they seem on the cusp of something big. But we hold them to a field goal chance, and then something beautiful happens. They miss it, the ball going wide past the goalposts. That sends a bolt of energy into the crowd.

We take the field, pumped. I do my job, like I've done since I was five. Since I was ten. Since high school. Since college. Since the start of the season. Drive downfield, throwing pass after pass from the pocket, my wall of Mack Trucks protecting me.

We reach the twenty, and a short pass to Jones sends him

running into the end zone to pad our lead. A lead we never look back on.

When the game ends, the crowd bursts into cheers. Horns blare. Whistles sound. Drums pound. We're one more game away from the playoffs. So close I can taste it.

On the field, a local sports reporter thrusts a mic at me, and I give my best "We just played all four quarters and stayed focused" kind of lines. When she walks off to find another player, my eyes drift to the stands, scanning, searching. They land on faces I know well, and the buzzing in my chest is like a note held long on a guitar. It shifts to a faster tempo when I see Violet. She's waving, her arms swinging wildly over her head, her chestnut hair blowing in the breeze. When she realizes she's caught my attention, she freezes, then jumps up and down in excitement. Something is happening. Something is building.

I follow my instincts, and they tell me to run over to the sides, find a security guy, and ask him to bring her onto the field. A minute later, she's escorted to me. I wrap her up in a hug and lift her high.

"You're all sweaty and dirty," she says, laughing.

"That's because I play hard."

"You sure do."

"Did you enjoy the game?"

"Loved it."

"Yeah?"

A smile curves her lips. "Every single second."

The noise in the stadium vibrates in my chest, a mixture of cheers, chatter, and fifty thousand feet pounding to the exits. But this conversation feels entirely private. Just for us.

So does the kiss she gives me next. She brings her mouth to mine, dusts her lips across me, and steals the breath from my lungs. I'm vaguely aware of the pop and flash of cameras capturing this moment. It doesn't last long, but the kiss feels like it's for me, not the lens.

And maybe it's the way my heart hammers after the victory, or maybe it's the taste of her lips, but it's enough for me to bring my mouth to her ear. "Hang out with me tonight."

She pulls back and looks up at me. "Yeah?"

I swallow and nod. "Yeah."

She has to know what I mean.

Ford insists on dinner first, taking the whole crew to a trendy new restaurant in Russian Hill, where he regales us with stories of the deejays the Clippers use on their chartered flights, and the time he took his superstar pitcher for the Yankees shopping at Target after midnight because that was the only time the guy wouldn't be recognized and the leftie simply wanted to pick out his own towels. "Orange with gray polka dots. Those were some *fine* towels," Ford says.

"When you finish his contract, be sure to get Cooper some pretty new towels at Target at midnight too," Trent says. "He wants pink with white polka dots."

Violet chimes in. "Don't make fun of polka dots. That sounds like an adorable combination."

Ford points at Violet, like he agrees with everything she's saying. "We should go all out for him, Vi. We will spare no expense. Hand towels, washcloths, bath towels. What do you think?"

Violet laughs, flicking her hair off her shoulder. "I think Cooper would love pink towels."

"Pink, orange, gray. Whatever." I shake my head as I look at Ford, my voice a touch more serious than usual. "Just don't talk about the contract like it's a done deal. We don't want to jinx it."

"Contracts aren't jinxed, my man. On-field superstitions are all well and good, but contracts are not part of the sphere of jinxing." Then he lowers his voice. "Besides, don't you worry. I'm still dancing, and trust me when I say I look good on the dance floor."

He raises his arms like he's got the moves.

"Just watch out for that overbite when you dance," I say, giving him shit since his teeth are pressed into his lips.

"Winning makes you feisty."

"You don't know the half of it," I murmur as I steal a glance at Violet across the table. She's chatting with my mom now.

Ford yanks me close. "Gotta say, it's so damn entertaining that she doesn't like you. She's pulling it off like a most excellent actress, with the pink polka-dot shit."

"Yeah, she is," I mutter, and then let his comment sink in.

Is he right? Have I misread Violet since the kiss at the

fountain in Sausalito when I felt the vibe between us shift? From the texts to the phone calls to the last kiss, I sure thought we were moving toward something more. Am I wrong? She agreed to hang out later, but maybe she only wanted to hang out *here*.

My chest tightens, and unease seeps into my bones during the rest of the meal. As we finish dessert, I replay the conversations I've had with her lately, trying to find the true meaning. Friends or maybe something more? More, or just friends like we've always been?

When the meal mercifully ends, Ford continues playing cruise director of my personal life when he says, "Hey, Vi, since I drove our boy to the restaurant, why don't you take him home?"

I know what he's up to. Violet valeted her car, and Ford figures someone will snap a pic or post a tweet about us waiting for the car together at the new eatery.

But he's also given me an excuse to leave with her without her brother thinking I'm up to something. I'm not technically up to something. I simply don't want the night with her to end, and I'll find out soon if she feels the same way, or if Ford is right.

Ford heads out first, grabs my bag from his car, and hands it to me. As I take the bag, I wince, my shoulder tight from the game.

The valet does a double take when Violet asks for her car. I tip my chin. "Hey, man." The guy beams and races to find her vehicle.

I grab a twenty from my wallet and tip him well when he returns. Then I settle into the passenger seat as Violet drives. When she turns on Fillmore, I roll my shoulder back, trying to loosen the muscles.

"You okay?"

"Just sore."

When we reach my home, she doesn't pull to the curb and say *have a good night*. She pulls into the narrow driveway, and I grin as I reach into my bag to grab the garage opener. I hit the button. Anticipation threads through me as the door rises. She pulls into the garage, and I want to punch the air because the night isn't ending.

"You didn't want to park at my house the other night," I say.

She swallows. "It was easier not to then."

"Is it easier to park here now?"

"I'm not sure if it's easier, or simply what I'm doing."

And I'll take that as a good sign. I'll take that as the sign that Ford was wrong tonight.

I tell myself to just let the night unfold. We go inside, and I drop my bag in the hallway, heading straight for the freezer in my kitchen. I grab an ice pack and wrap it around my shoulder.

"Does it hurt a lot?" she asks.

"Standard war wound."

She gives me a look. "Seriously. Are you injured? Are you being the big tough guy who doesn't let on that he's hurt, then plays through the pain?"

I scoff. "No. I'm not injured. This is just normal soreness. This is how I usually feel after a game."

"Gee, I wonder why. Could it be throwing thirty-yard passes with regularity while linemen try to mow you down wears on the body?"

I smile. "But it's nothing a beer and an ice pack won't cure. Do you want a white wine?"

She says yes, so I grab a bottle I think she'll like, then a glass. As I unscrew the cork, our eyes meet. Hers glitter with something—anticipation, maybe? I don't know what's happening, but I also know *exactly* what's happening.

Something.

That's what my gut tells me. That's what my instincts say. And those are the tools I rely on when I'm in the zone. I let them guide me now.

Something's been crackling between us for the last week, ever since she won me. Since I visited her salon, invited her to the game, and texted. Since she sent that photo.

As she leans her hip against my island kitchen counter, looking like she belongs here, wearing her number-sixteen jersey with a smudge of dirt streaked across it from when I hugged her after the game, my mind narrows in on one thing—her body.

How she reacts to the way I stare at her. How her lips part. How her cheeks grow pinker.

"You're almost in the playoffs," she says, her voice wobbling more than usual, as if she's a bit nervous.

"*Almost* being the operative word." I crack open a beer, hand her the wine, and toast. "To almosts," I say, my voice echoing in my quiet home.

"To almosts," she replies, and the air between us crackles and hums.

I turn on some music on my phone, and even though I'm tempted to crank up my favorite rock anthems, I find something that better sets the tone. Then I want to smack myself for going for mood music.

"Are you trying to put me to sleep?" she asks, laughing.

I wink. "Just making sure you're paying attention."

"Put on the good stuff," she says, and I switch to a playlist that starts with "Rolling in the Deep" by Adele.

"I love this song," she says, her face animated as she taps her foot against the floor.

"I know. That's why I picked it."

I adjust the ice pack as she sings the first few lines, then I join in for the chorus, using the beer bottle to sing into, while she cranks up the volume courtesy of her wineglass turned microphone.

"We would kill it in a karaoke duet."

"But I insist we sing 'Islands in the Stream.'"

"I accept your insistence," I say, as I refill her wine and grab a second beer.

We make our way to the living room. Violet tips her chin at the Christmas tree in the bay window. Red ribbons and silver ornaments hang from the plastic branches, along with ceramic candy canes and green felt mini-stockings. Blue and white lights flicker on and off, set on a timer for the evenings. "You set up your tree. It's adorable."

I give her a look. "Violet, how long have you known me?"

"Twenty years. Why?"

I gesture to the perfectly appointed tree. "Do you really think I pulled that off? Lined up ornaments with that kind of pinpoint precision?"

"Let me guess. Mama Armstrong did it?"

I laugh. "You guessed correctly. The whole nine yards."

"Tell Mama Armstrong she's a masterful decorator. Oh wait, I'll tell her myself when she comes by for her color."

I flop on the couch, adjusting the ice pack.

Violet kicks off her shoes and joins me, tucking her feet under her. "Does it hurt still?"

"Not really."

She arches a brow as she takes another drink of her wine. "Not even a little?"

I hold up my finger and thumb as the music shifts to "Wonderwall." "Okay. A smidge."

She puts her wineglass on the coffee table and waggles her fingers. "Let me help."

I put my beer on the table too. "Ooh, is this where we play quarterback and physical therapist?"

She rolls her eyes. "Is the team's PT your fake girlfriend?"

Violet cracks her knuckles, sets a hand on my shoulder, and tells me to face the other way. I turn so I'm looking at the stark white wall and the framed prints of Italy and Spain, New Zealand, and Australia, all the places I want to go someday. I release the ice pack, letting it fall to the floor. Her hands curl over my shoulders, and my reaction to her touch is instant.

I groan because it's so goddamn good as she digs her fingers into my flesh. "Tell me about meeting the players' wives."

"They were fantastic," she says, and as she recounts her time in the suite, I sink into the magnificent sensation of her hands on me, her thumbs driving into my muscles, her fingers kneading my flesh. The way she touches me sends sparks through my body as if an electric current sizzles under my skin, spreading into my every molecule.

While I'm on edge like this, everything in me buzzing toward her, I close my eyes and images flash. All the ways I want this night to go. How good it feels to have her hands on me. How dangerous it could be to get closer. Her brother. Our friendship. Whether she feels the same way. My contract. The pact. My focus.

But then I think about how I feel with her. How my heart bounced around in my chest when she watched me today. How warmth radiates through me when I see her texts. How her lips feel sliding across mine.

I remind myself that I take chances all day long. I play a risky, violent sport for a living. I can either stay safely in the moment of this impromptu massage, or I can run into the fray.

I choose risk and all the possibilities of reward.

I lift my hand to take hers, running my thumb along her

wrist. Her breath hitches. Her hands still. She stops moving as I glide farther up, brushing my fingers from her wrist to her forearm. She trembles.

I don't rush it. There's no one stopping us. No line coming after me, trying to take me down. It's only us, here in my home. No agents, no photographers, no Maxine. No one else.

I run my thumb back down over her palm to her fingers. I thread mine through hers and clasp. She squeezes back, her breath rushing against my neck. And it's then that the moment unfurls into something else entirely.

To something unquestionable.

I cover her hand with mine, and in one strong move, I pull her around me and onto my lap.

Her eyes widen, shining with longing. They lock with mine.

"What are we doing?" she asks, her voice so goddamn breathless it's like an extra dose of an aphrodisiac after I've already consumed the whole bottle.

I bring my face nearer, my forehead touching hers. "*This.*"

Then we kiss, and it's the first kiss that belongs solely to us.

CHAPTER 19

This kiss is ours, and as my lips crush hers, she melts against me. We sink into this, lips, tongue, teeth. Heat, hands, arms.

I lean back into the soft couch cushions and bring her closer, kissing her the whole time. She loops her hands in my hair, sliding her fingers through the strands.

We kiss as if this is what we've wanted all along. A private kiss. My hands cup her cheeks, and I hold her face as my kisses do the talking.

It's you.

You're what I want.

Stay.

Part of me should be shocked that these thoughts trip through my brain. But then, I'm not surprised at all. My head's always been in the game with her. My heart has tried to get in on the action from the start.

From the moment she kissed me onstage at the auction, it felt right. Now, as we kiss on my couch, tongues tangling and lips sliding, our kiss feels inevitable. I tug her closer, craving more of her taste. She presses against me, her chest to mine, her legs sliding around my thighs so she's straddling me.

I curl my hands through her hair, loving the way the soft strands spill over my fingers. As I slide my tongue inside her lips, she whimpers. It's so fucking arousing. I kiss her deeper. Her taste goes to my head, short-circuits my brain.

The sounds she makes are killing me—little murmurs, sighs, and needy gasps. I want to swallow them whole, give her everything she needs.

With a rough hold on my hair, she yanks me closer and kisses me so hard the world sizzles into a white-hot blur. Then she bites down, her teeth scraping my lip, and I groan.

My Violet has a rough side. And I like her rough. She lets go of my hair, slides her hands up my chest, and curls them over my pecs through my button-down shirt. She presses hard, like a stop sign.

Her breath comes in harsh pants. "What are we doing?"

"Kissing like we can't stop."

"I know," she says on a sigh, her breath fluttering over my face. Her eyes are hazy, as if she's drunk on this kiss. Drunk on me. But she needs something too. Reassurance? Confirmation?

"What do you want, Vi?"

I watch her, tracking every move. She swallows, breathes out, and brings her hand to her hair. She brushes it from her cheek, looks down, then back up. Her eyes pin me. "I need to know something."

"Yes?"

"Do you want me?"

"Are you kidding me?" I scoff, grinding up against her. It's unmistakable how much I want her.

"I know. But do you want *me*?"

"God, yes." I brush the backs of my fingers across her soft cheek. "You have no idea. How can you think I don't?"

"I just need to know it's me, and not because I'm a warm body."

"Give me more credit than that."

She covers her face with her hand. "I didn't mean it like that. I just want to know…"

I peel her hand off her face and make her look at me. "That I want *you*? That I want this gorgeous, funny, sharp, clever woman who keeps me on my toes and takes no shit from me?"

She smiles. "Yes."

I press a soft kiss to her lips. "It's you."

She curls her hands over my shoulders, taking a deep breath. "I don't want to get hurt."

That feels like the heart of the matter. She's afraid, and I hear it in her voice. "Are you afraid I'll hurt you?"

She nods and bites her lip as if she's holding something in. Her worry curls around my heart, charges through my body. Wanting her is simply a fact in my universe. It's gravity. It's the moon spinning around Earth. I'm barely thinking of our history, of all the ways our lives overlap. I'm only thinking of the next few minutes, and how good I can make her feel.

I lift her chin so she looks me in the eyes. "I won't hurt you. I want to make you feel good."

"You do make me feel good," she says, clasping my cheeks in her soft hands. "That's what's freaking me out."

I drop a kiss to her nose then dust my lips across hers in a promise. "Let me make you feel even better."

She shivers as she ropes her arms around my neck. Her eyes glitter with lust. "What would you do?" Her voice is feather-soft, an invitation.

With her on my lap, looking at me as she plays with the ends of my hair, my entire body hums. I bury my face in her neck, blazing a trail of kisses that makes her squirm as I lick a path to her ear then back to her lips, whispering against them, "I want to kiss you…*everywhere*."

That last word hums between us. It slips back and forth between our mouths. With my lips, I press *everywhere* into hers, and she kisses it back to me.

"*Everywhere*," she repeats, her mouth sliding over mine. Her voice is raspy; the word sounds as if she's been hypnotized by it. It sounds like a prayer.

"Will you let me?" I ask, my fingers straying down her body to the hem of her shirt.

She sits up straight. "What about you? Your vow of chastity?"

"The way I see it, if I keep it in my pants, I can still touch you without breaking the vow."

Her eyes drift to my crotch. "I can't touch you?"

I shake my head. "This isn't about me."

"Cooper."

"Violet."

"Are you sure?"

"Look, I want to be totally blunt—my dick isn't coming out to play. But what part of *I want to kiss you everywhere* involves my dick? None of it. The things I want to do to you, I want to do with my tongue and my lips. Will you let me?"

She inhales sharply. "Will I let you? How is that even a question?"

"You still haven't answered me," I say as she slips off my lap and scoots backward along the couch, moving her head toward the armrest. I slide her along the rest of the way, laying her flat across the cushions, setting a pillow under her head. I straddle her, my palms by her shoulders. I raise an eyebrow. "Do we have a yes, Violet?"

"Are you really going to do this to me? And I can't touch you?"

"Do you want to touch me?" I ask, dragging my hard length between her legs. She's so warm already, and I can feel the heat of her arousal through our clothes.

She answers with a lift of her hips against me. She loops her arms around my neck. "I do want to touch you."

I bring my mouth to the hollow of her throat. I lick her there, drawing her taste into my mouth, then kiss along her neck, sucking on her jaw until her body arches into me again and again, begging me.

"Another time for me. Let me touch you," I whisper.

"Yes. God, yes. Please."

We stop talking about getting hurt, and who's touching who, and what any of this means once I unbutton her jeans. I tug them down her hips, and each inch is a revelation—of flesh, of curves, of femininity.

"My God, it gets better and better." Her purple panties are tiny, with illustrations of zebras on them. They're unbearably sexy and ridiculously adorable at the same time. Like her. I love a good pair of black lace underwear, but I love these because she's not trying too hard. She is sexy, and she is sweet because she wears purple panties with zebras.

"Those are some damn cute panties," she says.

I place my hands together in prayer. "Please God, I've been a good boy. Let me help pick next time you go shopping."

"Let's see how good you can be," she says, a naughty glint in her amber eyes.

"Challenge accepted."

I peel her jeans down the rest of the way, savoring the view of her bare legs. She kicks off the jeans, and as I drag my gaze along her long, lush frame, my hands tremble. I want to do right by her. I want to worship her and make her feel adored.

As I crawl back up her body, my hands trail along her legs, tracing a path up the soft flesh. She shudders in the wake of my touch, then gasps when I drag a finger across the damp panel of her panties. My cock is thick and begging to come out. But that's not in the cards. Tonight is for her pleasure and hers alone.

"Can I convince you to take this shirt off?" I say, tugging on the end of her jersey.

She gives me a saucy look. "Doesn't it turn you on to see me in your number?"

I rise onto my knees and drag a hand over the bulge in my jeans. "Yes. Fucking immensely. But you know what else turns me on?"

"What?"

"Tits. Specifically, your tits. And I want to taste them and suck on them before I kiss my way down your body and settle between your legs, where I plan on introducing you to my tongue. And my tongue is very much looking forward to making your pussy's acquaintance."

She laughs. "My God, when did you become so dirty? Wait. Don't answer. I don't want to know."

I wiggle an eyebrow. "You don't like this side of me?"

She reaches for the bottom of her shirt, tugs it off, then grabs her tight tank top and shucks that off too. She's down to a pink bra and purple panties, and I'm about ready to burst. I'm so turned on, wanting her so much. I ache everywhere.

"I love this side of you, actually," she says as she reaches her arms behind her and unhooks her bra, letting it fall to the floor.

The heavens part. Angels sing. Her tits are glorious. Perfect teardrops, rosy nipples tipped up, asking to be licked.

"There is a god," I murmur as I lean in to suck on a nipple.

"Cooper," she says, starting my name like an admonishment then turning it into a long, low moan of pleasure. "*Cooper.*"

"You have world-class tits," I say when I come up for air, palming those beauties. "They're fucking astonishing."

"You've been checking them out?"

"I have been an admirer of your breasts for a long, long time. They're my happy zone."

She smiles and laughs. "Play with them, then."

"If I'm dreaming, I don't want to wake up."

I'm a devoted aficionado of racks, and honestly, I could spend an entire day, hell, a week, staring at breasts. I've often lamented the lack of paid jobs in this area, and in my future utopian society, this sort of ogling work will indeed warrant financial compensation. For now, I'll gladly accept a volunteer assignment gazing at these beauties.

I lavish praise on her gorgeous globes with my tongue. "So sexy," I murmur as I lick. "So delicious." I pinch her nipples. "So perfect." She writhes under me, moaning and groaning and grabbing my head in the valley of her tits. She's as turned on from this as I am.

I move down her body, drop my head between her legs, and kiss her sweetness through the panel of her panties. I can taste her arousal through the cotton. I can feel it on the tip of my tongue. "I don't think you can wait either."

She rocks her hips up into me. "Cooper," she begs.

"Yeah, baby?"

"Take them off."

I close my eyes for a second, letting the sheer sexiness of those three words imprint on me. When I open my eyes, I peel her panties to her ankles, and she helps kick them off. There's something intensely erotic about the way she moves. How she lifts her hips so I can tug her clothes down, making it easier for me to undress her. Like she trusts me. It's such a small thing, but it says we're in this together.

I see it in her eyes, too, as I slide my hands up her legs and gaze at her face. Her golden-brown eyes are trained on me—wide and guileless. At one point, she licks her lips, flicking the tip of her tongue over them. I reach her inner thighs, parting them, absolutely in lust with the view of her glorious pussy. One brunette landing strip and the rest is smooth. And there, right there, is where I want to be.

She glistens. My throat burns as my hands inch closer. The sight of her arousal, all silky and wet, is so ridiculously enticing.

I lower my face to her legs and kiss the inside of her thigh. She quivers. I kiss the other thigh. She shudders. "Does that hurt?"

"No," she murmurs.

I slide my tongue close, so close, right along the edge of her pussy, teasing her. "This?"

"God, no," she says, lifting her hips, seeking me.

"I told you I won't hurt you."

"I know. I didn't mean like that."

"I know what you mean." I press the gentlest kiss to her clit. She draws a sharp breath. "But I want to show you I'll do the opposite."

"Show me."

I skim my hands under her thighs and wrap my arms around them, my shoulders settling between. "Open your legs more for me."

She spreads wider, and I'm in heaven at the first taste.

She's so slick and wet, from the way we kiss, how we talk, how we touch. I explore all that sweetness with my tongue, lapping her up, flicking the tip against the delicious rise of her clit. She grabs my hair, clutching it like a lifeline, holding on so damn hard.

And then I bury my face between her legs, licking and sucking and kissing. Devouring.

She's mostly quiet at first, and I register that she's a soft moaner. I grin wickedly. Because now I know this private detail. Violet is a moaner, and I love that. It's like I've been given the secret keys to her body. I have the code, and I'm unlocking her. She's a rocker, too, because soon she rocks into my face, holding my hair like a pair of goddamn reins. I fucking love her abandon. I love how hot and wet she is, how good she tastes, how her noises turn to feral groans when I bring my mouth to her clit and suck hard on that gorgeous little diamond of pleasure.

Her noises turn into something else. My name. "*Cooper*," she calls out, and it sounds husky, raspy.

I lick her faster, learning her cues, discovering how she likes it. I bring a finger to her center, sliding across her slickness to see if she wants to fuck my finger, too, and she goes wild as I slide into her, her legs clamping tight around my head like a vise, and I love it. She tugs my hair harder.

"Please," she whimpers hoarsely, then it turns into a chant, like a plea. Her hands grip harder, she thrusts faster, and my world spins further away from me.

She's so close, and I'm so turned on. A blast of pleasure ricochets down my body, an overwhelming reminder of how much I want to be buried inside her. I'm practically dry humping the couch, I want her so much. I want to fuck her and kiss and touch her and do everything to her.

But I can't. So I kiss her pussy that way. So she knows I want it all. I devour her sweetness.

"Coming," she cries in the faintest voice, and then I grip her ass and drink her as her taste floods my tongue, making me high—higher—on her.

When Violet comes, she detonates. She writhes and pants and screams, and it's beautiful and primal. She can't stop saying my name, and it sounds intoxicating on her tongue. "Cooper, oh God, Cooper, oh God, Cooper."

Yeah, I like this chant. I like it a lot.

I slow my moves, easing her down with a final soft kiss. Then I move away from her sensitive clit and kiss her hip bone, her navel, up to her breasts. She cradles my head between them, lacing her fingers through my hair.

"Cooper, this is my happy zone," she says softly.

"Mmmm. Me too." I look up and meet her gaze. Her eyes are hazy. Her cheeks are flushed. Her expression is one I want to remember forever—my woman, thoroughly satisfied. "Can I do that again?"

"You better," she says playfully.

"How about now?"

She gives me a look like I can't be serious. "Now?"

I nod enthusiastically.

"Really?"

"Yes, really."

"Please," she says her voice beautifully desperate, then she pushes me down her body. That move right there, her hands shoving me back to her sweetness, is my new favorite part of the night, as she makes it patently clear where she wants me.

I return to her, and I kiss her once more, going slower, taking my time, learning how she likes it when she's already had it once. I work her up to a second time, kissing, licking, building, gliding, until she flies off the edge once more, thanks to my fingers and my mouth and my dirty desire to taste her pleasure all over again.

Afterward, I scoot next to her on the couch and wrap an arm around her. She sighs and snuggles against me, her naked body pressed to my clothed one. "You're like a limp noodle," I murmur, loving her postorgasmic state of bliss.

"My noodleness is all your fault," she teases.

I move her hair off her neck and press a gentle kiss to her soft skin. Another sweet sigh is my reward. The lights of the tree are flashing blue and white against the window when "Wrecking Ball" begins, and I groan.

"C'mon, karaoke king. Sing it with me," she says.

"You know how I feel about Miley."

"But this song. It's so epic. Just the chorus at least?"

And seriously, with her naked in my arms, how can I not do her bidding?

A little later, she gathers her clothes as if she's going to leave. I furrow my brow. "What's this?"

"Don't you want me to go?"

I sit up straight. "Um, no."

"You don't?"

"Seriously? Why on earth would I want you to go?"

"Because…" She flaps her arms, as if she's gesturing to us and what's happening.

"Because…you can't fly home? Are you trying to fly, Violet?"

She laughs and rolls her eyes. "I just figured…"

"That I'm a playboy who'll kick you out," I say, and grab her waist and tackle her.

She laughs.

"You forgot I can tackle," I say, tugging her under me on the couch. "I don't just throw. I can tackle, and pin you, and keep you."

"Yeah?"

With her under me, I stare into her eyes. "Can you stay?"

"You really want me to stay?"

I roll my eyes. "No, I'm lying. Get out."

She tries to swat me, but I pin her arm. "Cooper."

"Stay. Just stay."

"Why do you want me to?"

"I want you to sleep next to me. Why is that so hard to understand?"

"Okay, I get it, but I don't have my sleep shirt. I don't want to break the routine, and I don't want to sleep in something I wore all day, especially since it's kind of dirty after you hugged me."

"You say all this like I don't have a perfect solution to that problem."

Thirty minutes later, she's in my bed, wearing nothing but one of my jerseys. Honestly, if there's a sexier sight than her in my bed wearing my number, I won't believe it.

CHAPTER 20

My day off is glorious, even though Violet leaves before the sun rises. She dusts a quick kiss to my forehead, whispering, "I need to open the salon by eight."

I'm so exhausted from playing ball yesterday, as I am every Monday morning during the season, that I barely manage to drag my ass out of bed to say goodbye when she takes off. I put on my game face a couple hours later when I hit the links with my boys on a crisp December morning.

That's when the real pretending comes in. Ironic that I'm not faking a single moment with Violet, but now I need to act like I didn't do unspeakable things to my best friend's sister when I meet him for a 10:00 a.m. tee time.

Thank fuck Trent and I aren't playing solo, because it's hard to look him in the eye. Some voice in the back of my head tries to speak up, telling me that sooner or later I'll need to come clean with him. Trent is my rock. He's my solid, steady best friend in the whole damn world. I grew up with him, sneaked beers with him, shot hoops with him, and leaned on him. Hell, I was the best man in his wedding two years ago, and Violet was a bridesmaid. And damn, did she ever look stunning in a pale-yellow dress with little straps that showed off her shoulders.

There I go again. Drifting back to her. I chase away thoughts of the woman I want and try to focus on being in the moment with my friends. Today's not the day to fess up.

Jones adjusts his glove as he chats with his brother. Nearby, Rick and his best friend from college down their morning coffee, while Harlan ambles over to us, along with his brother-in-law. This is our regular crew, and we try to play once a month.

"Hey, man, any word on the contract?" Trent asks as he finds his club.

"It's anyone's guess. The GM might be waiting to see if we make the playoffs. I'm trying my best to keep it out of my mind."

"The real judge of a quarterback is whether he takes his team to the postseason," Trent says absently. He takes a few practice swings as if he hasn't just hit the nail on the head with regard to the waiting game I'm playing with the GM.

"Don't I know it," I say, a small prickle of nerves skating up my back. I'd really like to know if I'm going to be in San Francisco after this season. It's entirely possible the Renegades won't pick me up, and I'll have to fly where the free agent skies take me. Baltimore, Buffalo, Houston, New Orleans—who knows? Tension winds through me. I'm a lucky bastard to play in my hometown, and I don't want to give up seeing my friends and family this often. I raise my gaze to my teammates. I love these fuckers too. I want to stick with them. I want to take them all the way into January and beyond.

"Guess that means you'll be keeping up the dog-and-pony show with Violet for a little longer?"

My golf bag is suddenly the most interesting thing in the universe, and I take my sweet time hunting for my driver. "As long as we have to, I guess. You cool with that?"

"I'm cool with it. Even though it's really fucking weird to see you with her."

I look up. "Because I'm such an asshole, right?" I say with a mischievous grin.

"You're a total dickhead."

"But seriously. Why is it so weird?" I press him, expecting him to make another playboy comment, like he did at his bar. But that's not what he says.

"You've never gone ass over elbow for someone You're married to football, Coop." Then he strolls to the tee at the first hole.

I stand, unmoving, smacked upside the head by a hefty dose of reality. I've never been head over heels, and that's why my breakup with Kelly in college didn't faze me. Briefly, I wonder if my pretend breakup with Violet will hurt when it comes. Immediately, my chest twists at that unpleasant thought. *Breakup* and *Violet* are two words that shouldn't occupy the same sentence, and if I let my mind wander in this direction, I'm going to play a shitty game of golf.

I want to enjoy the hell out of my day off, since I enjoyed every single second of my late night.

I've just started to the tee when Jones stops me with a strong hand on my arm. He nods to Trent. "He has no clue how you really feel?"

"What?" I ask, brow furrowed.

"How you feel about his sister," he says out of the corner of his mouth.

I give him a blank look.

Jones laughs. "That's priceless. That expression on your face. Almost like you believe your own bullshit."

"My expression is that you're about to ruin a beautiful game of golf."

His chuckles continue. "You might be able to fool someone who doesn't *want* to see you're nuts for his sister, but you can't fool me. I heard how you talked about her to Jillian. You're in so far over your head."

I level him with my gaze. "And I saw the way *you* looked at Jillian. Think you might be in over *your* head?"

Now his expression is blank. "What are you talking about?"

"C'mon. You know she doesn't date players."

Jones rolls his eyes. "Don't even try to change the subject to matchmaking games."

"Watch me change it again." I point to the green. "Time to take my shot."

"But you know, Jillian is a badass babe," he says.

I grin and nod in acknowledgment.

I'd have to say the same is true for Violet, and when I'm done losing terribly at golf, I take off for Sausalito.

CHAPTER 21

When you're raised solo by a strong single mom, you learn certain things. How to live on a budget—ramen is your friend. How to do laundry at a very early age—if you hear my mom tell the stories, I was separating whites and darks at three years old. How to treat a woman—don't show up out of the blue without a gift.

That's why I stroll into the hair salon on Monday afternoon with a bouquet of violets. They're stunning, a rich royal purple, and they're tied with a silver ribbon.

"Hello, Sage," I say with a broad smile to the receptionist with the metallic-colored hair.

She giggles. "Hi, Cooper."

"I'm looking for the lovely lady who runs this shop."

"I'll get her for you," she says with a huge grin, her bangles jingling as she rises. "She's nearly finished with a cut."

"I'll just wait, then," I say, and make my way to the white couch.

But before I can park my ass, the click-clack of heels echoes across the floor. "You look gorgeous, Dani. And you are going to have the best time on your trip. I can't wait to hear all about it," Violet says to a customer, and when I hear her voice, a strange feeling erupts in my chest, like bubbles. I'm a goddamn soda bottle near her. Maybe that's what's going on with this odd sensation, like my world is suddenly effervescent.

"And you know I'll tell you everything. I always do," the woman replies.

I turn to see Violet hugging a high-cheekboned blond whose hair falls in pretty curls over her shoulders. I suppose I should admire Violet's handiwork, and how lovely the woman's 'do looks. But my eyes are on the brunette and that little black skirt she wears, paired too seductively for my own good with black boots that reach her thighs.

Those thighs.

My face fits so fucking well between those thighs.

And now my dick is sitting up and taking notice.

Focus on her face, idiot.

But that only intensifies matters because...those eyes that glitter, that skin that glows, those lips curved in a surprised but happy smile...

The bubbles are gone. Now I'm just burning with lust.

"Hi. I wasn't expecting you," she says as her client leaves.

I hold out the bouquet. "I brought you flowers."

Violet's smile grows even wider as she takes them. "They're gorgeous."

"Like you."

Sage giggles, and from a nearby salon chair, an audible sigh falls from a customer's lips as another stylist snips her locks.

Violet brings the flowers to her nose and inhales. "They smell sweet."

Like you, I mouth, just to her.

A pink flush spreads over her cheeks. "Let me get water for them. Follow me back?"

"Of course."

As Violet escorts me through the salon, a few heads turn, and a woman parked under a hair dryer snaps her gaze to us and widens her eyes. I'm all smiles as I follow the most beautiful woman in the room, the town, the whole damn city. The view is stupendous. Her ass looks fantastic in that tight skirt, the fabric hugging her curves deliciously.

"I have a vase somewhere in the utility closet," Violet says, glancing back at me as she walks past the shampooing sinks. She flashes me a smile that says we have a secret. That secret is I know what she sounds like when she comes on my lips.

My dick twitches with the fond memory of last night, making his presence in my pants even more noticeable. Cocky bastard. We reach the back of the salon and turn down a short hallway. I peer into one of the low-lit rooms and do a double take when I see a massage table in an empty room. "I didn't know you did massage here."

"Full-service spa, baby," she says, stepping ahead of me to reach for the doorknob of what I presume is the utility closet.

I call an audible in my head, though, changing the play right here on the line of scrimmage. I reach forward, grab her free arm, and tug her back.

She nearly stumbles, but I steady her, then pull her into the massage room.

"What are you doing?" she whispers as I close the door.

I grab the flowers and set them on the massage table.

"What I've been thinking about since you left this morning," I say, as I walk her back to the wall beside the door, line up my body with hers, and kiss her.

Fuck, she tastes good. Like lip gloss and spearmint. I kiss her rough, with a singular goal in mind—kiss the breath out of her. My plan works. She slinks her arms around my neck and angles her lush body against me as she gives herself over to this kiss. I get lost for a minute in her taste, in her lips, in the feel of our mouths crushing together.

When we separate, she blinks, licks her lips, and says, "Wow."

"All day. I've been thinking about that all day." My voice is rough, full of need.

"You have?"

"So much."

"Me too," she says, then tips up her chin, asking for more.

I grab her chin and bring her face closer. My lips are millimeters from hers, and for a few seconds I let this moment extend and unfold, our lips so damn close, nearly touching. Wanting and waiting. Then I slam my lips to hers, hungry for her. So damn hungry and greedy. I could kiss her all day. I could kiss her all night. I don't want to stop. Because there's so much of her to kiss. So much skin and flesh. I travel along her jaw, kissing her there as she gasps and moans and sighs my name. I push against her harder, grinding my hips into her body, and she pushes back. I bend slightly at my knees, finding a better angle, then rub my hard-on against her, right fucking there. "I've been thinking of how you taste. How you felt on my tongue."

"Oh God, me too," she says, rubbing shamelessly into me, her voice like a confession.

"Yeah? What do you think about?"

She drags her finger over my top lip. "These perfect lips. The way you went down on me." She cups my cheeks, stares into my eyes. "Mostly, how I felt when I looked down my naked body and saw this pretty face between my legs."

The world goes up in flames.

Hot lust floods my veins, and my groin aches—just fucking aches for her. "That's so fucking hot. I loved tasting you. I fucking loved making you come. Can't get it out of my head. The way you sound. The way you move."

"How did I sound?"

"Like you were desperate for me."

She moans. "I was. I still am."

I can't resist. I inch my hand under her skirt, rubbing my fingers against the cotton panel of her panties. She's soaked, beautifully wet for me, and I need to feel all this slick heat. Need to touch her. Judging from her instantaneous reaction to my fingers—how she rocks against me—she needs it too.

"Let me," I rasp out.

She glances at the door, worry etched in her eyes. "I have an appointment in ten minutes."

I flick my finger against her swollen clit through the panties. "Baby, I don't even need that much time."

She bites down on her bottom lip, holding in a cry. "I shouldn't do this at work," she manages, a feeble protest.

I drag my finger across her center. I'm fucking relentless. "Say the word and I'll stop."

No words come. Only whimpers. Only murmurs. Only gasps.

I bury my face in her neck, licking her skin to her ear. "You're the boss, Vi." I slip a finger inside her panties, and the blood rushes straight to my dick. She's so soft and so wet. "No one knows you're in the empty massage room, getting your sweet little pussy fingered by me."

She sinks into my touch, whimpering my name. The way she says *Cooper* thunders through my body. It's pure, liquid lust.

I grind against her, letting her feel my hard length. "All day long. My golf game was total shit. I'd line up a shot and think about the way you taste. I'd take a swing and remember how you moved against my mouth. You're on fucking repeat in my head," I say as I stroke her, my fingers sliding across all that heavenly sweetness.

She rocks with me, moaning, "I can't take it. It's so good."

"You've been thinking about coming again, Vi?"

Her eyes squeeze shut. Her breath rushes fast. "So much."

"Are you glad I stopped by?" I thrust a finger inside her, feeling the way she clenches me tightly. So fucking tight that I burn. My skin prickles with heat. My body floods with nothing but longing for her. I add a second finger.

Her mouth falls open and her head lolls back, hitting the wall. "So glad," she says, panting as she fucks my fingers.

I growl her name. "I jacked off to you in the shower. God, it felt so fucking good."

Her eyes snap open. "What were we doing? When you came?"

"I was fucking you, Vi. I was fucking you hard. Your palms were against the wall. Your hair was in my fist. I wasn't a gentleman in the least."

"Were you rough?" Her voice is colored with excitement.

"I gripped your hips and pounded into you, and I fucked you hard until you screamed my name."

She moans my name now, as if she's demonstrating how she'd sound. She dips down on me, grinding into my hand as I rub my thumb over her sensitive clit. "I got off to you too," she blurts out. "This morning after I was home."

"Yeah?" I ask, and this turns me on even more. I didn't think it was possible to be more wound up than I am right now, but picturing her with her legs spread, fucking her own fingers, does the trick. My entire body is strung tight with this raging desire. "What was I doing?"

"You wouldn't let me touch you. But I wanted you so much, and I begged you to come on me."

My brain goes haywire from her dirty mouth. I'm white-hot in every damn molecule in my body. I rub my hard-on against her hip just for the barest relief as I finger-fuck her. "You want to see that? That gets you off?"

"I want to see you naked," she says, and her voice is the most desperate sound I've ever heard. She grinds and rocks and thrusts, and all I can think is how much I want the same things with her. How absolutely fucking much I want this woman under me, over me, beside me. *With me.*

"You will, baby," I say, as I crush my mouth to hers, kissing her right when I know she's about to shatter. As I kiss her, I feel as if I'm devouring her pleasure with my mouth, as if I'm swallowing whole the sounds of her orgasm as she comes on my hand.

A minute later, when she seems to float down from her high, I say with a grin. "By the way, I got you another gift."

"You did?" Her voice is raspy.

"I thought you might need these," I reach into the back pocket of my jeans and hand her a pair of bikini panties. Green with a giraffe print on them.

Her eyes widen. "They're adorable." The meaning fully registers. She brings her hand to her mouth. "Cooper, did you come here knowing you were going to make me come?"

I shrug happily. "What can I say? I was optimistic."

After I leave, I tug my Giants hat low and drop on my shades, feeling like a fucking orgasm dispensary, and I couldn't be happier, even when a man with a beer belly and a dark mustache stops me. "Cooper Armstrong?"

"Hey there," I say with a smile, going into friendly-with-the-fans mode, since I don't know this guy from Adam.

But he seems to know me. He extends a hand. "I'm Ren Watling. I own this building."

Dickhead.

"Nice to meet you, Ren," I say, since he's Violet's landlord. I shake his hand.

"Business has been great. I'm thrilled. I hope you come around more often."

My lips twitch in a smile. "I hope to come around more often too."

Later that night, after I cook myself a dinner of salmon and green beans and study the playbook, my phone dings with a text message.

> **Violet:** Thank you for the afternoon delight. By the way, do you like my new giraffes?

When the multimedia image loads, I find myself with a shot of Violet from the waist down in her new panties and nothing else.

Giraffes are my new favorite animal.

CHAPTER 22

When practice ends on Tuesday, I shower at the training facility, put on jeans and a nice navy-blue button-down shirt, and grab my keys. I'm meeting Jillian and Violet at the Children's Hospital in forty-five minutes, so I make my way toward the players' lot. But before I can leave, a herd of elephants sounds behind me, shouting my name.

I spin around to see two frazzled intern types. One is a skinny guy with a beaky nose, and the other is a tall dude with a military-style haircut.

"Coach wants to see you," the skinny guy shouts.

"He asked us to find you," the military guy adds.

"Okay," I say, as a fleet of nerves launches in my chest.

I take a deep breath and smile. *Don't let on that you're as nervous as a reality show contestant who might be cut.*

I walk alongside them, making idle chitchat as we head down the corridor. *And now, on this week's episode of* Passers on the Chopping Block *is none other than Cooper Armstrong.*

We round the corner to Greenhaven's office, and every step feels like I'm one step closer to the guillotine. Last summer, I watched a docu-special on NFL training camps where the head coach of the Los Angeles Devil Sharks called a defensive back into his office and let him go on camera.

"I'm going to release you, Troy," the coach said in a coolly even tone.

The defensive back simply nodded and thanked the coach for the opportunity.

My chest ached watching that, a throbbing sympathy pain. Troy could have been any of us, at any moment, on any day.

Like today.

My heart lodges in my throat, beating painfully with a wish to stay.

Ironic how the game itself rests in my hands on any game day, but my own fate isn't mine to hold. All I can do is lift my chin high when we reach the wooden door with GREENHAVEN etched into the plaque in simple white letters.

"Here he is," the skinny guy says, pointing to the coach, who's on the phone.

"There's the coach," the other dude says to me, also stating the painfully obvious.

The coach motions for me to come inside. The chorus boys walk away as I cross the threshold into the decision chamber.

Will he stay or will he go? Only Greenhaven knows if Armstrong will get the ax.

Greenhaven holds up his finger to signal he's nearly done with his call. "It'll be done by five, I trust," he says firmly.

My shoulders tighten.

"I don't want any trouble this time," he adds, in that rough voice that terrifies three-hundred-fifty-pound linemen and two-hundred-twenty-five-pound quarterbacks alike.

He cracks a smile. "Thank you. Let me know when it's done."

He hangs up the phone, clears his throat, and strides around his desk, leaning against the front of it.

"Sorry about that. I was ordering a gift for my wife."

I blink, knitting my brow. "Oh."

"Emily loves antique tea sets, and she saw one a few weeks ago when we were in wine country on a day off. I'm having it sent to her at the house, but when the delivery company stopped by earlier, no one was there, even though I left instructions…" Greenhaven stops and waves a hand in the air. "Who cares? Bottom line—I want to make her happy."

"Of course. I'm sure she'll love it, sir."

Just rip off the Band-Aid, man.

He hasn't even asked me to sit down. Isn't he supposed to issue his directive from the power pose behind the desk? Instead, he's leaning all casual-like, and I have no fucking clue what he wants.

"I think she will too," he says then takes a breath and scratches his chin. "In any case, Emily asked me to find out if Violet has any eating restrictions."

I shake my head in surprise. "Excuse me?"

He laughs and waves a hand like he needs a conversational do-over. "Wrong order of info. First, she wanted me to invite you and Violet over for dinner, and second, she wanted to know if Violet has any food restrictions."

Relief pours through every vein in my body. My shoulders relax. A smile occupies all the real estate on my face. "She doesn't have any, sir. And thank you very much. Dinner sounds great."

He claps me on the back. "Excellent. I'll get you a date shortly."

He says goodbye and returns to his desk, and I'm dismissed with a dinner invite instead of a pink slip.

Except he didn't give me a date, and now I'm left wondering if the dinner will happen if we don't win this weekend.

CHAPTER 23

Shane's light-blue cast is propped up on the cushy couch. The curly-haired thirteen-year-old isn't even my teammate, but he shouts encouragements as I work the controller. "Go long!"

"I'm trying, man." I jam on the Xbox thumb stick, aiming the on-screen ball at the receiver, but my shitty-ass screen-self throws a pick instead. The cornerback intercepts it and runs straight into the end zone.

"Dude! Did you see that?"

The triumphant cheer comes from Tina, a ten-year-old with glasses who just had her fifth corrective surgery on her right foot. She's a huge Renegades fan and wears a number sixteen shirt that could double as a dress. Shane, meanwhile, is recovering from a broken leg, courtesy of a car accident, and he's sporting a sweatshirt.

Joining us is Carlton, who looks sharp in his eye patch, since he had retina surgery. He's on my team here at the Children's

Hospital, since the kids figured he'd need the extra help, given he only has half his vision.

Turns out I'm the one who needs help. My dirty little secret? I suck at *Madden NFL*.

Violet, however, rocks. She takes over for Shane and proceeds to march her team downfield and straight into the end zone. "Take that," she shouts.

I stick out my tongue.

She laughs at me.

We've been here for a few hours already. After the hospital administrator gave us a tour of the new wing, and I visited as many patients as I could and signed as many casts as possible, a group of kids convinced us to play Xbox in the hospital's game room here on the third floor. It didn't take much convincing, to be honest. This is my favorite part of these kinds of visits. Chill time with the kids in the game room. The walls are a bright yellow, the TVs are huge, and the video games are plentiful. Jillian has parked herself in a quiet corner of the room, tapping away on her phone. That's her job—to be here if needed but to fade into the background if not.

"Can't we switch to *NBA 2K*? I can school all of you at basketball," I say.

Violet laughs then pats my shoulder. "But you know I can beat you at that too."

I scowl. "Apparently, my girlfriend has been practicing video games behind my back."

Violet's eyes widen when I say *my girlfriend*, and I flash her a smile. She feels like my girlfriend. For real.

Shane laughs, and Carlton cracks up. "Cooper, you're terrible at *Madden*," Carlton says in his pipsqueak nine-year-old voice.

A nurse knocks on the open door. A redheaded girl with bright-blue glasses stands at her side. "Hi there. This is Natalie. She's eleven and she had a fantastic day," the nurse says with a cheery smile.

Immediately, I pop up from the couch and head to the doorway. "Fantastic days at hospitals are the best days," I say.

Natalie lifts a hand to wave. "I got the results of my one-year scan today."

My eyebrows rise. "That so?"

She nods and smiles, showing two missing teeth. "The doctor said I don't have leukemia anymore."

Violet gasps.

I hold up a palm, and Natalie high-fives me. "Best news ever," I say with a huge grin.

"That's amazing, Natalie," Violet says with a wobble in her voice. She clears her throat, speaking evenly now. "What are you going to do to celebrate? Do you want to hang out with us?"

Natalie nods, then looks at her parents in the hall behind her, who gesture that it's okay for her to join us.

"Natalie, do you like sports?" I ask as she enters the game room.

She nods enthusiastically. "I like ice skating and gymnastics and roller derby. I went to the roller rink last week, and I had the best time. The roller derby girls were there, and I decided I want to play roller derby."

"What would your roller derby name be?"

"I would be Smashalie."

I crack up. "That is most excellent, Smashalie. I don't think we have roller derby on the Xbox, but I would love it if you want to be my teammate in *NBA 2K*."

But Natalie has very little interest in the video games. Ten minutes later, she puts down her controller and turns to Violet on the other side of her on the couch. "Are you one of the nurses?"

She shakes her head. "No, I'm here with Cooper."

"Are you his sister?"

She laughs. "No." She lowers her voice to a whisper. "Don't tell anyone, but I'm his hairdresser."

Natalie's eyes widen. "He has a hairdresser?"

She nods my way. "Of course. How else would we make sure his hair looked so messy all the time?"

"His hair is super messy. But yours is pretty. Did you do your own hair?" Natalie asks, pointing to Violet's coffee-colored hair, twisted up on one side in a small silver barrette.

"I did," Violet says. "I can pretty much do any style you can imagine."

Natalie raises her hand and touches her own hair. It's a little longer than her shoulders. "I didn't have hair for a while. But I have some again now."

"You have gorgeous hair." Violet stops, considers it, and says, "Have you ever worn a French braid?"

Natalie shakes her head. "I tried, but they're hard to do. Can you actually do a French braid?" she asks with complete wonder in her tone.

"I can do two French braids. One on each side. If you wanted three, I could even do that."

Out of the corner of my eye, I see Natalie raise two fingers, then whisper, "I really want two. The roller derby girl I liked had two French braids."

Soon, I lose track of the game. Instead, I can't take my eyes off Violet. She and Natalie have moved to a corner of the couch. Violet is kneeling by Natalie's side, her fast hands lacing chunks of red hair into a neat, tight braid down one side of the young girl's head. When she reaches the end, I take a closer look and see Violet has looped the bottom through with a French braid she'd already woven down the other side. *Holy hair skills.*

Violet grabs her phone, snaps a picture, and shows the back of Natalie's head to a girl who, a mere year ago, didn't even have hair.

"I look like a roller derby girl now," Natalie says in awe.

"You're Smashalie," Violet declares.

My heart expands in my chest, thumps hard against my rib cage, and I know that this is the moment when I want to take Violet home with me. It's not because she's sexy. It's not because she's clever. It's because she's good.

She's so good that I want to find a way to turn this pretend relationship into the real thing, because it already feels that way for me.

CHAPTER 24

When we leave the hospital, I swear I'm ready to say, "Be mine. Screw this pretend stuff."

After Jillian says goodbye and takes off for the training facility, Violet and I head to my car. I take her hand, and like I did the other night at my house, I decide to just go for it. "Hey, Vi. Would you ever want to go out on a date—"

"Cooper Armstrong. Can I just ask one question?"

I whip around and nearly groan when I see a local sports radio host known as Todd the Talker striding across the asphalt and cutting in. Todd invited me on his show earlier this year after a weekend when I played like crap, and he pointedly asked, "Why should we, the fans, consider you anything besides the insurance plan that didn't pan out?"

To his credit, a few weeks later, he was the first to declare I'd turned the ship around. "What can I do for you, Todd? I didn't expect to see you here today."

He thrusts his cell phone at me, so I guess he's recording this.

I also surmise he's not going to tell me how he found me, but I remember another reason I don't like social media since I suspect he follows the team's social and a photo has already been posted from my visit here today. "Is it true the Renegades are waiting to see if you make it to the playoffs before they re-sign you?"

I flash a practiced smile at the sandy-blond dude with a chipped front tooth. "That's entirely up to the GM."

"If you don't make it, we hear that New Orleans is first in line to sign you as a free agent, given its woeful quarterback situation. Would you go to New Orleans?"

"New Orleans is a great town."

"So, does that mean you're going to New Orleans?"

I laugh. "You'd be better off talking to the team or my agent. I let them handle the negotiations. My job is to throw the ball and get it to the end zone."

Todd is relentless, even in the parking lot, even by the passenger door of my car, even with Violet next to me. "But if you don't land a wild-card slot, what happens then?"

I draw a breath. "My focus is on the game. That's where it needs to be all season long anyway. And that's where all my attention belongs. On the game."

Todd glances at Violet and makes a move to thrust the phone at her. I give a quick shake of my head and wrap an arm around her shoulders. "Thanks, Todd. Good luck with your story."

Once inside my car, Violet lets out a big breath. "He's a little, how shall we say, aggressive."

"Understatement of the year." I drag a hand through my hair and heave a sigh.

"You okay?"

I shake my head. Then I nod. Yes. No. Maybe. I rub the back of my neck. "Just wish I knew what was coming next."

"I can imagine."

"I *get* that this is part of the business, but I don't know where I'll be next year," I say, turning to meet her eyes. A million thoughts swirl in my head. Her business. My business. The landlord. The contract.

"Maybe it's best if you focus on football then, Cooper," she says softly.

I flinch. "Are you breaking up with me?"

She laughs and shakes her head. "No. I'm in this for as long as you need me. I meant the other stuff."

I frown. "You're cutting me off from giving you orgasms?"

"Ha. Do I look like a masochist?"

I pretend to give her a thorough once-over, appraising her. "Nope."

"More like the opposite these days," she says, nudging me with her elbow. Then, her expression turns serious. "I mean, I don't want anything to get in the way of your focus. So why don't we wait till after you make the playoffs to talk about dates and all that jazz?"

Her meaning is crystal clear. Orgasms are good. Dates are bad. But does that mean she's erecting a wall, or simply keeping me on track? I don't know if she's putting me off from looking ahead because she doesn't want what's next, or because she only wants sex.

The trouble is, the more I try to puzzle it out, the less likely I am to do what I need to do. And that's follow my own advice. *Focus on football.*

I give a crisp nod and a salute. "Sounds like a game plan."

She looks at her watch. "I should return to the salon."

"I thought it was your day off."

"It was. But we've been so busy, I can't really take a whole day off, so I need to handle a few appointments this afternoon or we'll be slammed."

I point behind me to the hospital. "You did this for me?"

"Of course I did it for you," she says, her sweetness making it harder to concentrate on orgasms only. But those are my new marching orders. I turn on the ignition, reminding myself to zoom in on what matters most. Her business. My business. Not the unknown business of my heart.

I start to back up, then I tap the brake. "Before we hit the road, I have one question. Does focusing on football mean I can't tie you up tonight when you get off work?"

"You want to tie me up?" she asks, her voice suddenly a little breathless.

"I would very much like to give you another orgasm. I find it helps my focus on football immensely."

Her lips curve up in a smile. "I'll take one for the team, then."

CHAPTER 25

I work out, shower, make dinner, watch game film, study the playbook, pack for our cross-country trip to Baltimore where we will kick unholy ass on the gridiron on Sunday, and text Violet to ask if she's hungry. An emoji face holding a fork and a knife is her answer. I pack up some food for her and drive to her home, knocking at eight thirty sharp.

"Don't laugh, but I have to be in bed by ten thirty," I tell her when she opens the door.

Her lips twitch in a grin. She chuckles and pats my cheek. "It's so cute that you have a bedtime."

"When you meet Greenhaven, you'll understand why we all follow his rules. Dude is intense." I shut the door behind me and hold up a soft cooler packed with food.

"Are you feeding an army?"

I eye the gigantic red lunch bag that's, admittedly, more suitable for a day of fishing than delivering dinner to a woman. "Pretty sure this is just for you, but maybe I'll keep it for myself."

"What did you bring?"

"Protein, protein, more protein, and broccoli."

She mimes gagging. I walk past her to the tiny kitchen, where I unpack the bag and set a Tupperware dish of stir-fried chicken on her counter. "I lied. It's stir-fry and veggies. Come and get it."

She pants like a dog as she trots into the kitchen. "Yum. I love your chicken stir-fry."

"I know." I watch as she opens a drawer and grabs some utensils. She's wearing black leggings and an emerald-green top that's sparkly and hangs low and loose. The scoop neck affords a fantastic sneak peek of the tops of her tits.

She hops up on the counter, takes the Tupperware, and digs in. She smiles as she chews, then rolls her eyes in delight. Her bare feet swing back and forth, and she looks so utterly, delightfully happy that it makes my chest ache in a whole new way. A good ache. A warm ache. One that makes me want to get closer to her. All because she's...eating adorably?

What the fuck is wrong with me? I'm sporting a goofy grin. I better wipe that shit off my mug right about now.

I lift my chin. "Thanks again for coming today. You were great with all the kids, especially Smashalie."

"I loved it. That girl is cool. I want to go to her roller derby games." She takes a bite of the chicken and then gives me a mischievous little look. "Want me to braid your hair sometime?"

I drag a hand through my locks. "Somehow, I doubt even you could braid my hair."

"I did learn on Trent," she says as she spears another forkful. I arch a brow. "Seriously?"

"Remember in fourth grade when he refused to cut his hair?"

I snap my fingers. "That's right. He wanted to be a rock star."

She taps her shoulder with the end of her fork to indicate the length of Trent's rocker locks back then. "Mom let him go one year without cutting it. He was my crash-test dummy."

I shake my head in amusement. "That is basically the best dirt ever."

"You're not going to tell him, are you?"

"No, I just like knowing it. Why? Did he swear you to secrecy?"

She brings her fingers to her lips in an *oops* gesture. "I think so." Her expression turns serious. "He doesn't know about *this*?"

I step closer and plant a kiss on her neck. "You mean *that*?"

She shivers. "Yes. *That.*"

"Of course not. Besides, there's nothing to tell, right?" I wink. She laughs, but the sound fades quickly. "Did you mention anything to him?"

"God, no."

"What about Holly, though?"

"Holly honors the friend code," Violet says.

"Are you sure?"

She gives me a look as if I'm nuts. "She hasn't said a word."

"And you do know he's her husband?"

She stares at me. "Yes, I am aware. And she didn't take a vow before God and family to tell her husband all his sister's secrets. Like I said, she honors the code."

"But she knows that I'm here?"

Violet sets down her fork. "Are you asking me if I specifically texted her and told her *hey, guess what, Cooper's coming over tonight*? The answer is no. If she knows generally that you gave me several stupendously magnificent orgasms, the answer is yes," she says with a proud lift of her chin.

I smile. "Stupendously magnificent?"

"I might have mentioned your talents."

"Excellent."

Violet laughs. "If my brother knew about your skills, that would be an issue, but as long as I'm praising your oral and manual talents to my sister-in-law, it's all good?"

"I'm simple like that." I take a beat. "Besides, it's different with Trent."

"I know," she says, her tone slipping to a more serious note.

It's different because I have no clue how he'd feel about me being here. I don't know how he'd react if he knew my relationship with his sister has sailed into uncharted waters. And I have no idea what he'd say about the way my heart seems to take on a different shape when I'm near her. A new and wholly unfamiliar shape.

But I know this much—I don't want to think about Trent tonight. "I don't want to talk about him anymore."

"Funny, I don't either."

She leans over and drops the Tupperware in the sink and glances at the clock on her microwave. "Ticktock. Bedtime approaches."

I put my hands on her thighs, nudge her legs open, and wedge myself between them. "Yes, and I need to do bad things to you before I leave for the coldest place on Earth."

She quirks an eyebrow. "Is Baltimore that cold?"

"Hell if I know. It's not California, that's for damn sure. All I can say is thank the good Lord for domed stadiums or I would be screwed in the NFL. I'm too warm-blooded."

She runs a hand down my arm. I'm wearing a black T-shirt. "You are. Also, do you know it kind of turns me on to know that I'm touching the arm that everyone is going to be talking about on Sunday?"

I laugh. "You can lick it and kiss it too."

She purses her lips. "I'm so lucky."

I mimic throwing a football, and she grabs hold of my upper arm. "Seriously," she says with a sigh. "You're a gunslinger."

I puff up my chest. "Why, yes, please inflate my ego more."

She runs her hand from my bicep down to my forearm. "I'm not trying to inflate your ego here. I'm honestly just amazed at what you can do with this simple body part."

"Wait till you can see what I do with other ones."

Instead of tossing a zinger back my way, she presses a kiss to my bicep and lets her soft hair fall against my skin. Goose bumps rise on my arm. *This woman.* I run a hand through her hair. "What are you doing to me?"

She meets my eyes. "I don't know. What *am* I doing to you?"

She waits for me to answer.

I brush the backs of my fingers along her cheek, answering in my head.

Everything. She's doing everything to me—hitting me everywhere—mind, body, and straight in the heart with an arrow I'm not even sure she knows she's aiming in that direction. But only a few hours ago, she made it clear we needed boundaries. Our playbook should be simple, not complicated. This isn't a quarterback option; this *is* an easy down-and-out pass.

That's why I turn her question around on her. "What I'm doing to you," I say as I scoop her up, wrapping her legs around my waist, "is taking you to your bedroom."

She squeals and ropes her arms around my neck, holding on. With her hooked around me like a koala, I carry her out of the kitchen and turn down the hall.

"Bedroom is that way."

I roll my eyes. "Yeah, I figured, since the hall only goes one direction."

"You've never seen my bedroom."

"Do you need to go hide teddy bears and Justin Bieber posters before I go in?"

"Don't be silly. I did that before you came over."

When I reach the door, I push it open with my hip. I stop and stare, as if I've entered a wonderland. A den of femininity.

Her bed claims most of the room, and above it shines a string of lights shaped like lotus flowers. On one wall, she's hung a black-and-white photograph of a cobblestoned street. Paris, I think. On another, she's hung a simple illustration of a black cat against a pink background. One more is covered in small frames with image of perfume bottles. It's all so pretty and so her.

"Looks very you," I say softly as I stare. "I feel like I've been given the keys."

She loops her hands tighter around my neck, saying nothing, almost as if she's holding in words, and maybe emotion too. My eyes roam the walls, then the bed, and then I do a double take.

Gently, I lower her to the bed, let her go, and walk to the head of the bed. She watches me as I reach for the silky purple fabric. I give it a tug. A scarf is tied to each bedpost at the top.

"So that's what you did before I came over."

She nods as she nibbles on her lips. "You did say you wanted to tie me up."

CHAPTER 26

They say a photograph is worth a thousand words.

I've never been more tempted to take a photo in my life. But I want to experience all one thousand words that this moment is worth. And then some.

Violet lies naked on her bed, her arms stretched above her head, her right wrist bound by a purple scarf, her left by a red one. The lights from the lotus strands cast a pretty glow across her skin.

I run my hand down her neck, between her breasts, along her stomach. She arches into my touch. My fingers make their way south, teasing at the soft curls of hair, then dipping lower. Her mouth falls open, but before I spend more time in the *V* of her legs, I stand beside the bed.

"Want to know why I wanted you tied up?"

"Because you like me tied up?"

I laugh as I lift my hands to the hem of my shirt. "That, and to reduce temptation."

She narrows her eyes. "Seeing me naked and trussed up makes you less interested. Gee, thanks, Coop."

"No," I say roughly as I tug off my shirt.

Her breath hitches. "Oh shit." She stares at me with wide eyes. "You're…"

Yeah, this is why I work out. This is why I run. This is why I lift weights. For *this* moment. For the look in her eyes. For the heat in her gaze as she stares at my chest, and as she ogles my arms.

"You're torturing me," she whimpers.

"How am I torturing you?"

"Because I can't touch you, and your body is unreal."

I raise a hand to my pec, drag it down my chest, over the grooves of my abs. I drop my hands to my jeans and undo the first button with a pop.

"Cooper." Her voice is a plea.

"Yes, Violet?"

"Why can't I touch you? You're stunning."

Every early-morning workout was worthwhile. Every bench press has proven its value.

I'm not a narcissist. I don't need praise. But I'm so goddamn satisfied that she likes what she sees.

Wait.

Make that *lust*.

She *lusts* for what she sees.

"You're pretty stunning yourself," I say as I unzip my jeans.

She squirms on the bed, her hips lifting. My dick hardens

more as I watch her try to somehow pull me closer with the way she offers herself. I push my jeans down my hips to my thighs, then all the way off. Nothing but black boxer briefs. She struggles against the scarves as she stares at the outline of my erection, straining against the fabric. "I want to touch you."

"I know," I say, my voice dry. "I want you to touch me. But you tempt me too much."

"That's why I'm tied up?"

I step closer, the outline of my cock inches from her face. She turns toward my hard-on, which is pointing at her.

"Yes, because if you touch me, Vi, I swear I'll lose my mind with pleasure. If you touch me, I'll have you on your hands and knees so fast so I can fuck you."

She throws her head back and nearly howls. "Oh God."

"So this is how it's going to be. You can look, but I'm the only one who can touch."

She narrows her eyes at me. "That's not fair."

"Baby, it has to be this way," I say, imploring.

"I know."

I hook my thumb into the waistband of my briefs and then wiggle a brow. "Did you want me to take these off? I'm not sure."

"*Please.*"

I push them off, and my cock springs free, jutting out.

Her jaw falls open. "Are you for real?"

A smile tugs on my lips. "Pretty sure I am."

"Oh my God," she groans as she stares at me. "You have the most perfect dick."

I bend to her and run my finger across her top lip. "You have the most perfect filthy mouth for such a good, sweet girl."

I grip my dick, running my fist up and down my length. I close my eyes, shuddering, because it feels really fucking good to get some action, even with my hand, the only body part that's touched my dick in months. But for the first time in all that time, I have an audience. I'm not alone. I stand by the head of her bed, and I stroke my cock mere inches from her face. She writhes, twisting onto her side as she moans my name.

It sounds like pure porn on her tongue.

I run my left hand along my chest, over a nipple, pinching it as she stares. Then down between my legs, gripping my balls, which are heavy and aching.

She moans as I stroke and tug. I moan too. Then I let go so I can get on the bed. I straddle her, clamping my hands on her hips.

"Are you going to…"

I shake my head. "No. I'm not going to fuck you tonight. I'm going to come on you. Like you wanted."

"Oh, Jesus."

I move up her, kneeling over her stomach so I can fuck my fist as she stares.

"Feels so much better when you watch me do this," I groan as I stroke from base to tip and back.

Lust surges inside me, barreling down my spine as I devour

her with my eyes. My God, she's so stunning, all curvy, sexy, and soft.

Her gaze never strays. She watches with a wild abandon, her amber eyes glossy with desire that matches mine. She nibbles on the corner of her lips, so hungry, so greedy. And I can't wait. I need to know how her lips taste on my dick.

"Kiss the tip," I whisper hoarsely.

She nods savagely, and I shift forward, planting a palm on the mattress by her outstretched arm as I rub the head of my dick across her lips.

She darts her tongue out instantly, flicking it over the head, and I growl in pleasure. A drop of liquid beads at the tip, and she licks it up greedily. Her eyes are hooded as if she's savoring my taste. She opens her lips more, trying to entice me to fuck her mouth. Desire nearly strangles me. It practically lassos all my restraint to the ground. But I stay in control, fucking her with my words instead. "You want to suck me off, baby?"

"You know I do."

I rub the head over her top lip, loving—*fucking loving*—her tongue on me. "I want your mouth on me so bad, Vi," I tell her as I keep up my pace, gripping my fist tighter as I stroke my shaft.

"Let me," she begs.

Another drop of my arousal spills from my dick onto her lips, and her tongue hunts it out instantly, lapping it up. I rub the head against her bottom lip. She flicks her tongue out once more, and I'd really like to feel her all over me. That's my cue to pull away from her far-too-tempting mouth.

"Don't go," she says in a sexy, needy whimper as I move down her body.

"I'm right here." I settle above her pussy, my hand working my cock, stroking, tugging, driving her wild. Driving myself wild.

My muscles tighten everywhere. Tension expands inside me, overtaking me with a wicked intensity as I jerk harder, faster.

I'm all for masturbating. I'm all for pleasure. Orgasms of every variety rock, including solo flights. And while I'm dying for her to get me off, this will do just fine for now.

This will do more than fine.

Because pleasure consumes me. It camps out in my body, fills me completely as I shuttle my fist tighter, rasping out, "Where do you want me to come, baby?"

"My tits, my belly, my face, anywhere."

"Oh fuck," I groan, closing my eyes as my world burns white-hot and everything blurs into the pleasure that shoots down my spine, climbs up my thighs, obliterates all my senses as my body jerks and I come on her stomach. All the fuck over her beautiful, sexy, soft belly.

I groan her name, getting out only the first, seductive syllable. "Vi," I grunt as I squeeze the last drops onto her skin.

My shoulders shake, and when I finally get a grip on reality, I find she's breathing hard, panting, lifting her hips, and staring at the evidence of my pleasure on her body. She murmurs my name as if it's all she's ever wanted to say.

Her voice goes to my head. Sinks into my heart. Reminds me that I'm in so deep.

I try to clear my head. I tell myself to focus on the here and now. On my job this second. "Let me clean you up," I say, then I climb off her and head to her bathroom. I grab a washcloth, wet a corner with warm water, and return to erase my orgasm from her skin. I find the laundry basket in the corner, filled with her clothes, and I drop the washcloth on top and shoot her a naughty grin. "Thanks for letting me come on you."

"You dirty man," she says. "You dirty, clever man, finding a loophole to keep your pact."

I lift my chin, then drink in her body with my eyes. "I am pretty clever. And now I have another idea."

"What are you thinking?"

"How I'm going to make you come."

"Any way is fine with me."

I arch a brow. "Any way?"

"Any way at all."

"Do you have a vibrator?"

"Do I like chocolate? Do I like music and sunsets and puppies?" She nods to the nightstand. "Top drawer."

I slide open the drawer and grab a pink one with a dolphin attachment. I hit the on button, and the shaft takes off, vibrating at Mach speed. "Down, Flipper," I say, then adjust the speed. I settle myself between her legs, sitting cross-legged so I can play with her. "Wider, baby."

She parts her thighs, letting them fall open for me. A groan rumbles up my chest as I admire the sight in front of me. She's so wet, so aroused, and I'm going to fuck her.

Well, this dolphin is. "He's my backup."

She strains against the scarves. "Please."

I rub the head of the shaft against her hot, wet center. She shudders when I touch her, breathing hard. Then, her eyes travel down my chest. "I looked up shirtless pictures of you last night."

I startle, surprised by this admission as I press the head against her wet folds. "You did?"

She arches into my touch. "I wanted to remember what you looked like."

As I play with the vibrator, stroking it against her wet heat, I ask, "What did you find?"

Her words come out in a rush. "Training-camp shots. Sponsor shots. None of them do you justice."

I push inside, and she cries out, thrusting up against the pleasure device. It's only a few inches inside her, and she's already trying to fuck it. As she rocks into it, she keeps talking, as if she's confessing. "I used to love watching you take your shirt off in high school."

"You did?" I slide the vibrator deeper into her, and she gasps, taking it all. I flick on the dolphin, rubbing her clit with it. With my free hand, I widen her legs even more.

"*Yes*," she cries out, and it's both a reply to my question, and the answer to whether she likes how I'm touching her.

"I fucking love that you were watching me," I say as I push the shaft in her, hitting deep, then stroking it out.

She parts her lips, but she can't even seem to form words. She's moaning and groaning and grinding into the vibrator, and she's so clearly close to shattering. She slips into some kind of exquisite torment, the look on her face both anguish and bliss. Her eyes squeeze shut and her lips fall open as she seems to chase her pleasure.

My dick is steel again, and I'm already turned on beyond reason. Her hips rise over and over as she fucks the toy, and I fuck her, and I wish it was me inside her. My mouth on her mouth, her body beneath me, feeling her grip me, feeling her come on me, coming inside her.

Her mouth turns into an *O*. Then she twists her hips, crying out in pleasure. "Oh God, oh God," she pants, moaning, tossing her head back and forth, the picture of erotic bliss, and I can barely take it. I can barely withstand my own lust as she comes undone before my eyes, her hands tied, her hips lifting, her lips parted. Coming for me. Beneath me. Because of me. I want more of this. I want all of this.

I am on fire for her.

I slide the vibrator out of her, turn it off, and toss it on the covers. Then I do the riskiest thing in the world. I untie her. First one arm, then the other, and in seconds we are wrapped around each other, two hot, sweaty bodies, sliding together. I'm kissing her wrists, making sure they don't sting, and she's naked and rubbing against me.

"They don't hurt," she says and pulls her hands free from my grip to bring them to my face. "It only feels good."

"I wanted to kiss you at prom," I blurt out, picking up where we left off in our mutual confession.

"You did?"

"So much. You were so pretty. We were slow dancing to one song, and I wanted to thread my hands in your hair and kiss you." She presses her soft breasts against my chest. My skin burns with desire. She's so close to me. She's all over me. She's everywhere, and I want to feel all of her.

I groan as I yank her impossibly closer, my cock pressed to her thigh, her pussy rubbing against my other leg.

"I would have let you," she whispers, her words sending a sharp, hot thrill through me.

"Yeah?"

She nods, kissing me, claiming my lips. "You could have kissed me then. You could have kissed me anytime. I wanted you to kiss me at my brother's wedding when you danced with me."

I close my eyes as my palms slide up her back and into her hair. "I wanted that too," I murmur, then curl my hands around her head and bring her closer, slamming my lips to hers and kissing her till we are both senseless, mindless, boneless.

We're side to side, and rubbing against each other. Flesh to flesh. Skin to skin. All heat, and desire, and something more. Something that's so damn dangerous. My heart feels as if it's going to fucking explode in my chest. It hammers wildly for this woman, and I can't stop touching her. My hands are everywhere. My lips are all over her mouth, her jaw, her neck. Her fingers roam my body, touching, exploring, searching.

We hunt for ways to get even closer. Our kisses are hungry and greedy. We are two desperate people who can't get enough of each other. When we kiss now, it feels like making love, and I'm losing control. I'm losing my mind for her. All this nakedness, all this heat—it's combustible. I tug her closer, pushing my hard length against her mound. As we move, my cock slips between her legs.

I groan so loudly it's deafening to my own ears. Because the sensation is dizzying. I'm not inside her, not even close, but like this, it's absolutely electrifying to feel her slickness against my hardness. I thrust once, my shaft gliding across her.

She moans, a long, sexy *ohh*.

It nearly breaks me. I'm so ready to flip her to her back, hike her legs over my shoulders, and sink into her.

One more thrust. One more deliriously good slide against her.

Then reality smacks me hard.

I can't fake fuck her. I certainly can't fake fuck her without a condom. I won't play with fire, and this is a burning-down-the-forest level of danger.

I freeze, willing my hands to stop moving along her flesh, forcing my body to disengage from hers. I curse up a storm, then I do what I've been taught to do to avoid a hit I can't handle—get out-of-bounds. I jump out of bed, moving away from her.

"Shit, Vi." I drag my hands roughly through my hair as I grab for my clothes. "You're too tempting. I want you too much."

She looks chastened. "What does that even mean?"

I yank on my boxer briefs. "If I stay for another minute, I will be fucking you. I will be fucking you all night long. I won't want to stop." I drag a hand through my hair roughly. "I need to get it together." Squeezing my eyes shut, I try to will away this raging desire. When I open my eyes, I breathe out hard like a bull.

She reaches for a sheet and pulls it to her chest, covering her beautiful body. "That better?"

I grab my jeans. "It's worse and it's better. I'm sorry. I'm sorry if I seem like an ass."

She sighs. "Let me walk you to the door."

Two minutes later, she's in a short, satiny robe, her hair a wild mess, her cheeks glowing. I'm dressed and both satisfied and blue-balled. But I have a job to do, and I can't let things with her go any further. There's too much at stake.

I cup her cheek. "I leave tomorrow. I'll be thinking of you."

She shakes her head. "Don't think of me. Think of destroying Baltimore."

My God, she's a perfect football girlfriend.

I mean, fake girlfriend.

Fake girlfriend who I nearly real fucked.

CHAPTER 27

Violet: I have great news. I signed the new lease. All is well in Hairlandia.

Holly: Yay! So, what does that mean for the little game of k-i-s-s-i-n-g in a tree?

Violet: I honestly don't know. I have this feeling, Holly, that once the contract is done...

Holly: He's going to drop you like a hot potato?

Violet: Yes.

Holly: Don't think that. He's wild about you.

Violet: He's a twenty-six-year-old professional quarterback with a winning record, scads of women throwing themselves at him, and an excellent shot at the playoffs. His contract is in flux. He's not looking for a commitment from a woman. He's looking for a commitment from a team.

Holly: Sweetie...

Violet: It's the truth. I'm taking what I can get. I'm savoring what this is. I know it won't last. It just can't.

Holly: Why?

Violet: He's already in love with the game, and I'm not sure he has the room for anything else.

Holly: You're not a thing.

Violet: I know that. But I also understand and respect his priorities.

Holly: You don't have to be so levelheaded and tough about this, sweetie.

Violet: But I do have to be strong. If I'm not, my heart will break.

CHAPTER 28

After a dinner out with the guys in Baltimore on Friday, we stroll through the lobby of the team hotel, heading straight for the elevator banks. I avoid the hotel bar at all costs, and I don't make eye contact with any of the football groupies.

As we turn down the hallway, Jasper and his wife are walking toward us. "Gentlemen." Jasper flashes us a smile that shows off gleaming white teeth. "Good to see my stars"—his eyes drift to the elevators—"heading upstairs."

His meaning is clear. He has no patience for the guys picking up the groupies, even though it's often a part of the game.

"We like to get our beauty sleep," Jones offers, speaking for the four of us.

"How wise," Jasper says in his smooth voice. He raises a hand to scratch his jaw, and his three Super Bowl rings nearly blind me.

"I hope you all have a great game Sunday," Vera chimes in, then she motions to me, signaling she wants a word. I step aside.

"I keep meaning to tell you," she whispers, "how devastated I am that you have a girlfriend." Then she smiles. "I'd been hoping to finally convince you to join my client list."

I smile too, thinking of Violet. "She's great."

"And I'm so glad that you-know-who settled down. But, fair warning. I ran into her in the restaurant."

Tension spreads through my whole body. I haven't seen Maxine since the auction. I kinda hoped she'd be out of my life forever. Not that she was ever in it. But still.

"Thanks, Ms. Scott. I appreciate the tip," I say.

She rolls her eyes. "Vera, darling."

"Thanks, Vera," I say.

Then she waves goodbye and rejoins her husband while I jog to catch up with my guys.

And I nearly smack into Maxine as she rounds the corner. She's dressed to the nines in a red sequined top and black jeans with towering heels.

"Hey, you! I was just getting a nightcap," Maxine says. "But then, I don't have to be on the field bright and early for practice."

The hair on the back of my neck stands on end. Is she coming on to me again? "Bright and early," I say with a forced smile, since tomorrow is Saturday, and it's a light workout day before the Sunday game.

I hear footsteps behind me and thank God we're not alone, as it seems Maxine has no idea of the term *personal space*. Still, I don't look behind me—I keep my eyes on the prize of the elevator. Maxine waggles her fingers at me. "Are you sure you have to go to bed right away?"

"Positive," I say, worry sliding down my spine.

"Just one drink?" she continues, stepping closer, getting into my space.

With a gulp, I shake my head. "No, thank you."

"But I've given you such great coverage on my show," she says in a purr that feels like a lie.

I don't even know how to respond to her tit-for-tat implication except with a muttered *thanks*.

"I'd hate to stop covering you so enthusiastically...so if anything changes, you know where to find me, *Mister Randall*."

I freeze.

The sound of footsteps recede.

Then Maxine turns and walks off, leaving her intentions floating loud and clear. *Mister Randall?* I guess she's not dropping the *I'm her husband* bit.

I take off, finding the guys stepping into the elevator. Once inside, I breathe a sigh of relief and rest my forehead against the panel. "Is it me or is she...?"

But I trail off. I'm not sure what's going on with her. Or what lines she's crossing. If any. All I know is I feel uncomfortable as fuck around her.

Harlan pats my back. "Saw what just went down. Sucks, man."

"Yeah, it kind of does," I say, and that's when the wrongness of her hits me in full force—it's one thing for random women to come on to me. But she's a media personality who's borderline threatening me.

But I don't know exactly what could or should be done about that. Maybe it's best to put it behind me.

When we reach our floor, I give a quick wave good-night and head to my room. The door clicks shut behind me, and I wash my hands, brush my teeth, and undress. When I'm down to nothing, I grab my phone and contemplate texting Violet.

We've only texted a few times since I left, and most have been from her of the *go team* variety. But I want her to know I'm thinking of her, so I send one.

Cooper: Sleep well in your lucky jersey.
Violet: I will 😊

I turn off the light, and I don't wake up until my phone rattles on my nightstand in the morning like the world is ending. I rub my eyes, stare at the screen, then sit bolt upright when I see who's calling.

Jasper Scott.

I answer immediately. "Yes, sir?"

"Cooper, can you meet me in my suite before practice?"

"Yes, I can, Mr. Scott."

Fifteen minutes later, I'm showered, dressed, and heading into the great unknown. It's a little terrifying.

No, a lot.

CHAPTER 29

In my nearly four seasons with the team, I've spoken to Jasper on only a few occasions, and I've never been called to his office. Not once. Now, as I wait for the shining silver elevator doors to whisk open, I have no clue what to expect.

When the elevator arrives with a soft whoosh, I step inside, my feet leaden, my chest hollowed. The doors close, and I swipe my key card across the security pad and press the button for the top floor.

As it rises, I can't shake the feeling that I'm screwed. That I did something wrong.

When I reach his floor, I try to psych myself up with reminders that I can handle this. I stare down linemen, I scramble in the pocket, and I throw pinpoint passes under fire from the toughest defensive coverage. Chin up, chest high.

I find suite 1200 and raise my fist to knock. Before I can even rap, the door opens. Maxine leaves, head down.

Ice-cold dread fills me from stem to fucking stern. Shit.

Does Jasper know I lied? Did he figure out I faked a romance to escape Maxine? Did Maxine just put two and two together and blab it all? Maybe.

She doesn't even look at me, though, as she goes. *What the hell?*

Jasper smiles, showing no teeth. He wears navy slacks and a crisp button-down, and holds the door open. "Thank you for coming, Cooper. Especially on such short notice."

"Of course, sir," I say, heading inside as Maxine retreats down the hall.

The suite is quiet. Only the hum of the heater echoes as we walk from the foyer around the corner. Vera is here, perched on a couch in the sunken living room, her hands folded in her lap.

"Please, have a seat," Jasper says, indicating the chair across from his wife.

Is Vera pissed I'm not joining her matchmaking agency?

Jasper sits in the yellow chair across from me. "Can I get you anything? Coffee, tea, water?"

I furrow my brow. The owner is offering me a beverage? Maybe I'm dreaming. Maybe it's still the middle of the night, because this is a topsy-turvy world. "I'm good, sir."

"Excellent." He rubs his palms on his pant legs, almost as if he's nervous. "You might be wondering why I called you here."

Ya think?

I nod. I can hardly speak.

He takes a deep breath, sighs, then gestures to his wife. "Vera told me what's going on."

My stomach churns as I wait for her to reveal my dirty little lie.

But when Vera meets my gaze, her expression is elegant, professional. "I told my husband about the remarks Maxine has been making on her show. And I overheard some of what she said to you last night. I thought I lost an earring so I doubled back and heard her inviting you out for a drink, as well as the other things."

I sit straighter, girding myself for whatever is coming next.

"And I told him how she behaved at the auction. So we decided to pull our sponsorship of her show. Effective immediately."

My jaw comes unhinged, and I try to speak. To say *holy shit, thank you.*

Vera continues. "We won't be associated with that kind of unwanted attention. It's gone beyond a funny sort of joke about a celebrity. It's completely inappropriate. And we won't be a part of it. We have resources on the team to help you if you need any. Counseling, if that's something you want."

Wow. "Um, thanks. I think I'm okay, though," I say, since truthfully, last night was the only time she went too far, and I handled it. I take a big breath. "Thank you, though. For stepping up like that."

Except, what if they figure out I don't deserve the support? What if they know I lied about Violet at the auction?

"Of course. It's what we do for our players," Jasper says, then sighs deeply, like he's relieved to be finished with that unpleasant matter. "But that's not the only reason we called you in."

Shit. There's more? "Okay," I say tentatively.

Vera leans forward. "Now, I know you and Violet have known each other since you were kids, but since your relationship first came to light at the auction, I'd love to showcase the two of you on my social media. For my agency."

I blink, unsure why the hell she would. "But we didn't use your agency," I say, pointing out the obvious.

Vera waves a hand airily. "Of course not, darling. I'd never claim you did. I simply want to showcase you as an example of the kind of love I can bring to my clients. As relationship goals. I can see you're in love with her, and it's so wonderful."

I squeeze my eyes shut and open them again. Once more, the room is upside down, right side up, tipped on its side. "I'm in love with her?" I ask, but then I realize those words shouldn't come out in the form of a question.

And not just because of my audience. That's because it's not a fucking question. It's a fact of my existence.

"I'm in love with her," I repeat, this time with the certainty I feel inside. In my heart.

As soon as I say it, I can't seem to stop saying it. It frees me. It rips the weight of confusion off my shoulders. Everything that's been happening with Violet crystallizes in one bright, clear moment. "I'm completely head over heels for her."

I am absolutely smitten with my best friend's sister, who I've known nearly my whole life.

"I can tell," Vera says, a soft smile curving her lips. "And, she's quite in love with you too."

My eyes widen to the size of pizza pies. "What?"

Wild hope takes off inside me, strapping my heart on to a rocket of hope. Violet's in love with me too? There's no way. That's too much to ask for. That's like winning the Super Bowl.

Vera's eyes twinkle. "I saw you two kiss. And I've been following your romance. It's a little magical." She turns her gaze to her husband, who smiles adoringly at her.

"A lot magical," he adds. "And we're glad we can assist with removing any tension Maxine may have caused in your personal life."

The team owner and his wife just went to bat for me. To prevent an uncomfortable situation with a radio host.

But what have I been doing?

Hiding everything.

"I'm glad we could chat and properly take care of matters," Jasper says.

And when I'm dismissed, I realize that's exactly what I need to do too.

CHAPTER 30

It takes all day to work up my nerve because I'm about to do something my agent would deem utterly insane.

That's why I don't call Ford. There wouldn't be enough yoga classes in the Bay Area to calm him down if I told him my plan.

Besides, when I'm on the field and see safeties swarming the guy I'm about to throw to, I can't find a new target if I'm looking to the sidelines for instructions.

I have to lead the team.

I have to be the one to lead my own damn career.

When the pregame team meeting in the hotel conference room ends that evening, I don't leave with my teammates. I walk over to Greenhaven and ask if I can have a word. He turns away from his assistant coaches and tells them he'll be right back. We head into a private room off the conference area, and he shuts the door.

"What can I do for you, Cooper?"

My first name. There it is again. That's who I want to be for him. But I can't be that guy if I'm lying. I clear my throat. "I wanted to thank you for the invitation to dinner with your wife."

He nods. "Of course." He takes a beat, studies my face, and reads me loud and clear. "But you didn't need to pull me aside for that."

"No. I didn't." I take a deep, fueling breath. "I'm not really involved with Violet."

His brow furrows. His eyes register surprise. I think this is the first time I've ever seen Greenhaven flummoxed. "You're not?"

"I am, but I'm not."

"You might want to explain that better."

"Something happened at the auction. Someone wanted to bid on me. And I didn't want that person to win. So Violet bid, and when the host of the auction saw us onstage, she figured we were together, and I didn't correct her. I said she was my girlfriend, and we kept it up."

He raises an index finger like a professor making a point. "But you go around with her like you are with her. You stopped by the hospital, she kissed you at the game last week, you post those pictures on your feed…"

"You see my Instagram?"

"I'm aware of what my players post on social media. Are you saying it was all a lie?"

That word cuts straight through my chest, a sharp knife

to my heart. Nothing has felt more true than my feelings for Violet. "I'm saying it started that way. I did it to make my life easier, but then somewhere along the way, I fell in love with her." I hold up a hand. "I know that doesn't excuse the fact that it started as a ruse. I'm not trying to make it all okay. The kiss on the field was real. At least to me, it felt real. Going to visit the kids was absolutely real, and to tell the truth, that's probably when I knew in my heart I was in love with her." I swallow and push past my fear that I'm upending my chances with the team.

His lips twitch. "A man doesn't look at a woman the way you look at her without it being real."

I flash back to the day in his office. To the gift he ordered for his wife. To the way he talks about Emily. This man is still madly in love with his woman. That must be what he sees in me when I look at Violet, when I talk about Violet.

"It is real. For me, at least. I have no idea if she feels the same. But I needed you to know the full truth. I want to carry this team. But I want to do it as a leader, not as a liar. And if I ever come to your house for dinner, I don't want to be the guy who sits down at your table with you and your wife unless all my cards are on the table too." I spread my hands in front of me, gesturing to the imaginary table. "These are my cards."

He nods, the wheels in his head turning, it seems. "I appreciate you showing them to me."

And that's it. That's all he says.

"Now, if you'll excuse me, I need to return to the coaches."

I leave, having no clue if I just blew up my future with the Renegades.

CHAPTER 31

"You did *what*?"

I sink into the chair in Jones's room. "I told him everything."

He drags both hands through his dark hair. "What in the actual fuck?"

"I know, right?"

"No, I mean what in the actual fuck are your balls made of?"

I laugh, the first good laugh I've had all day.

He gestures to my crotch. "Are they steel? Are they titanium? Are they some new fucking substance cloned from the DNA of the toughest badasses in the world? Special Forces guys and paratroopers and bounty hunters?"

"Maybe just pure stupidity."

Jones shakes his head. "Nope. Not stupidity." He claps his hand on my shoulder. "You're a steely-eyed missileman, and I will follow you into battle."

I give him a look. "You can't be serious, can you?"

"Dude, I have motherfucking chills. Look at me." He holds out his arms, and yup, the hairs stand on end.

"This is weird. I'm in your hotel room, and you're showing me the hair on your arms."

"Because you're like a Navy SEAL, man. You march in there, you see the commanding officer, you tell him the whole truth, so help you God. And you leave without him telling you what he thinks. You have the biggest cojones I've seen."

"You've been checking out my cojones, have you? You peek in the showers, right?"

He gazes heavenward. "Why do I compliment him? Why?"

I smile. "Thanks, Jones. I needed this. I feel a little insane right now. I texted Ford afterward and told him, and his only reply was Go kick Baltimore's ass tomorrow, you fucking superstar. I have no clue what that means."

Jones furrows his brow. "Do you want me to play text message interpretation with you?"

"No," I say, shaking my head.

"I'm going to do it anyway. It means a cigar is just a cigar. It means go kick Baltimore's ass tomorrow."

I hold up a fist for bumping. "That sounds like a plan."

"It's an excellent plan. It's precisely what we're going to do. Because you're not insane. You're a field general. You're the motherfucking quarterback."

And that's what I do the next day against the enemy. I lead the team down the field as fifty thousand raving Baltimore Cougars fans boo us like we're the Ebola virus.

And I don't care.

I'm all business from the first possession when I take the snap, hand off to Harlan, and we earn a first down.

From there, I do my goddamn job with blinders on, tuning out the crowd, tuning out the noise, listening only to my head and gut. I call an audible when I see their defense switch from man-to-man to zone coverage. My receivers change routes, and several seconds later, I lob a pass to Jones in his smelly socks. He grabs it fluidly, darts around the safety, and takes that prize another twenty yards.

The rest of the drive is clockwork. A short pass to McCormick on second down. A handoff to long-haired Harlan, and then the bastard shows off his quicksilver feet, darting, dodging, and taking the ball right into the end zone.

It's a beautiful start, and I high-five him.

Our defense holds them to three, but when we get the ball again, their line nearly mows us down, and we barely get into field position. But we manage, and when Einstein spits out his bubblegum, he sends the ball soaring thirty-seven yards between the goalposts.

I bump fists with him when he comes off the field, grab some water, and watch the defense. Greenhaven glances my way and gives me a nod.

I can't decipher what that means, and I decide to stop trying.

I stop thinking about everything I can't control. Violet's feelings. My job situation. Ford's state of mind. Trent's potential reaction. Where I'll be next year. The one thing I can control is what happens on the gridiron, and when we get the ball back, I am in the zone. Namely, the end zone.

Twice.

As the team trots to the locker room at halftime, I'm one of the last guys to head inside. I'm keenly aware that someone's right behind me, and that gruff-voiced someone determines my future.

"Cooper."

It's Greenhaven. He takes two big strides to catch up, and we walk side by side through the tunnel. "Did I ever tell you the story of how I met my wife?"

"No, sir."

"I met Emily at a barbecue thirty years ago, when I'd first started with Phoenix. I wore a team jersey. As I flipped a burger on the grill, she asked if I was a Phoenix fan."

I look at him, waiting for him to continue.

"She was the most beautiful woman I'd ever seen. Know what I told her?"

"No, sir."

"I told her I was an assistant coach on the team."

I furrow my brow. If memory serves, he wasn't the assistant coach thirty years ago. Assistant coach is a key position, one he worked his way up to. But that wasn't how he'd started. "You weren't, though, right?"

He shakes his head as we walk, our footsteps echoing. "Not in the least. Know what my job really was?"

"What was it, sir?"

"I was the assistant to the coach," he says with a lopsided grin.

I dare to let a smile spread on my face, since there's a world of difference between an assistant coach and the assistant *to* the coach. "Is that so?"

"Have I mentioned how pretty she was?"

"I believe you did."

"But she was more than pretty. She stole my heart. I think that's why Emily forgave me when I admitted on our second date that I'd fibbed," he says as we reach the inside corridor of the stadium. He stops and clasps my upper arm. "I appreciate your candor. And I value it, Cooper."

Then he strides into the locker room, where he gives his halftime speech to *keep it up*, and that's exactly what we do.

We're on fire the rest of the game, scoring a field goal and two more touchdowns. A calm, focused energy fills me with each drive. When the clock ticks to nothing at the end of the fourth quarter, the Renegades erupt with elation because we fucking made it to the playoffs.

Holy shit.

That's when the emotions explode. That's when exhilaration overwhelms me. We punch the air. We hug it out. We shout and hoot and holler. There's still so much more work to be done, but for now, I let myself enjoy this moment, even though I can't believe we pulled this off. Three years of warming the bench, a terrible start to the season, and here in late

December on enemy territory, we're celebrating a wild-card spot and a kick-ass record.

Later, when the cameras stop rolling and the cheers die down, there's one person I want to call first.

CHAPTER 32

I call my mom.

Obviously.

Who else would I call first?

She's the reason I'm here. She's the reason I have a chance at the postseason. She's done everything for me.

"Hey, Mom, if I win the Super Bowl, want me to get you another house?"

She screams in excitement, so loudly I pull the phone from my ear. Then, she laughs. "Just a new Coach handbag and my favorite Chinese food, please. And I knew you'd make it to the postseason, sweetie. I just knew it."

"Funny how a lot of people say that, but you actually said that when I was seven," I say as I make my way toward the stadium exit, pressing the phone closer again.

"And eight, and nine, and ten, and so on. When will I see you again?"

"I'm heading back tonight. I can try to stop by tomorrow,

but it's a tight week since we're the Thursday-night game of the week."

"You know where to find me, and you also know how to get me tickets on the fifty-yard line for Thursday night, so why don't I plan on seeing you then?"

"It's a date."

"Besides, there's someone you should see first."

"Yeah, who's that?"

She laughs. "Might it be a pretty little lady who you've had your eye on since you were a teenager?"

"I have no idea what you're talking about," I say as I near the exit.

"Right. Sure. Keep telling yourself that. Incidentally, I always knew there was something real between the two of you."

My chest twists when she says that. "You did?"

"I did," she says with a smile in her voice. "I could tell you two liked each other. I could tell at the game last week, and I could tell back in high school."

I want to believe every word she's saying, but I also don't know if I can.

"Mom, I'm not sure it's real for her."

"Nonsense."

"I'm serious. I don't know if she'd get seriously involved with a guy like me."

She scoffs. "You mean handsome, talented, rich, kind, and good?"

I laugh. "More specifically, I meant someone who's married

to football. That's what Trent said about me last time I saw him. Do you think it's true?"

"In many ways, you are, and that's not a bad thing. What would be bad is not letting her know how much she means to you."

I heave a sigh. "Why are you always right?"

"It's a gift. It comes with being a mom," she says with a light laugh.

I tell her I love her, then I hang up and open Violet's contact info.

Telling Violet how I feel isn't as simple as it sounds, though. How do I convince her there's room for both her and this other great love in my life? But more so, how do I even know if she wants to make room for me in her life? Not to mention, what the hell do I say to her brother?

I'm not sure I have the answers, but maybe the cross-country flight will give me time to sort them out. For now, I want to hear her voice.

I call her as the security guard opens the door that leads to the lot with our bus. She answers on the second ring. Her voice is a little hoarse. "The time you threw the touchdown pass in the fourth quarter against Baltimore in the game that sealed the wild card. That's my new favorite play of the season."

I laugh, remembering when we first played boyfriend-girlfriend *Jeopardy!* "Funny, that's mine too," I say, mouthing a *thank you* to the security guard. I stop in my tracks when something wet lands on my forehead. Then my cheek. Then my hair. "It's snowing."

"It is?" she asks with wonder in her voice. We don't get snow in San Francisco.

I hold up my palm. "Holy shit. These are some fat flakes. I had no idea it was snowing. Guess that's what happens when you play under the dome."

"By the way, your play under the dome was amazing. My voice is shot from screaming in excitement at the TV," she says.

"You sound like a frog. A sexy frog. Speaking of, can I see your sexy frog-ness when I return?"

"Ribbit," she says by way of answer.

"I take it that's a yes."

She croaks out a yes.

"Good. There's a lot I have to tell you. Lot of stuff that went down here before the game. Things I learned."

"Oh," she says, her tone suddenly heavy.

"It's not bad. But it's better shared in person."

"I understand."

I reach the bus. "I'll let you know when I land. It might be late, though."

"I'll either be awake or asleep," she deadpans.

I laugh. "Yes, those would be the two options."

As we say goodbye, something seems different in her voice. As if it's missing some excitement. Some enthusiasm for me. Maybe I'm imagining it, maybe I'm reading too much into one short phone call. I tell myself it'll all be clear when I see her. But as I sink down into a plush seat on the team bus, I find myself wondering if maybe this is more one-sided than I thought. Perhaps it's been pretend for her all along.

The snowflakes attack the tarmac, building aggressively into a huge-ass snowstorm that grounds our flight for the night. We can't take off on Monday morning either. By then, the manager of operations is dealing with fifty-three cranky, big-ass players who want to return home because the one thing we like best after winning is our routine.

Living in limbo in Baltimore on a short week is not routine at all.

We pass the time practicing, playing Ping-Pong and video games, and watching game film at the hotel. We finally take off late Monday night, and by the time we land on the West Coast, it's the middle of the night.

I text Violet an emoji of a bird landing, and then foolishly hope she'll reply with *come over* or *I'm waiting on your porch in my birthday suit*, but it's three in the morning and my phone, understandably, is silent. An hour later, I'm home, where my bed and I spend eight hours together before it's time for a late practice and playoff prep all day Tuesday and into the evening.

I'm not complaining. This is where I want to be right now in my career.

But I also want to be someplace else. Someplace clear with her. When I leave the training facility late that night, it's too late to see her. If I see her now, I won't get enough rest, and I'll play like crap. So I don't ask if she's free now. I text to ask when I can see her tomorrow. She replies that she has an early afternoon on-site appointment in the city tomorrow with a new client, so she can meet me at my house before.

Before.

Why does that word feel so fucking ominous?

Because it's not *after*.

Because it's not open-ended. Because it tells me what I need to know. She's sandwiching me.

I'm not the end to her day.

CHAPTER 33

I open the door, prepared to be tough. Prepared to handle the *it's time to end this* speech that she surely plans to hurl in my direction on her pit stop to her appointment.

But that strategy flies onto the street when I see her. She stands on my porch, a December breeze whipping her dark hair around her face. A black skirt is painted on and her boots are so tall she looks like she can slay dragons in them. A leather jacket completes the sexy-as-a-rock-star look.

Her lips shine, like she just slicked on gloss.

For a split second, I read her like I'd do another team. Like she's the enemy. In those eyes I find determination, hardness, an edge that wasn't present the last time I saw her.

But then her gaze wanders, drifts down my body, and maybe she's inventorying me like I just did to her, taking in my jeans, bare feet, and charcoal-gray Henley shirt.

When she returns to my eyes, the cool veneer is gone. In hers, I see heat.

I see a spark.

But neither one of us says anything, and it feels as if we're facing off. Like something happened when I was out of town. Or maybe something happened when I bolted from her home last week.

She breaks the silence, raising her chin. "Your hair is a mess. You still need a trim."

I run my hands through unruly locks. "I'll make an appointment. Unless you're too booked."

"I'll see if I can fit you in."

That feels like the operative phrase. Like she's fucking fitting me into her life.

"You're welcome anytime. Besides, the lease is signed. Woo-hoo!" She thrusts her arms in the air in victory, and I smile, then lift her up in celebration. A soft sigh escapes her lips the moment we touch, and that's all it takes. I carry her inside, shut the door with my foot, and push her up against the back of it. I hear the faint sound of my phone ringing on the couch, but I ignore it.

Then it happens. All at once. Our lips crash together. We kiss fiercely, like we're ravenous. Her scent—peaches and cool December air—intoxicates me. It unravels me. All my plans to talk to her, to tell her how I feel, become secondary to the heat of her body. To the feel of her soft, sexy lips. To the way my pulse spikes and my blood heats being this close to her.

Talk. What's that? I can't even string words together. All I can manage are grunts and growls. This is primal. This is physical. This is so fucking intense as I push against her and kiss those lips that own me.

I thread my hands through her hair. "Vi, I thought about you so much."

She breathes out hard, nodding as she drops her purse to the floor. "Me too. You, that is."

I push her skirt to her hips. My gaze drifts down, and my throat is dry. She wears pink panties with white foxes on them.

I can't speak.

I've been reduced to nothing but muscles and blood and heat and desire. That's all that works in me, and it's working in overdrive. My hand slides between those gorgeous thighs, then across her panties, and I'm done.

She's so fucking wet.

"Need to get these off," I mutter, and she nods vigorously. "Yes. Off."

I kneel, tugging her panties down, helping her step out of them in her high-heeled boots, while she shrugs off her jacket. She wears a pink sweater, and I could fucking die. She's so sexy. She's so pretty. She's so mine.

But she's not mine.

She's only mine for now, and I'll take what I can get. As soon as I stand, she grabs at the hem of my shirt, and I yank it off.

I pat the back of my jeans for my wallet, but it's on the kitchen counter. Besides, I'm honestly not sure I have a condom in it. It's been months since I needed one.

"Vi," I say, heavily. "I don't think I have a—"

"—I do."

She grabs her purse and snags a condom in five seconds flat.

"You're prepared," I say, surprised for some reason that she's carrying.

She levels me with her gaze, her eyes intense and her tone brutally honest, it seems. "Cooper, I've been prepared for this since the first night at your house. I've been ready for a long time."

Those words grab hold of me, touching my heart, rekindling my hope. I try not to read too much into them, but they feel so true. I take the condom from her hand as she lets go of her purse, and I kiss her once more. "I've been ready for a long time too," I say softly.

A desperate *oh* comes from her, and I sweep my thumb over her lips, almost as if I can catch the sound, hold it close, keep her.

I look down to tear open the condom when I feel a hand on my shoulder. "Are you sure? The superstitions and all that stuff?"

I don't know the answer, but I also don't care. "I don't care. You're all I want." I unzip my jeans, push them to my hips, and roll on the condom as she watches with wide, hungry eyes. My phone bleats again from the couch. "I don't care who's calling. I don't care about anything else right now."

"I don't care about anything else either," she says in a breathless rush, and I know we said we'd talk after the game,

I know there are so many things to discuss, but I need this woman more than words.

I need her right now against the door.

God bless her high-heeled boots. All I have to do is bend my knees slightly and we line up. I rub the head of my cock against her sweet, hot pussy. She trembles, and I shudder. I'm not even inside her, and I'm shaking. I'm fucking shaking with desire.

She loops her arms around my neck, and I look into her eyes. I nearly tell her right now that I'm madly in love with her. I bite back the words, murmuring only a desperate "you're so beautiful" as I grip the bottom of her thigh, hiking her leg up and over my hip.

A shuddering gasp is her response, and then I sink into her.

The most sensual *oh* I've ever heard falls on my ears. It sweeps over my whole body.

And I know. I just know. Nothing compares to this.

This is heaven.

I still myself before I'm all the way in, sensations rocketing inside me, but it's more than just the physical. It's the overwhelmingness of this moment. I've thought about this. I've imagined it. I've longed for it.

Now it's here.

"Vi," I whisper, and that one syllable comes out reverently.

"Oh God," she whimpers, and her body goes softer in my arms, as if she's falling into me. She's paradise, so warm and tight, and she grips me so intensely I feel like I could come now. That's not permissible, though, so I squeeze my eyes shut and count to three. I push in deeper, and she wraps her leg tighter around me. She whimpers as I nestle my cock all the way inside her. The sound she makes sends shock waves through my blood.

I stroke into her, heat blasting through all my cells, sparks flying across my skin as I look at her, as I stare into those eyes that don't stray from me either. Nothing has ever felt like this. This good. This intense. This necessary.

With one hand holding her leg firmly, I raise my other hand to her face and grip her chin.

She gasps, and it almost sounds like a cry. Like a wonderfully needy plea for me.

The world slows.

The city fades to a distant blur.

Time ceases to matter.

Her eyes stay locked with mine, and I swear, I fucking swear, she's unmasked right now. I can see everything in her eyes. She looks at me like she feels all the same things I do. I see my emotions reflected as she holds on tight.

"Vi, baby. It's never been like this."

"I know." Her voice sounds as if it's breaking.

I thrust, and a shudder racks my whole damn body. "Never."

She swallows, keeping her gaze on me. She has to feel it too. She has to know. She has to get it. This isn't sex. This isn't a wild fuck against my door. This is two people who are meant to be together.

I pull back, then push back in. I do it again, filling her all the way and stilling myself inside her.

She bites down hard on her lip, and her back bows, her chest pressing against me. It's the most seductive thing I've ever seen. Pleasure spikes in me as I move in her. As I stroke. As I fuck. As I watch her, my hand tight on her jaw, her eyes locked on me. At one point, I go so deep, she nearly screams, then her eyes float closed.

That won't do. "Look at me," I demand.

She squeezes her eyes, then opens them. "I'm looking at you. I can't stop looking at you."

"Fuck, baby," I mutter as I yank her closer, fucking her hard and deep. "Do you feel it?" I rasp out as I stroke into her.

She manages a desperate nod. "I feel it all."

Her head falls back, her neck stretched long and inviting, her words landing on my ears.

So good.

So close.

More.

Deeper.

You.

Coming.

Oh God, I'm coming.

She trembles. Her shoulders shake, and she cries out in pleasure. That's enough for me. I need nothing more. I'm there with her, my own orgasm insisting on appearing right fucking now as my thighs quake, and my balls tighten, and I come hard and deep inside her, filling the condom.

I groan for what feels like minutes. She does too. We pant and moan and come down from the highest high. My hand is still curved on her face, gripping her jaw, and when I let go, I realize I've held her so hard, I left fingerprints on her chin. "You okay? Did I hurt you?"

She shakes her head. "No." Her voice is like a feather. "It only feels good."

Gently, I slide out of her and excuse myself for the bathroom. After I toss the condom, clean up, and zip my jeans, I return to the living room, but she's not there. Her purse is gone, too, and my heart stops beating. Fear takes over, and I actually look out the bay window to see if she's pulled off a dine and dash.

I spot her green car parked right outside, and another car pulls up in front of it.

Why the hell would I think she's taken off? Maybe because we still haven't talked. We still haven't figured out what we're doing.

Her heels click across my floor, and I turn around, my breath coming fast. "I thought you left."

She narrows her eyes. "I'm not going to just take off without saying goodbye."

"I know. My mind is making things up."

She hooks her thumb in the direction of one of the bathrooms. "I was straightening up. I have an appointment. Remember?"

"Right, yeah." I scrub my hand over my jaw, trying to

make sense of the emotions steamrolling me. "Do you need to go now?"

She looks at her watch as she moves closer to me. "I should leave soon. I have a couple of updos for a Christmas party."

I lean in and give her a kiss, lingering on her lips. "I have to go to the team hotel tonight." We always stay at a hotel the night before a home game. It's the team rule, so we don't have to worry about spouses, girlfriends, sick kids, or cars that won't start in the morning. "Let's figure out a time to see—"

A wild knocking sounds on my door.

She arches a brow. I peer in the peephole. Just outside, Ford grins as if he's won the lottery.

CHAPTER 34

"Who's the man?" Ford holds his arms out wide. His smile extends to Pluto and back.

"You're the man?" I ask playfully, gallons of hope rising inside me. If he's here, that means one thing. One awesome, amazing thing.

He claps me on both shoulders. "You. Are. The. Fucking. Man."

Anticipation bursts in my chest. "And why am I the man?"

Ford stops and gives Violet a cheek kiss. "Hello, beautiful. Wherever are my manners? Good to see you."

"Hi, Ford. Why is Cooper the man? Are you going to tell him?" she asks, practically bouncing on those skyscraper heels.

My agent raises his right arm toward the ceiling, like a warrior issuing a battle cry. "Four years. Four beautiful, amazing, incredible, make-it-rain years."

My jaw comes unhinged. It falls to the motherfucking floor

when he says the dollar amount. It's mind-boggling. It's staggering. I slide my hand through my hair. "Holy shit."

"Holy fucking multimillion-dollar-face-of-the-team-starting-quarterback-for-the-next-four-years shit."

Ford punches the air several times, and Violet throws her arms around me. "I am so proud of you. This is amazing. This is incredible. You deserve everything," she says, her voice bubbling over with excitement. She sounds like champagne. Like diamonds. Like all the stars in the sky.

I'm floating. I'm in shock. "Thank you," I say, surprised I can even get those words out because I'm too stunned. Too overwhelmed. Ford already banked me life-changing money when he negotiated my rookie contract. This is many-lives-changing money.

I walk to the couch and sink down because I'm not sure I can stand anymore as I process this news.

"Don't sit. We need to go out and celebrate. We have points to review. We have things to discuss. Get up, brother," Ford says.

Violet sets a hand on his arm. "I think he needs a little time to process this."

Ford turns to Violet, pressing his hands together. "Speaking of time, how can I thank you? You were amazing. You were incredible. Thank you for everything you did. And guess what?"

"What?"

Ford waves his arms as if he's flying. "You're free now. You don't have to pretend to like this guy anymore."

She narrows her eyes. "What do you mean?"

He shoots her a look. "He told me you were never into him in the first place, and that's why it's all the more amazing that you pulled this off. You were so believable. Kind of ironic, though, that in the end, our man went all Boy Scout and told the truth that you guys were never a real thing."

Violet snaps her gaze to me, her voice wary. "Cooper, what is he talking about?"

My brain is sluggish, still processing the shock and thrill of this news. "I told the coach the truth before the game."

"What did you tell him?" she asks tentatively.

"That it was all smoke and mirrors," Ford says, waving his hands like a magician.

"Smoke and mirrors?"

"Fake. False. Made-up. Whatever you want to call it," Ford adds, like he thinks Violet doesn't understand words.

"I know what smoke and mirrors means," she says to Ford, then turns to me. "I just don't understand why you'd say that."

"I didn't want the coach to think I was a liar," I say, the words coming out slow since my head is a swirl of numbers and deals and life-changing news. But even in this daze, I try to explain what went down as best I can. "I didn't want to earn the job under false pretenses. I wanted him to know the whole truth."

"What is the whole truth?"

I part my lips to speak—to tell her nothing is false with her—when an alarm sounds from inside her purse. She grabs her phone and mutes the noise. Her shoulders tense, and she mutters something about her appointment as she heads for the door.

"Vi," I say, standing and walking to her. "But I also realized—"

She turns around. Her eyes brim with sadness, but her voice is resolute. "I can't be late, Cooper. This is a new client, and I can't take a chance."

I nod. Of all people, I understand how sometimes—even most of the time—business has to come first. "We'll talk later?"

She offers a smile, but it feels forced. Or maybe confused is the better term. Because fuck, I am too. This offer should be the greatest moment on the business side of my career. The chance to step into my own. To have security and a bright, bold future. But as I look at Violet, suddenly the contract isn't the most important thing. I want a future with her. She's the thing I can't live without.

I grab her hand. "I'll call you later. I promise."

She swallows and nods tightly. But she says nothing, almost as if she doesn't want to chance speaking. She turns on her heel, walks down my steps, and leaves. I don't look away, not yet. Finally, when she's in her car, I turn around to see the smiling face of my agent. I want to ask him how I can negotiate my way back into her heart.

But he's not the guy who knows those answers.

Instead, we spend the next few hours reviewing the deal over a fantastic steak dinner, and he offers to take me to the team hotel, but I have sixty minutes before I'm due there, so I ask him to drop me off at Trent's bar instead.

Trent nods at me from his spot behind the bar. "Well, well, well. If it isn't the king of San Francisco."

I wave him off, like the adulation is all too much. "Please. I insist on a parade now everyplace I go."

He tosses a dish towel in my direction. It lands on the wooden counter. "You came to the wrong place. In fact, you might have to pay for drinks now."

I feign a look of shock. "Money for food and drinks? Never heard of such a thing. By the way, what are you doing behind the bar?"

"I like to help out now and then. What the hell are you doing here?" He looks at an imaginary watch. "Don't you have to go to your nun cloisters and put on blinders like a horse before the Kentucky Derby, so no one can see you?"

"Something like that. I have thirty minutes before I have to be at the hotel. If I'm not there, it'll be lights out," I say, slicing a finger across my neck.

"Really?"

"No. But yes, I need to follow the rules." I slap my palms on the counter as if it's a drum. "But also, the team offered," I say, then tell him the amount, and he blinks about five million times.

"That's insane."

"I know. It's ridiculous. It hardly feels real."

He grabs a glass and pours from the tap. "So you came here for a celebratory drink before your last game of the season?"

I shake my head and draw a deep breath. "I don't drink before games. I came here for something else."

He sets the glass down. "My potato skins recipe is under lock and key."

"Dude, you told me years ago the secret was how long you bake the cheese."

"Dammit."

I glance behind me. His bar is full of too many ears. "Can we go to a table in the corner?"

"Ooh baby, I thought you'd never ask."

I roll my eyes. Trent waves over another bartender to cover for him, and we head to a quiet table. Funny, the last time I was here he told me the notion of me being with his sister was absurd on account of my supposedly straying eyes.

Looking back on this last season, I can say with certainty I'm not a playboy at all. I've been with one person, and she's the only person I want to be with ever again. I stroke my chin, like I need to steel myself for a tough conversation. But honestly, there's nothing hard about what I have to tell him. When you speak from the heart, you don't need a dose of courage to get the words out. You just need to open your mouth.

"A funny thing happened while I was pretending to be involved with Violet."

He cocks his head to the side. "Yeah?"

I nod. "It's not pretend."

"It's not?" he asks hesitantly.

I lean back in the chair, hold my arms out wide. "I'm in love with her."

He knits his brow and rubs his ear like he has water in it. "What did you just say?"

"I'm wildly fucking in love with her. Like, to-the-moon-and-back shit. Like rest of my life, no one else, she's the one. The sun and all the stars in the sky."

"Wow. Did you just have a brain transplant from a poet or something? Because this is not you."

I rub my hand over the back of my neck. "I know. But now it is me. Because that's what happened. And the truth is, I think I've been falling in love with her for a long time, and this pretend deal brought it all to the surface."

He blows out a long stream of air. "Does she know?"

That's the biggest issue. "She knows I like her. I'm not sure she knows I'm in love with her."

He frowns as if he's still trying to make sense of this. "Are you looking for my blessing, or something?"

I laugh and shake my head. "Actually, I'm not. And I hope you can respect that. I love you, man, and I don't want to lose your friendship, but I can't take a chance on her slipping through my fingers. So, I hope you approve, and I'm telling you first, but I want to let her know, and I'm planning on making it crystal clear."

He takes a deep breath. "What's your plan?"

"That's where I need you most. There are a few details I need you to oversee. Maybe Holly too." I quickly outline what I have in mind. "I want her to know how much she means to me. Will you help me?"

He stares at me with intense brown eyes, as if he's hunting for the truth in my face. "You'll treat her right?"

I nod. "Like a queen."

"You'll be good to her?"

"Every day."

"You love her?"

"More than I love football."

He shakes his head, amused. "I never thought the day would come."

But that day is here. "I was bracing for you to give me a hard time," I say with a relieved sigh. "You were pretty pissed after the auction."

He holds up a finger. "Correction. I was pissed when I thought you hadn't told me what was going on. Now you're telling me, and I appreciate it."

"So you don't think I'm just your dickhead, playboy, asshole friend who doesn't deserve your sister?"

He laughs as he scrubs a hand over his jaw. "You'll always be a dickhead and an asshole, but you're my friend, and you're a good guy. If you're telling me that the sun rises and sets with my sister, then you damn well better go get your woman." He shoos me off. "Get out of here and take care of that phone call."

When I arrive at the hotel, I call Violet and invite her to the game tomorrow. "Please tell me you can make it."

Her voice is cool, like she's holding back emotion. "You want me there? As your fake girlfriend? I don't understand why when Ford made it clear we were over."

"Ford handles my business. He doesn't handle my heart. There are things he doesn't know."

"And you don't want to tell me those things now?"

I move the phone away from my ear and stare at the picture of her on the screen. "No. I want to see your face. I want to see you in person. I want to tell you in person. The whole truth. Like I told the coach."

She sighs heavily.

I can't let her get away. "I don't want you there as my fake girlfriend. I want you there as you. As *my* Violet. Okay?"

She takes a beat.

"Do you trust me?"

"I do."

"Please come."

"I'll be there."

When she hangs up, I text Jones and tell him to gather the guys. I grab something for Rick that I picked up at the store on the way over, a little gift for Jones, then an item I snagged from the front desk. I drop them in a plastic bag from the hotel. Ten minutes later, I meet them in Jones's room.

They're assembled, parked in chairs around the table.

"To what do we owe the honor of this impromptu team meeting?" Jones asks.

I place my palms together. "Gentlemen, we are going to cut Harlan's hair tonight."

Harlan sits up straight, his hand shooting to his long hair. "Blasphemy. What are you talking about?"

"Dude, we're winning," Rick adds.

I reach into the bag and toss him a pack of Big Red. "Time for cinnamon gum tomorrow."

Jones smirks. "Let me guess. You have new socks for me next."

"You know it," I say, dipping my hand into the bag and tossing him a pair of my own freshly cleaned socks.

"What in the ever-loving hell?" Harlan asks.

Jones stands up and taps Harlan's skull. "You can't figure this out?"

Awareness dawns on him. "Ohhhhh." Harlan looks at me. "You fucking horndog."

I shrug and hold my hands out wide. Had I broken the pact before we clinched, I might have felt worse. But I don't, for many reasons. "Guys, we don't win because of rituals. We win because we play like a team. You guys have had my back all season, and I've had yours. But we don't win because of smelly socks, or pink bubblegum, or uncut hair."

"Or you not getting your dick wet," Jones mutters.

I smirk. "Exactly. We win because of how we play, and how we play together. As you can surmise, I broke my superstition.

So, the way I see it, you three can step out on the field tomorrow doing what you've always done this season. Or you can have my back, and start a new ritual with me. Like a team."

Jones pumps his arms at his sides and grinds his pelvis. "Cooper can't keep the snake in the cage, boys. And if the snake is out, the socks are clean, the King of the Jungle's hair gets cut, and the gum is a new flavor."

We put our fists together and knock as a foursome.

Harlan sighs. "Since Violet's not here, which one of you assholes is going to cut my hair?"

The three of us shake our heads.

"Seriously? You're all too chicken to cut hair?"

"If you have clippers, I'll give you a buzz cut," Rick says, rubbing his hand over his own short hair. "But fair warning. I'd probably slip and shave your eyebrows too."

Harlan sighs. "Thanks, but no thanks, Barber Rick."

"Wait," Jones says, grabbing his phone. "I have an idea. I saw Jillian here earlier."

We all make obscene gestures in his direction. He doesn't care, though, since he's convincing the team publicist to play stylist for the night. Moments later, she arrives with a cheery smile on her face.

"Edward Scissorhands at your service," she says as she marches into the room.

She wets Harlan's hair and snips off a few inches as I tell them the rest of the plan for tomorrow. Jillian coos and says she can't wait.

I can't either.

CHAPTER 35

Some say the games you play after you clinch are meaningless. I say there are no meaningless games. I'd like to think the fifty thousand fans at our stadium, and the millions watching the Thursday-night game of the week, would agree. Our final bout is against a team with a losing record, the St. Louis Thunderbolts. But they don't play that way. They play tight and tough and close.

We do too. Rick chews the Big Red and kicks a field goal. Jones wears fresh-as-a-daisy socks and compiles seventy-nine receiving yards and two touchdowns, while Harlan, with his newly shorn locks, gets his feet in the end zone. As for me? Well, let's just say that freeing the snake hasn't hurt my game. I'm not perfect, not by any means. I fumble a ball, miss several passes, and get sacked twice. But I play well enough—like someone who can anchor a team for the next four years, which is exactly what I plan on doing.

And when we win tonight, we lock down a 12–4 record for the regular season, and a stadium full of happy fans.

I'm stoked for the victory, but that's not what I want most to win tonight.

Fortunately, one of the benefits of my position on the team is that the sports reporters usually seek me out first. Tonight, Jillian makes sure of it. As soon as the game ends and the media hits the field, Jillian sends Sierra, the reporter who emceed the auction, to interview me. The perfectly coiffed and polished redhead is working tonight for the network carrying the game, and she's exactly who I want to speak to right now.

I steal a glance at the sidelines, hoping to catch a glimpse of Violet. But the field is too crowded, the stands too stuffed with fans. I can't make her out, and I have to trust that Trent and Holly are doing their part, right next to my mom, who's here too. Their job? Don't let Violet leave, and make sure she tunes into the postgame on her phone.

Sierra fires off a few standard game questions, and I answer Crash Davis-style, then she switches gears. "And now, for the talk of the town. Word is you're re-upping with the Renegades, and they've offered you a four-year contract. Can you tell us more about that?"

I flash a smile as I answer. "I couldn't be happier to stay, and none of this would be possible without an owner like Jasper Scott, who's committed to putting the best team on the field, and to Mike Greenhaven, who knows exactly what to do with that team. I'm grateful to the owner and the coach and the entire organization for giving me the chance to stay on."

In my peripheral vision, Jillian motions to Sierra, giving her some kind of signal to ask the next question. "And is there any particular reason that you want to stay here in San Francisco?"

I can't help it. I grin like a man in love. I'm not sure what Violet will say to this public declaration. But I think I saw it in her eyes yesterday when I made love to her against the door. A look then that said she felt the same wild beating in her heart that I felt in mine. That I still feel when I think of her.

For now, I say goodbye to the Crash Davis school of media relations and speak from the heart. "It's about a woman. Sometimes that's what makes a man want to stay. I love the fans, I love the city, and I love that my family is here. But more than that, there's someone in this town who I'm madly in love with."

Sierra's green eyes light up. "Do tell."

I'm not going to confess on national TV all the details of how we started. All anyone needs to know is the woman they think I'm with is the woman I want. "I hope she wants to stay with me. I hope she wants to be with me for a whole lot longer than the contract I just signed." Now I turn to the camera, since I'm not talking to Sierra anymore. I'm talking to the woman I hope is watching on her phone at the fifty-yard line.

Behind me, teammates and reporters stream across the field, while fans cheer as they make their way out of the stadium. But my world is small now. My words are for one person only. "Violet, I've been falling in love with you since high school, and it's not stopping. I fall more for you every single day. I want you to be mine, to keep being mine, every night. I don't want this to end. Ever."

Sierra brings her hand to her heart and gasps. "That is

so sweet. I love it when the quarterback falls in love with the hometown girl and stays with her."

"That's exactly what I hope is happening in my life." I glimpse a commotion on the sidelines. I don't even try to rein in a smile as a sweaty, dirty Jones, still in his uniform, escorts Violet onto the field. That was his job. To go to security in her section, and then bring her to me.

Violet has never looked prettier as she race-walks to me in her jeans and a Renegades sweatshirt. She's smiling, and she looks as if she's crying too.

She picks up the pace, but I won't let her run to me. I need to run to her.

"Thank you, Sierra. I need to see my woman."

And I go running to Violet, scooping her up and wrapping her in my arms. I gaze into her eyes and tell her face-to-face what I told the whole world. "I love you so much."

"Shut up," she says, but she's grinning.

"You want me to stop talking?"

"Never," she says, sniffling as she cups my cheeks. "I'm so in love with you, and you better have meant every word."

I laugh, and happiness floods every corner of my body. "Every. Single. Word." I press my sweaty forehead to hers, then pull back. "I am so ridiculously in love with you, they're going to need a new word for it. I want you to pick out pink polka-dot towels with me, and sing Miley Cyrus, and beat me in *Madden*, and I want you to be mine. I want you all the time, baby. When I said since high school, I meant it."

Tears stream from her eyes. She purses her lips, then says in a soft, broken voice, "When I said since second grade, I meant it."

I blink, and now I might be officially stunned. "You did?"

She nods. "I've had a crush on you forever, Cooper." It hits me—that's why she said she was worried I'd hurt her, because she's been holding on to this feeling for so many years. "And I never thought this would happen. I never thought you'd feel the same."

"Why wouldn't I? You're amazing."

"I think when you've been in love with someone your whole life, it's just hard to imagine you'd be so lucky that he'd love you back."

"Get used to it. You're getting lucky with me, and you're getting lucky on a regular basis. And this love? It's only growing stronger. I love you in every single way," I say, planting kisses all over her gorgeous face, kissing away her tears.

"It's the same for me. I've felt this way about you forever, but since the auction, it's gone into the stratosphere. I've loved getting to know you more, even when it was pretend. Because it was never pretend for me."

"You want to get to know me more tonight? There are some parts that you don't know well enough, as far as I'm concerned."

She laughs and presses a kiss to my lips. "I want to get to know all of you so very well."

"How would you feel about coming over tonight? And spending Christmas with me? And going out with me on dates, and putting up with me when we lose, and putting up with me when we win, and letting me do whatever I can to help you with your business so I can support you, too, as you go after your dreams?"

Her bottom lip quivers as she nods. "I would say you really ought to take me out of here very soon because there's a good chance I'm going to do indecent things to you on the field."

"You better do indecent things to me," I say, and then I kiss her under the lights of the stadium, and judging from the bright pops and flashes, this picture will be splashed all over social media in about thirty seconds.

And it's all real.

It's the most real thing I've ever felt, and I make sure she knows that as I kiss her in front of fifty thousand fans.

CHAPTER 36

Tonight, I don't need ice for my shoulder. I don't need a beer to smooth over the moment. I don't even bother with music. Once we're back at my house, I take her to my bedroom, prepared to strip her naked.

She gets in the first word, though. "Unzip your pants."

I wiggle my eyebrows. "I can do that," I say, obliging her request.

She pushes on my stomach, indicating I need to get my ass on the bed.

I sit on the edge of the mattress, she drops down to her knees, wraps her hand around my dick, and sucks.

"Holy fuck."

Instantly, my hands find their way into her soft hair, and I groan as she goes for it. There's no playing around here. Violet doesn't tease or toy. She takes me deep as she licks my cock, and I grip her head harder.

"That's so good, baby. Have I told you how much I like blow jobs?"

She shakes her head, since her mouth is full. Quite full.

"I'm not going to tell you, then. I'm going to show you by letting you do that to me as much as you want."

I can feel her try to laugh against my dick. Then all laughter ceases, and I give in.

Heat pools in my groin as she licks and sucks. For a couple minutes, I let myself get lost in the feel—and the view. The woman I adore is on her knees, sucking me off as if it's all she's ever wanted. She makes me feel like a rock star, like a goddamn king as she introduces me to the joys of her mouth. But it's too good, and the last thing I want is to come before she does.

I stop her, gently tugging her face up. "I'm going to be blunt. I want to spend a ridiculous amount of my life with my dick in your mouth, but right now, I need you naked and under me."

"Have it your way." She crosses her hands over each other and tugs off her sweatshirt. Soon she's wearing nothing, and I get into the same outfit as well. She scoots back on the bed, and I climb over her.

"Hey, gorgeous," I say, and then before she can protest—not that she would—I bring my face between her legs and kiss her sweetness.

Instantly, she arches up into me. "Why can you do this to me and I can't to you? Are you going to have all these rules again?"

I laugh lightly. "No rules. Except this one—you come first and, ideally, more than once before I do."

Really, how can she protest that? She doesn't, because I make it worth her while. I lick and kiss and suck until she's rocking against my mouth and coming on my lips.

When her moans subside, I'm above her, my chest pressed to hers. "Hi."

She blinks open her eyes and smiles woozily. "Hi."

I kiss her neck, her throat, her ear, then meet her lips, whispering a kiss over them.

She says my name again, and this time, her voice grows more serious. "Cooper."

"What is it?" I ask as I reach for a condom from my wallet. I snagged some from the hotel last night.

"I'm on the pill. And I'm negative. Are you?"

"I am."

There's a code among pro athletes. Wrap it till you're married. But this isn't about the wear-a-glove code. It's about trust and respect. It's about who I'm giving my heart to.

When I look into her bright eyes, I see everything I could ever want in this life. She's not going anywhere, because I'm never going to let her get away from me. I don't want more than the two of us right now, and I know she's the only one for me. I know she'll be here when my career is over, because she was there before it started. She'll be here, because I can see forever in her eyes.

I rest on my forearms, settle between her legs, and sink into her.

We both moan at the same time.

It's so good. It's so intense. It's everything.

I take my time, building and pushing and savoring. I watch her, cataloging every intoxicating reaction. I love the way her lips part, how she breathes out hard when I swivel my hips, how her face is the picture of exquisite torment when I thrust deep into her.

She grabs my ass, and I slide her knees up her chest. I make love to her like that. With her pinned beneath me, saying my name, breathing my breath, kissing my lips.

Her gasps come faster.

Her noises grow louder.

Her moves become wilder.

She rocks up into me, widens her legs, takes me deeper.

Everything in me crackles. Pleasure snaps in my body. Desire flows hot in my blood. I'm dizzy with want, ravenous with the need to be as close to her as possible.

In seconds, she's crying out in bliss, saying my name, chanting God's name, calling out incoherent moans of pleasure, and sending a whole new wave of electricity sparking across my skin. As the aftershocks shudder through her, I rise to my knees, grab her hips, tug her down harder on my cock, and go wild, thrusting, pounding, letting go until the world slips into pure pleasure and my climax obliterates me, as I come inside the woman I love.

The woman I plan on loving for the rest of my life.

After, as I collapse on her, then roll to the side, I find myself wondering how it's possible to just know. To know with absolute certainty that you're with the person who makes you not only happy, but better.

Because I know I've found the one I want. I don't want her to doubt my love. I run my fingers along her cheekbone. "Hey, Violet. You want to know something?"

She turns to me, her cheeks rosy and glowing. "Yes, I want to know something."

I wrap an arm around her. "You're stuck with me."

She laughs. "Is that so?"

"Yep. I don't plan on letting you go. Ever, basically."

"I can live with that."

"You should live with me," I say.

She arches a brow. "You're already inviting me to live with you?"

"Vi, I plan on loving you for my whole damn life. I don't need to mess around with stages and steps and taking things in some kind of orderly fashion. You're an eighty-yard pass, and I want to get into the end zone with you."

She rolls her eyes. "That sounds incredibly dirty."

"Yeah, it does."

"Hey, do you want to know something?"

"I do."

She runs her hands down my chest, over the planes of my abs. "Why did the football go to the bank?"

"Why?"

She wiggles her eyebrows. "To get her quarterback."

I crack up. "You've got him. You've absolutely got him."

"I'm keeping him." She slinks a hand over my hip and around to my butt, squeezing. "After all, you do have the best butt in the NFL."

———

Two days later, she wakes up with me on Christmas morning, and I give her one of many gifts. A key to my home. She already has the key to my heart.

CHAPTER 37

Holly: I'm waiting...

Violet: For what?

Holly: For my *You were right*.

Violet: Hmm. What were you right about?

Holly: *Scrolls back through previous texts. Reminds Violet.* Ahem. "He's wild for you." So, yeah, I was right.

Violet: Well, I mean, sure. Fine, I am hanging at his house right now and he just made me pancakes.

Holly: I was right. I was so, so, so right. Say it.

Violet: You totally predicted the pancakes.

Holly: I predicted it all!

Violet: Did you?

Holly: Girl! I did. And now look at you—happy as a gal getting served pancakes. That is the sign of true love.

Violet: Love is pancakes.

Holly: It is.

Violet: Well, I suppose I should say "You were right."

I'm still kind of amazed. The guy I've crushed on since second grade is as in love with me as I am with him. This is better than pancakes.

Holly: Enjoy them anyway.

Violet: I will. Want to know why?

Holly: Why?

Violet: Because you were so, so, so right.

Holly: I told you so. 😊

EPILOGUE

A FEW DAYS AFTER CHRISTMAS

Ah, this is my favorite view.

"You can cut my hair all day," I say, smiling like the cat that ate all the canaries as Violet snips my hair, trimming the messy strands at her salon.

"You dirty man," she chides.

"You like me that way," I say, setting my hands on her hips.

She stops snipping and gives me a look. "You can't do that when I cut your hair."

"But the rest of the time I can, right?"

She laughs. "Possibly."

She finishes my haircut, and that evening, we go out on a date. Violet jokes that it's the charity date she won from the Most Valuable Playboy auction. I don't like to think about how the other dates from past auctions went. They were one and done. This date is the start of the rest of my life.

That's why I make sure it's different. We meet the whole crew at my favorite karaoke bar in Japantown, in the heart of the city. Trent and Holly wave from a table by the stage, since they arrived first. When Violet and I sit, Trent shakes his head, gesturing to us. "Still getting used to the two of you together," he says, but he's smiling.

Violet wiggles her eyebrows. "Let me help you with a little trial by fire." She turns and kisses me hard in front of him. She's loud, too, making lip-smacking sounds.

"Get a room," Trent says, tossing a napkin at us.

When Violet wrenches away, she grins at her brother. "Did that help you? Or do you want to take a picture to hang in your home?"

"Damn. You two really are perfect for each other," Trent says.

Holly runs a hand through his hair. "I told you so. They were meant to be."

A few minutes later, my good friends McKenna and Chris show up.

The bubbly McKenna wraps Violet in a warm embrace. "You guys are adorable. Also, I had a feeling he always liked you," McKenna says.

"The feeling has always been mutual," she replies.

More friends join us, and soon Trent, Holly, Jones, Jillian, Harlan, Chris, McKenna and Rick work their way through standards like "I Want It That Way," "Hooked on a Feeling," "Love Shack" and, of course, "Livin' on a Prayer."

Yes, I let Jones have my song, because I take my turn with Violet. We sing together, belting out "Islands in the Stream." We're no Kenny and Dolly, but if you listen to the words, you'd be hard-pressed not to fall deeper in love. It's one of the most upbeat, happy love songs ever written.

Which makes it perfect for two people who are *"disgustingly cute"* as Jones shouts to the stage.

"No, they're *ridiculously adorable*," Jillian corrects.

That's us. We're those people onstage, singing a popular love song as if no one else is around, as if we're going to go home and rip each other's clothes off, then make pancakes together the next day.

Come to think of it, both of those things sound like great ideas, so that's what we do.

Violet roots from the fifty-yard line in all my playoff games. She shouts the loudest and cheers the hardest when we win the wild-card round in an absolutely epic trounce. She goes nuts in the divisional round, and I'm running on the most exhilarating adrenaline I've ever felt when we kick ass with a fat victory.

But our quest splinters in the championship game against Los Angeles. It's a tight match against our rivals, and we lose by three measly points.

Not gonna lie. It stings. It hurts.

But there's always next year.

When I drive to the coach's home a week later, Violet

fiddles with her bracelets in the passenger seat, and I set a hand on her wrist. "Relax, baby. Greenhaven isn't that bad, I swear."

Violet shoots me a look that says *you've got to be kidding me*. "I'm not worried about the coach. I want his wife to like me."

I laugh. "She'll love you."

And she does. Because Violet is pretty freaking fantastic. She brings a set of antique teacups that she found in a store in Noe Valley, as well as a bottle of wine. No surprise—both Mike Greenhaven and his wife, Emily, think Violet is the bomb. At dinner, Emily pours the wine and raises her glass. "To next year."

"To next year," we say in unison.

It's both a toast and a fervent wish.

Having it all is a pretty tough feat to pull off, and I remind myself that in the scheme of things, I've already come out grossly ahead this year. New contract, fat payday, amazing team, strong playoff performance, and the best part of all—someone who loves me and would still love me even if I didn't have any of those things.

Maybe next year I can add a ring to the mix.

For now, I have everything I need in the woman I come home to at night and wake up to in the morning.

ANOTHER EPILOGUE

A FEW MONTHS LATER

"Go, go, go!" Violet thrusts her arm in the air when Smashalie scores a point.

Turns out the little girl was serious about roller derby. She took it up after her last appointment and joined a junior league that Violet and I happen to fully sponsor. My signing bonus was pretty damn sizable, and I decided to donate it to charities and youth programs in the Bay Area. The Children's Hospital is using it for services and research, and Ford is helping me funnel money to worthy programs for kids. That includes sports for girls, but also some sports programs for kids who might need a little extra help, whether after battling cancer or having corrective surgery. I want to give them every chance to reach their fullest potential.

So here we are at the roller rink, watching a bout as Smashalie and her teammates cruise around the oval.

"What would your roller derby name be?" I ask Violet.

She screws up the corner of her lips, looks to the ceiling, then at me. "I'd be the Purple Snipper. Don't you think?" She pretends to cut with scissors.

I grab my crotch. "Ouch."

"Lavender Cutter?"

I seesaw my palm. "Mildly better."

She snaps her fingers. "The Lilac Shredder!"

"You're brilliant," I say, pressing a kiss to her forehead.

"What about you? Would you be Best Butt in the NFL? Rock-Hard Cheeks?" She squeezes my ass.

"Steel Buns."

She shakes her head. "Nope. I'm keeping the butt nicknames for myself. You're the Gunslinger." She runs a hand down my right arm. "Yes, the Gunslinger made all this happen."

And, honestly, that's one of the things I'm most proud of. That I've been able to give back. And I've done it with Violet. That's always been one of our shared passions, finding worthy causes that help kids. That's why I chose this spot instead of the beach, a mountain hike, a picnic, or a basketball arena. That's why there is no Jumbotron, no cameras, no flash mob. I researched ideas. I googled clever strategies. I approached this moment like I was prepping for a game, studying all the options, deciding which plays to use.

In the end, though, I want today to feel authentic to who we are as a couple.

I turn to the woman I adore. "Hey, Violet, I wanted to ask you something."

She tilts her head, waiting, her lips quirking up in a soft smile.

I move quickly. Always have. I drop to one knee and flip open the box I've had in my pocket. Her eyes widen. "You're my best friend, my lover, and my favorite person in the universe. You are more precious to me than anything else. And I know our love will outlast everything. Will you marry me?"

She clasps her hand to her mouth as she whispers the loveliest word I've ever heard—*yes*.

Tears stream down her cheeks as she kneels with me, still nodding, now sobbing, and holding out her hand. I slide the ring on her finger, and it's perfect. Honestly, it's one of the biggest rings ever made. You can't be the quarterback's wife and walk around with a tiny diamond.

"I love you, Cooper. So much you have no idea."

"Oh, I do have an idea. A very good idea. I think it's pretty damn close to how much I love you."

She brushes a kiss on my lips. "Some days I still can't believe it's real."

"And I'll spend a lifetime showing you how real my love is."

She threads her hands through my hair, and we kiss, kneeling on the floor of the roller rink.

When she breaks the kiss, she lifts her hand and gazes at her ring. The way I see it, even if I don't have a ring, there's no reason she shouldn't.

Besides, there's always next year.

FINAL EPILOGUE

VIOLET

One year later, I walk down the aisle at his mom's home in Sausalito. We hold our wedding on the deck overlooking Richardson Bay, all of San Francisco in the distance. There, I marry the guy I've crushed on for more than two decades. He's my love and my best friend. Plus, he makes me pancakes and he makes me happy. Sometimes, life just works out better than a crush. So much better.

BONUS PREQUEL TO
MOST VALUABLE PLAYBOY

When he wrapped his arms around me and pulled me close at my brother's wedding, my heart beat faster. When we danced into the night, my mind raced far ahead, entertaining all the possibilities I'd longed for. And later, when Cooper told me he'd won the starting quarterback job before he shared the news with anyone else, I started to believe we could be more.

But I didn't want to lose him as a friend, so I chose to focus on him solely as my buddy. That worked well enough for a while.

Until that night, in front of everyone, when he shocked my world to its core.

MOST IRRESISTIBLE GUY
A PREQUEL NOVELLA TO MOST VALUABLE PLAYBOY

CHAPTER 1

I can't stop staring at the best man.

As I walk down the aisle, strains of classical music rising in the church, my eyes are inexorably drawn to the man next to the groom.

That tux. That crisp white shirt. That bow tie.

Most of all, that smile. A grin I've never gotten over.

Clutching a bouquet of yellow tulips, I march. Hundreds of pairs of eyes are watching. Smiling. Tears welling.

Everyone loves a wedding.

My gaze is firmly fixed on the best man; the way the tux fits him, how it's snug against his toned, muscular frame, how his soulful brown eyes lock with mine.

Oh, God.

He's looking at me.

He's staring.

My heart skids in my chest, pounding painfully against my rib cage as his gaze lingers on me like he's taking a stroll up and down my body as I approach the altar. With every step I take, tingles spread down my bare arms, and for several brief and torturous seconds, I let myself imagine I'm walking to him and he's mine.

Mine to link arms with. To hold hands. To brush a kiss to his cheek.

This is a game I play now and then. I can't resist in this moment, even though I've learned how to live with this riot of emotions in my chest like a flock of birds soaring to the sky all at once.

I learned to live with this wild sensation in my chest because I have to.

Cooper Armstrong isn't my man.

Instead, he's my best guy friend, and he's my brother's best friend too.

He's someone I'm incredibly lucky to have in my life. He's supportive, and caring, and funny, and so damn easy on the eyes. When I reach the front of the church, I smile at him, then at my brother Trent, the groom. I take my place across from the best man. We turn as the wedding march begins and the bride glides down the aisle to marry my brother while I steal glances at his best friend.

When the vows are exchanged and the rings are slid on and when the groom kisses the bride, we all cheer. A wave of happiness rushes over me for my brother. He's marrying Holly, the love of his life. They walk back down the aisle as husband and wife, the crowd standing and clapping for the newlyweds.

Cooper and I follow, arm in arm.

He leans in close, his lips dangerously near my ear. A shiver runs through me, and I try to hide it so he won't know how he affects me, how he's always affected me. "Save a dance for me, will you, Violet?"

I give him a playful little smile, so he knows he's my friend, not the object of my desires. "I'll see if there's room for you on my dance card," I say, adding in a wink for good measure.

"Then I'll do my best to monopolize it."

He can have every single dance if he wants to, but I can't let him know that. I've been friends with him my whole life, and there's no way I'll jeopardize that for the dark-horse shot of something more.

CHAPTER 2

For the record, I've crushed on Cooper for a long time.

Okay. A crazy ridiculously long time.

Fine, let's call a spade a spade. Decades. Nearly two decades. After all, he was my first ever crush way back when I was in second grade.

Yup, I'm *that* girl.

But, in my defense, he is adorable.

And sexy.

And fun.

And sweet.

And smart.

He's the right mix of a little bit cocksure attitude, a lot of charm, and a canyon of determination. Plus, he's a total gentleman.

It's impossible not to like him.

My crush that launched in second grade only intensified when we were teenagers. I might have enjoyed watching him work out on the football field in high school. I definitely liked the view when he took off his shirt. And sure, I've imagined what it would be like to kiss him countless times.

But I've always kept my emotions in check. We're friends. Great friends. We've watched movies together, gone for runs along the water, broken bread at his mother's house. We've gone out with friends and sung karaoke together as a group—my brother and Holly, Cooper and me. For the record, I am most excellent at crooning "Sweet Child O' Mine," and Cooper kills it at anything Bon Jovi. We've also crushed it duet-style to Human League's "Don't You Want Me," and the irony of the title isn't lost on me.

We know how to have fun, and we've relied on each other over the years the way old friends—*good* friends—do.

Translation: I'm a big girl, and I've learned to live with this unrequited crush.

I've never even tried to *requite* it. He's too important to me to let words spill of how I feel. It's easier to be like this, like friends.

"Slice of cake?" I ask later that night as I grab a delicate china plate that's home to a mouth-wateringly fantastic-looking slice of wedding cake.

Cooper pats his belly. "I'm watching my figure."

I pat his stomach too. Flat as a board. Tight as a drum. Delicious as candy. I mean, I *bet* it's as delicious as candy and as lickable too. "You're right. If you have even one bite, you'll puff up, and you'll be sacked in the first game."

He rolls his eyes playfully. "Violet, don't be silly. I have to play to get sacked."

"You'll play. Sooner than you think." We sit down at the head table. My brother and his wife are circulating and chatting with other guests, so it's only the two of us right now. "Jeff Grant can't play forever."

Cooper scrubs a hand over his square jaw. "Some days, it feels that way. But I just have to keep waiting."

"You do, and it'll be worth it."

Jeff Grant is the starting quarterback for the local NFL team, the San Francisco Renegades. He's also one of the game's GOATs, as in greatest of all time. The veteran quarterback has three rings, impeccable statistics, an eye-goggling winning percentage, and a sterling reputation for coming back in crucial moments, including bringing the team from the brink and pulling out an astonishing fourth-quarter win in last year's Super Bowl after a fourteen-point deficit with ten minutes to play.

He is great. There is no debating it. As football fans, we're truly spoiled to have him helming the team.

But even so, I still want this guy next to me to be the one in the pocket, calling the shots, scanning the field, and marching the team down it, leading the Renegades to victory because I know that's what he can do.

"It seems hard to believe now, but Father Time will eventually catch up with Jeff. Just keep being patient," I reassure him.

Cooper shrugs. "Who knows when that'll happen." He

flashes a smile, letting me know he can't let his bench-warming status bother him. He's learned to be cool about his backup status. Drafted two years ago in the first round, he's hardly seen any playing time because Jeff Grant is not only amazing, he's also durable. It's been frustrating for Cooper to watch Jeff take all the snaps, but he's learned to be patient too.

"Soon," I say, as I take a bite of cake. "Your time will come sooner than you think."

"For now, I'm learning everything I can from the best." His eyes turn fiery, blazing with the kind of intensity I know he shows on the field. "And when I'm called up, I'll be more than ready."

"You will. Now, tell me what you're learning," I say, diving into the dessert for another forkful.

"You want to know what I'm learning from watching Jeff?" Cooper's lopsided grin is deliciously sexy and quirks up at the corner of his lips, almost as if he doesn't really believe that I want to know.

I tap his forearm. "Yes. I do. You know I love game talk."

"That's true. You have an endless appetite for football conversations. You could have been a sports talk host."

I shudder at the thought. "I detest sports talk shows."

He laughs. "Me too."

I stare at him pointedly, drumming my fingers on the table. "Well? Are you going to tell me stuff? Or is it top secret?"

Laughing, he leans closer to me. Closer than I'd expect him to be. Anticipation weaves through me. "I'll tell you, but you can't tell a soul," he whispers, his breath ghosting over my skin, goosebumps rising in its wake.

Damn body.

I want to tell my libido to calm down. But when Cooper inches near me and turns up the flirting dial, I don't know how I can rein in the hot, tingly tremble that's threatening to run through my entire body, just from being near him.

I can smell his clean, woodsy scent. His aftershave. His minty breath. I want it all, but I can't have it so I practice my best I'm-cool-with-this skills, the ones I've needed my whole life. "Oh, is this your secret playbook?"

"I'm learning strategy, confidence, but also some amazing new plays." His eyes blaze as he talks, and the golden flecks in his brown eyes seem to shimmer with excitement.

This is his playground, and he loves it.

I do too. I can't help myself. A rabid football fan, my love of the game is a part of me, and I can feel it in my bones. My passion comes from the strategy, the angles, the myriad ways the game can be played. I love trying to figure out what type of play a team will execute, how the defense will respond, and what risks the players are willing to take. Cooper and I talk about that as I nibble on the cake. As he dives into some of the plays, his eyes sparkle more, his expressions become more animated. I savor moments like this, to enjoy these conversations with my good friend.

He shakes his head, amused when I ask about a particular play-action fake strategy.

"Did I get the question wrong?" I ask, curious why he's laughing.

"No. You had it right. All of it. It's impressive."

"What can I say? I'm a junkie. I'll probably be more of one when you're the starting quarterback. I'll be cheering the loudest."

"At every single home game?"

I nod. "Consider it done."

"Yeah?" He says it almost as if he doesn't quite believe I'd be there.

"Of course."

A slow smile spreads across his handsome face, lighting up his features. "I'd like that."

I nudge him with my elbow. "You'd like that because you'd be the starting quarterback."

"Yes. But I'd like it because I like it when you come to the games."

My heart sits up, looks around, wonders if he really said that. If it meant something more. "You do?" I ask, my voice feathery.

"I always have. I like playing for you, Vi. You're my favorite spectator. Even back in high school I got a kick out of knowing you were in the bleachers."

My heart stutters, tripping a switch in me, the one that longs for him. I distract myself with another bite of cake. "Too bad you're too busy watching your figure, because this cake is delicious. You should consider giving into temptation."

He quirks an eyebrow. "You think I should?"

There's something borderline flirty in his voice. Something I ought to ignore.

"You should." Using the fork, I point to the cake. "This is heaven."

"Damn. You're making it sound too appealing." He grabs the utensil, dives into the cake with it, and takes a bite. He groans as he chews.

The sound of it is carnal, masculine, and too damn sexy for my own good. I should not be turned on by the sound of him eating a bite of cake.

But yet, here it is. A pulse beats inside me.

He sets down the fork with gusto. "And now I'm going to dance off this cake." He takes my hand and pulls me up.

"I'm dancing it off too?"

His gaze travels up my body once again, like it did at the ceremony. "You're perfect. But I still need you to shake it up, baby."

Baby.

Holy smokes, he just gave me an affectionate nickname. And he called me perfect. I'm not at all, but I adore his compliments.

I don't have time to soak them in since he guides me to the dance floor where we shake and shimmy through some fast numbers.

"Are you dancing off that one dangerous bite, Cooper?"

"Absolutely. Can't you see me get trimmer as we speak?"

A slow song begins, and I half expect we'll do that thing people do when they wander away from the dance floor.

But that's not what happens.

CHAPTER 3

He slides in closer to me, setting his hands on my waist. "You weren't going to take off for the slow song, were you?"

My throat is dry. My pulse hammers. "No."

"Good," he says, his voice soft, and the gentle sound of it makes me freeze, my arms in mid-air.

I know I need to put my arms around his neck, but I haven't been this close to him since prom. Cooper Armstrong was my date at prom. He was a freshman in college, I was a senior in high school, and he came back to town for that weekend. I'd been planning on going with my boyfriend but the guy broke up with me shortly before the big dance. Cooper swooped in and saved the day. He said he didn't want my dress to go to waste. He wanted me to wear it and to have a good time. I wound up having the best time with him.

"You can put your arms around my neck," he says tenderly.

I blink. "Sorry. I was kind of out of it for a second."

"That's okay. I have that effect on women."

Right. *Women.* I need the reminder. Cooper is a hot, single, eligible bachelor. He dates. He plays the field. He doesn't know I have a long-standing crush on him. He doesn't know I have feelings that run much deeper than friendship. We've never been together, even though in moments like this, with his hands on my waist and my arms slinking around his neck, something starts to feel inevitable in the way we touch.

Like we were meant to come together on this dance floor.

Only I know that's my foolish heart talking. Or my eyes, since they're busy drinking in the up-close-and-personal sight of this most handsome man, his square jaw, his messy brown hair that the hairdresser in me wants to get my scissors on and cut, but the woman in me wants to get my hands in and run my fingers through.

Most of all, there's a part of me every now and then that wishes we could have this. These long chats that unfurl late into the night and lead to more.

That lead to dancing.

To his hands on my waist.

To my fingers tiptoeing dangerously close to the ends of his hair. "Cooper," I say, chiding him. "Your hair is getting long. We need to cut it again."

He arches an eyebrow, pretending to think. "Know any good hairdressers?"

As if I'm also contemplating, I stare at the ceiling as the soft strains of Ella Fitzgerald cocoon us. "I do, but I wonder if she can fit you in."

"I'll just go to a barber."

I gasp. "Horrors. What a terrible thing to say. You can't take this pretty hair to a barber."

"So you'll fit me in, then?"

Anytime, anywhere.

"I'll do my best to get you on the books, and I'll give you a very nice haircut."

He moves in closer. "You give the best haircuts."

It doesn't seem as if we're talking about haircuts.

It doesn't seem that way at all.

His lips skate tantalizingly close to my neck, as his mouth comes near my ear. "As if I'd let anyone else touch my hair."

This time, I don't shiver. I melt. I'm molten all over, and I can feel the effects of his words everywhere in my body.

He inches even closer, and I do, too, like it's the next step in the dance.

An inch here, an inch there, and we'd be indecent.

I wonder if it's apparent to anyone else that the bridesmaid is thinking about doing filthy things to the best man and wishing, wishing, wishing he would take her home.

Wishing, too, she knew what the best man was thinking in this moment.

We're quiet as we sway, the twinkling lights scattering across the dance floor.

Like this, it feels like fantasy could slide into reality. It feels like we're one slip of the tongue away.

It might be the way his right hand curls tighter around

my waist. It might be the way he moves almost imperceptibly closer. It might even be the slightest rumble in his throat as the song nears its end.

Or it might all be in my imagination.

The music fades, and when a faster song begins, we break apart.

CHAPTER 4

ONE YEAR LATER

The chorus to Sam Smith's new single plays in my salon, faintly in the background, providing the soundtrack for my customers. With my high-heeled boots planted wide on the smooth tiled floor, I stand in front of Gigi, concentrating on snipping the last little uneven strands of her pretty blond bangs.

One last clip.

And there.

"You look gorgeous," I declare.

"Do I?" Her voice rises in excitement. She has a fifth date tomorrow night with a guy she thinks might be the one. He's a chef, a baseball fan, and he loves to send her good morning and good night text messages. She's told me everything about their budding romance during her half hour in the hot seat, since that's what people usually do with their stylists.

Just call me a priest, a therapist, a temporary best friend, as well as the wizard with scissors.

"You're going to knock that man to his knees." I spin her chair around so she can face the silver-lined mirror. Gigi smiles widely when she sees her reflection, fluffing her hair, running a hand over her smooth locks.

"You're a miracle worker."

I wave off the compliment. "Please. Look at the raw materials you gave me to work with. You're naturally beautiful."

"And now you've made me feel even prettier."

It's my turn to smile since I honestly love helping people feel beautiful about themselves. "I want a full report," I tell her as she leaves, then I spend the next few minutes chatting with the other stylists who work for me to see what they need at my salon in the heart of Sausalito, a little tourist town right across the Golden Gate Bridge from San Francisco.

I opened the shop two years ago, and I've expanded it in the last year. Heroes and Hairoines has taken a lot of my time, but it's been worth it since business is booming. But I haven't had time for much else in the past year, except the rare date here and there. A regular client set me up with her brother. Holly suggested I have coffee with a guy she works with. Both were nice men, but there were no sparks.

I have no complaints about how much time my business has demanded of me, and I don't mind working nearly every day past closing time.

As I walk past the sinks to the back of the shop, I check

my phone to see when my next appointment is. Five minutes from now. Just enough time to make a cup of tea. My phone dings, the alert for a news story. I swipe my thumb and stop in my tracks. My jaw comes unhinged when I see the headline on ESPN: Grant To Retire. Anticipation rises sky-high in me as I click it open and read.

> **Three-time Super Bowl champion and Renegades starting quarterback Jeff Grant announced his retirement today.**
>
> **"It's been an amazing run and I am lucky to have played for my hometown team and for such amazing fans. I know the team will be in good hands with the new starting quarterback, Cooper Armstrong."**

I squeal out loud. Excitement and effervescence run through me. I've just drunk a glass of champagne, devoured a mouth-watering truffle, watched a friend win the lottery.

One of my stylists turns to me, asking, "Everything okay?"

I must look like I've been dipped in a paint can of glee. "Everything is amazing," I tell her.

My heart skips and I want to jump for joy. I can only imagine how incredibly happy Cooper is, and I can't wait to congratulate him myself—this is what he's worked for his whole life. This is what he's wanted more than anything.

I start to tap out a text to him, when the receptionist sets her hand on my arm. "Violet, your next appointment."

"Thanks, Sage."

I tuck my phone away, and honestly, I'm glad I didn't have time to fire off a text. This calls for more than a text. I need to give him a phone call later.

I settle in at my booth and work on auburn highlights for Marissa, who tells me she's desperately trying to figure out why her husband is suffering from headaches. "They tend to get worse if he's in the kitchen, but they're fine when he's elsewhere in the house. Isn't that crazy?"

Today I'm playing the shrink.

"Not entirely. Is there anything in the kitchen that could be making him sick?" I ask as I wrap a section of her hair in tinfoil.

"My cooking," she mutters.

I laugh. "Maybe there's something going on with the stove. Perhaps something needs to be fixed with it."

And now I'm an electrician and a diagnostician.

She arches a brow. "You think that might be it?"

I smile at her in the mirror. "I think you look amazing with red highlights, and I have no idea why he's not feeling so great. But maybe check it out? Sometimes the answers to problems are under our noses and easier than we think."

An hour later, her hair is redder and she's tracked down a stove specialist, promising to update me in four weeks when she's back for her regular appointment.

I twist my index and middle fingers together. "My fingers are crossed," I say as I walk her to the door and hold it open.

I swear I'm seeing a mirage.

Cooper is at the door. His arms are raised in the air. His smile is as wide as the sea, and he strides to me, picks me up, and lifts me in the air.

CHAPTER 5

"Did you hear the news?"

I nod as his strong arms hold me tight. "I did. I told you so!"

He smiles as wide as the sky. "This is the one time I don't mind hearing 'I told you so.'"

"Then I'll say it again. *Told you so.*"

He sets me down and grips my shoulders for emphasis. "*Three years*, Vi. I've watched every single play from the sidelines with the exception of two games I started when Jeff sprained his ankle. Three. Whole. Years. And come September, I finally get my chance to start the season."

That champagne feeling when I read the news? It has nothing on the rocket ride I'm on now. It's not even *my* news. But it doesn't matter. I've rooted for Cooper my whole life. "I couldn't be happier for you. This is so amazing."

His hands curl tighter around me. "I wanted you to be one of the first people to know."

"You did?" This information sends a dangerous thrill through me.

"Hell yeah. You're one of the most important people in my life. I told my mom first, and I had to see you next. I knew you'd be excited."

"I'm glad you came here," I say, my voice a little softer, and even though I want to believe he's telling me because he harbors the same crazy, lifelong crush as I do, I know better. That wedding dance and the closeness I felt that night was a sliver in time. It hasn't been repeated, but our friendship has grown even stronger.

Now that my brother's married and busy with his wife, Cooper and I talk more. He's here every few weeks for his haircut, and when he comes by in the evenings, we usually grab dinner after. That's why he stopped by today. Because we're friends. Great friends.

I give his hair a quick once-over. "I don't think you have an appointment for a few days, but if you're going to be the starting quarterback, we need to give you a haircut."

He bats his eyes. "Think you can fit me in?"

"It just so happens I had a cancellation, so I can give you a quickie."

A laugh bursts from his mouth. "A quickie? Hell yeah."

I swat his arm as I realize my faux pas. "A quickie cut."

"Other quickies are fine with me, too," he says, a little flirty, a little dirty.

"Get over to the sinks," I say, trying my best to make light of the comment, so he won't notice the fierce blush radiating over my cheeks.

Quickie.

What was my brain thinking, letting that word spill out?

He parks himself in a chair at a sink, and I partake of one of my favorite things—shampooing his hair. He shuts his eyes and sighs contentedly as I scrub in the shampoo, lathering it up.

I take my time, making sure I don't miss a single strand, running my fingers through those lush locks, massaging his scalp.

I rinse his hair, my hands running through his hair one more time to get all the suds out.

Another soft sigh falls from his lips, and it makes my heart flutter.

If he were mine, I'd do this every few weeks, and then we'd kiss, and he'd bring me close, and we'd slink away for a little while.

I squeeze the brakes on the fantasy, shut off the water, and run a towel over his head. We head to my booth, and he sits in the black leather chair, where I cut his hair.

I have free rein to look at him, to study him, to touch the soft strands.

As I snip his locks, I pepper him with questions about how the news came down.

He tells me he heard from his agent, and tomorrow is his first press conference.

I rest my hand on his shoulder and meet his gaze in the mirror. "And you're going to look so handsome."

A grin crosses his lips. "Thank you."

I run my hands over his hair, enjoying this opportunity to touch him more than I should.

Maybe that makes me a pervert. It's only hair, really. But it's great hair. I relish the chance to make him look his finest, to take care of him in this small way I can.

I move closer, trimming the ends. His gaze drifts up in the mirror, his brown eyes locking with mine.

He says nothing. He simply stares at my reflection. I could be wrong, I could be reading something into nothing, but I swear there's heat in his eyes, maybe a little flicker of desire.

It makes my breath catch. My heart speeds up. My pulse hammers.

It's the same look I saw at the wedding. It's the look I see when our bodies move closer when we seem to connect in unexpected ways.

I stop snipping for a few seconds, trying to get my bearings. I want to know what's going on in his head.

But soon enough, it's time for him to go. As he leaves, I'm hit with the realization that I need to find a way to let go of this lifelong crush once and for all. I need to focus solely on the friendship, because that's the only thing that lasts.

CHAPTER 6

THE START OF THE SEASON

"Excuse me."

A burly, bearded Renegades fan tucks himself into his seat and lets us pass by his knees.

"Thank you so much," I say to him.

He nods and shouts, "Go Renegades!"

I pump a fist, and Holly and Trent behind me do the same thing.

The pre-game excitement hum is in the air, coursing throughout the stadium. The three of us make our way down the row and find our seats on the fifty-yard line next to Cooper's mom and her boyfriend, Dan. Cooper's mom gives me a big hug. She waves a foam finger and hollers, "Number Sixteen!"

A vendor tromps down the concrete steps, offering beer and pretzels. Another one from the next section over shouts out that he has sushi and wine.

That's San Francisco for you, and our beautiful new stadium has a little bit of everything, including gorgeous September weather.

No jackets required today.

I opt for a pretzel and Holly grabs beers for my brother and her.

Trent raises his cup. "Here's to pulling out a W."

I tap my pretzel against my brother's beer cup. "I'll nosh to that."

Cooper's mom joins in the toast with her blue foam finger. "Go Coop! You can do it."

The game hasn't even begun, and we're all a little overly enthusiastic today.

"Last week was only jitters," she adds, as she should know. She knows her son as well as anyone, and she's attended nearly every single game he's ever played.

"It was absolutely only jitters," I say, smoothing a hand over my Number Sixteen jersey. "He'll be great today. He's a star."

The announcer's voice booms throughout the stadium, like he's using two hundred megaphones and each word has ten syllables. "Welcome to the Renegades stadium for the first home game of the year."

"He's going to be amazing," Trent says, pumping a fist.

"He'll be great," Dan says, chiming in.

"Bring it, Coop," Holly shouts.

Okay fine, we're a tad more than overly enthused. We might be bordering on nervous. After all, last week's game bordered on abysmal, and Cooper played terribly. There's no way to sugarcoat his performance.

But it can't be easy replacing a legend.

Images of the players flash on the Jumbotron as the announcer shares the lineup. The visiting team is properly and soundly booed, and all the home team guys are cheered, including the last few guys announced.

Harlan Taylor, the star running back. Jones Beckett, the fantastic wide receiver. And at last, the guy I'm here for.

The announcer's voice thunders across the stadium like an echo from Zeus. "And your new starting quarterback in his first home game…Cooper Armstrong."

Everyone stands and cheers as the handsome new quarterback runs onto the field.

"That interception last week was a fluke," Trent says with a confident nod. "Today will be different."

"Today will be amazing."

I hold my breath. I don't think I will ever be able to let it out again. I'm making promises to the universe. Promises I have no right to make. I tell myself it's just a game. It's just football.

We're only behind by fourteen and he can do this, he can pull out a win. But as Cooper goes into the pocket at the end of the second quarter, scanning right, scanning left as Jones runs downfield, he overthrows.

My heart craters when the ball lands squarely in the open arms of the opponent.

The crowd groans collectively.

My heart breaks a little bit when the fans boo him.

"Bring back Grant."

"You suck."

"Go back to the bench, bench boy."

My jaw clenches, and I want to go personally reprimand every single naysayer in this stadium. "Mark my words," I'll tell them.

"Just you wait," I'll say.

But frustration wends through me, and I can also feel it from Trent, Holly, Cooper's mom, and Dan. We're all rooting for this guy so badly. We want him to succeed as fans, but mostly for him.

"Shake it off," says Trent, talking under his breath.

Cooper's mom waves that finger again. "You can do it."

When the third quarter begins and Cooper starts it with another interception, my heart sags once more. Even though he delivers two touchdowns after that, it's not enough and the Renegades finish with their second loss of the season.

Silence blankets the stadium as we leave, that clawing sense of potential doom hovering over us. I have to wonder what Cooper feels like. If he thinks he's letting everyone down, from the team to the coach to the fans.

I want to reassure him that he's not. That he's got this. And I know what to do. I know how to lift him up.

Later that night I send him a text message.

Violet: Why did the football go to the bank?
Cooper: I've been wondering that very thing.
Violet: To get his quarterback.
Cooper: 😁 Thank you. I needed that.
Violet: Hey, if you have any free time this week, can you meet me at the high school field?

He writes back, telling me he'll be there Thursday night.

CHAPTER 7

We don't need stadium lights. There is enough starlight tonight in Petaluma, our hometown.

Nearly twenty years ago, I met Cooper in this town when I was in grade school. I was riding my purple banana seat bike, and he moved a block over from my house. This is the high school we both attended, and this field is where I watched so many of his games, cheering from the sidelines.

I was never a cheerleader. *Please.* I'm not that kind of girl. But I still went to his games, and I shouted and clapped.

Tonight, I'm here to cheer in a whole different way. I have everything we need—a football and some music. I wait at the fifty-yard line.

When Cooper shows up a few minutes later, striding across the grass, his thumbs tucked into the pockets of his jeans, a gray T-shirt hugging his firm frame, he shoots me a curious look. "Are you my new coach?"

I toss the ball back and forth in my hands. "Nope. I want to play for fun."

He raises an eyebrow. "Are you holding out on me, Vi? Are you really a ringer for Brady?"

I flash him a big smile. "There's only one way to find out."

I turn on the playlist on my phone, cueing up Guns N' Roses' "Welcome to the Jungle."

"How apt," he deadpans.

"It is a jungle out there." I launch the ball up and down, then tip my forehead toward the goalposts at the end of the field. "Come on! Go deep."

"You're the quarterback now?"

I shimmy my hips back and forth. "Maybe I am. Thirty-six. Zone. Lion. Sail. Ten." I rattle off one of the plays he gave me at the wedding.

His eyes widen. "You remember the playbook?"

"I told you I love strategy. Now get your butt down the field and catch this ball."

Saluting me, he takes off, running a post route, as I launch the ball toward him. I don't have a cannon for an arm. That's why I picked a skinny post route. But I do manage the fifteen yards just fine, and he catches it beautifully.

Of course.

"Now if only I could've done that last Sunday," he mutters.

"You can," I say with enough confidence for both of us. "Now throw it to me."

He palms the ball, considering the options, it seems. He raises his face, meets my gaze, and calls out a play. It's an easy one, and I remember it from our talk. A simple, short route. I run a few yards as he lobs an easy spiral in my direction.

Even though I know he's not putting all of his strength into it, he can't help but throw hard. I haul it in, but I can still feel the punch that he packs as I grab it, the ball smacking me in the chest.

A cough bursts from my throat.

"Are you okay?" Cooper trots towards me.

I hold out my hand like a stop sign. "I'm fine. I can handle catching a football."

"And you caught it well. Too bad I can't get it to the receiver when I need to."

My eyes narrow and I march the final feet to him, stabbing him in the chest with my finger. "No."

"No, what?"

"No feeling that for yourself," I say firmly and crisply, shoving the football at him.

"I'm not feeling bad for myself."

"You are and I'll have none of it."

He heaves a sigh. "Fine, but you would too. Have you heard the crap they're saying about me on sports radio?"

I shake my head. "I don't listen to sports radio. And you shouldn't, either."

"Have you read what they say about me on the Internet?"

Another shake. "Stop googling yourself."

He raises his hands in surrender.

"I mean it. Get your head out of the Internet and focus on

the game. That's all you have to do. Just remember that." I tap his temple. "This is yours. This belongs to you. Don't let them in here."

A slow smile spreads across his face and he nods, taking it in. "You're right. This is mine."

"Your mind. Your head. Your best weapon on the field."

"Mine. All mine," he repeats like he needs to remind himself, then he shouts another play.

I follow his directions easily, taking the spot of his receiver, and we play like that for the next thirty minutes. Running easily, tossing balls, barking directions and audibles, and having a blast running into the end zone, arms raised, scoring touchdowns, pretending to kick extra points.

Until finally we flop down on the cool grass in the middle of the field and stare at the stars. I turn to him, and I'm delighted to see not only relief on his face, but happiness and confidence.

He looks my way and our eyes connect, his brown eyes holding mine longer than I expect.

"Hey you," he whispers.

"Hey you too." Tingles sweep over my skin.

"Thank you."

"It was nothing," I say, though I know that's not true.

I wait for him to look away, but he doesn't break the hold.

And my brain reassembles the scene. My mind says this is the moment in the script when they kiss. When the hero touches her shoulder, runs a finger along a strand of hair, moves in close.

But the better part of me, the stronger part, the piece of me I've kept in check since the wedding, rises to the surface. Reminding me. I'm here for the friendship. That's what's steady. That's what lasts. That's what I'll protect in the same way Cooper's offensive line protects him. I will guard our friendship fiercely because it means the world to me.

This is not the moment when friends turn into lovers. Instead, this is the time when he needs to know I'll be there for him always.

He taps my shoulder. The look in his eyes is soft and earnest. "It was everything."

My heart somersaults. My throat goes dry.

"I'm glad you had me come here tonight," he adds.

"Me too," I say, and it's wholly true, somersaults and cartwheels aside.

I let go of that swoopy, crazy feeling in my chest. I say goodbye to all the tingles and shivers. This is where I want to be right now. His friend.

I punch his shoulder. "Go get 'em, Tiger."

He does.

He turns the season around the next week, and the next and the next, putting the Renegades in playoff position by early December, and making the city fall in love with the new quarterback again—handsome, talented, good, and *winning*.

He's the most valuable guy on the team, and he's become the toast of the town.

When December coasts into San Francisco, it's time for the annual players' charity auction.

That means he needs me to work my magic.

CHAPTER 8

Cooper's hair is sticking up. He has some kind of crazy bed head look going on tonight. But that's part of his appeal.

So is his tailored charcoal suit, which makes him look completely edible.

Not for me, of course.

I'm over all those crazy crushing feelings.

My goal tonight is simple. Make the guys look good before the auction to raise money for the children's hospital. "We need to domesticate your lovely locks, Cooper. I think this gel will do."

I hold up a tube of hair gel, my silver bracelets jangling on my wrists, as I prepare to put the finishing touches on the stars of the team.

"What is that goop?" he asks suspiciously.

"Why this? It's called Goop for Guys. It's perfect for you."

We joke some more, along with the other guys here in the suite. They're all wearing three-piece suits, and damn, there's something so yummy about a good-looking man wearing a vest with a suit.

Something that gets my blood heated to hot.

But I'm not that girl anymore. I'm not longing for him like I have in the past. I can simply appreciate him as a man, while enjoying him as my buddy.

As I work on his hair, I eye his attire. "I like this. You rarely see anyone wearing a vest around here."

"Is that your way of telling me you're a vest woman?" he asks in a flirty voice that makes me want to flirt back with him.

Just for fun.

Not for anything more.

I laugh and whisper, "I'm an everything woman."

He blinks, like he's surprised I said that.

Hell, maybe I am too.

But even though there's some kind of energy and excitement in this room tonight, I know that's all it is. Maybe a year ago, I would've wondered if our friendship would catch on fire and make us both melt from the heat.

Tonight, though? I know we're solid, and we'll finish the evening as we started it.

I run my gel-covered hands through his hair, taming it for the camera since the auction is being carried live on local TV. Surveying my handiwork, I issue my pronouncement.

"You are one hot quarterback."

His lips part. He takes his time answering. "I am?"

I flash him a coy smile and pat his shoulder. "Of course you are."

If I were in the audience, I'd bid on him. Not that I'm a bidding girl, and I don't have that kind of money to play with, but he looks like a prize.

They all do.

I spin around, regarding the guys. Harlan, the running back; Jones, the receiver; and Rick, the kicker. "You boys are all so pretty."

Rick crosses his legs. "You want to bid on me tonight, Vi?"

I decide to have fun with them since I'm in that kind of mood. "It's all I can think about." Rooting around in my purse, I find my wallet and grab a few bills. "Will twenty dollars be enough for you?"

As the guys tease about whether that's too much to pay for Rick, Cooper tenses and scowls, almost as if he dislikes the idea of me bidding on Rick.

I point to Harlan. "How much for you?"

Another round of joking ensues, as well as more grumbles from Cooper.

I glance back at my friend. "Coop, are you as cheap as the others? Should I try for you?"

He scoffs. "I'm a premium kinda guy," he says, confidently. Then, with those brown eyes pinned on mine, he adds, "But if you wanted to bid on me, I'd foot the bill for it."

His tone is intense and serious. Like he means it, and I can't help but wonder if he's saying I should bid on him for some reason. I don't know why he would want that. Everyone will be bidding on him—he's the main attraction.

Soon, the auction is about to start, and Jillian, the team publicist, leads the guys out of the room.

I call out to Cooper, and he turns around. I walk over to him in my high-heeled boots that don't make me as tall as him, but do shoot me a little bit closer.

I raise my hand and smooth out a strand of his hair that's out of place. He's been part of this auction for the last three years, but this is the first time he's going out there as the team's starting quarterback. "You've killed every year as the backup. You'll kill it even harder as the starter, and you've been playing great the last three months."

He knocks on the wall. "Knock on wood. We need to keep playing great. And I know you're part of why I'm playing so well."

"Am I?"

"That night on the high school field was everything I needed to turn it around."

I smile. "I'm glad I could help."

"Vi, you did more than help. That was everything I needed to hear."

I beam, my heart soaring with contentment. "All right, tiger. Get out there." I straighten his hair one more time, then I adjust his tie, even though it's perfect.

He meets my eyes, his voice going a bit husky. "Does my tie look good?"

My stomach swoops. But I remind myself that it's a vestigial response. It's borne from the past, and I don't need to be anchored to those feelings. The ones I'm getting over. "Everything looks good. Now get out on stage. I'll be in the audience watching every minute, and I can't wait."

He turns to head down the hall then stops at the sound.

He groans. "It's Maxine."

And the bawdy, bold, kind of inappropriate radio host is singing "It's Raining Men."

CHAPTER 9

Ten minutes later the auction is in full swing.

The host, local TV reporter Sierra Franklin, is running the bidding and extolling the virtues of Jones. As she waxes on about his hands, I find Cooper backstage.

He paces, tension written all over his face.

I ask what's wrong, but he simply jokes about having Holly's friends bid on him when it's his turn. The comment nags in my brain, makes me wonder if something went down in the hall.

I touch his elbow. "Is everything okay? Did something happen with Maxine? You mentioned her right before you left the suite, and now you don't quite seem like yourself."

Before he can answer, Sierra's voice echoes from the on-stage mic. "And now we're getting ready to bring our starting quarterback on the stage."

Cooper whispers quietly. "I wouldn't use the term *okay* to describe my interaction with her."

The tension winds tighter, and I wrap my hand around

him, feeling protective of him. With that, he strides onto the stage, and I can hear everyone in the ballroom cheering and clapping for their chance to bid on the star athlete. While a part of me is thrilled the crowd is excited to see him, his comments worry me, and that part of me takes over. I scurry through the hotel and make my way to the ballroom, scrambling to watch his blind side.

The ballroom is packed, and I wedge my way through crowds of cheering women and men, laughing and clapping as Sierra interacts with Cooper on stage.

He gives her a peck on the cheek, and she clasps her hand to her face, saying, "I'll never wash this cheek again."

She gestures to Cooper and sings his praises before the audience. "And now, ladies and gentlemen, for the pièce de résistance, this year's starting quarterback, at long last, and the winner of the Most Valuable Playboy auction for the last three years in a row. After all, who wouldn't want to take this handsome and talented man out for a night on the town? Everyone loves the quarterback."

Truer words were never spoken.

Cooper smiles for the crowd, seemingly shucking off his backstage concerns, as he takes off his jacket and shows off how absolutely decadently delicious he looks in his pants, shirt, and vest.

Yes, I am a vest woman indeed.

He scans the crowd and finds me easily. I mouth, *Vests are hot.*

When he smiles, it feels like a private grin just for me.

Even though I know it's a friendship grin, and I'm completely cool with it being just that.

Sierra sings his praises, from his stats to his skills—six-foot-four inches, light brown eyes and dark brown hair, great cheekbones, talented in the kitchen, and a rock star at karaoke.

Yes, yes, yes.

I know all that cold.

Cooper launches into a few lines from his favorite Bon Jovi tune, and all seems well. I'm not so sure what he was worried about with Maxine, but she's nowhere in sight, so perhaps it's much ado about nothing.

When the bidding begins and my brother and Holly offer measly bids for fun, I figure there's truly nothing to worry about.

Until a flash of red catches the corner of my eye.

Maxine is here. She thrusts a jeweled hand high, and when her voice rises above the crowd, upping the bid from a paltry fifty dollars to a startling three thousand, I understand why Cooper was concerned.

She wants him.

Her hands are parked on her hips.

Her eyes are guns, aiming for him.

Chills skate down my spine as she stares at the quarterback, licking her lips.

"That's quite a large jump," Sierra says.

"And that handsome fellow is worth every penny," Maxine replies, her voice dripping with desire.

"Three thousand," Sierra repeats. "Do we have thirty-one hundred?"

A few others in the crowd jump in with higher bids.

But Maxine raises her price every time, staring at Cooper like she wants to eat him for breakfast, lunch, dinner, and a midnight snack.

She keeps outbidding everyone, determination in her tone.

Sheer certainty she'll win him.

And in that moment, the stark realization hits me.

I don't want her to get her hands on him. I know Cooper is no saint. I'm not trying to keep him pure for me because this isn't about me. This is about Cooper. I can read him. I can see something in his face. It borders on fear.

My friend. My guy. *Mine*.

Maxine stares at him, slashing an arm through the air and declaring five thousand dollars, eliminating pretty much anyone else.

Sierra's eyes light up. "Going once?" she asks, scanning the crowd, waiting for one last bid.

My brain whirs.

My mind races.

When I see Maxine wink at Cooper, I burn.

She thinks Cooper wants her.

I clench my fists, flashing back to what Cooper said to me about footing the bill.

I can't let Maxine win him.

She's gunning for the quarterback's blind side, and that does not fly with me.

I'm his left tackle. It's my job to protect him. I won't let him get sacked.

I make eye contact with him, tapping my nose, a signal.

"Going twice," Sierra says, her voice trailing off.

Cooper's eyes light up, and he brushes his finger on the side of his nose.

We are the only ones speaking each other's language. He wants me to do this.

My arm shoots high in the air. Like a determined woman who won't let anything take her guy down, I shout, "Ten thousand dollars!"

Sierra smiles crazily. "Do we have ten thousand one hundred?"

No one else speaks. No one says a word. I'm not sure if Maxine is shocked into silence or if everyone is.

But I think I am, too, especially when Cooper sweeps me up on the stage, and before I know it, he kisses me in front of the whole crowd.

FOR MORE BALLERS AND BABES, READ ALONG FOR AN EXCERPT OF *A WILD CARD KISS*, LAUREN BLAKELY'S SEXY FOOTBALL ROMANCE BETWEEN A SINGLE DAD ATHLETE AND THE WOMAN WHO GOT AWAY.

CHAPTER 1

KATIE

I wasn't one of those girls who imagined her wedding day from the time she was small.

Or at any time.

I didn't fantasize about walking down the aisle and into the arms of the Prince Charming of my dreams.

No way.

For one, I was agnostic about the existence of Prince Charming. And two, I was emphatically atheistic about princesses.

Didn't believe in being one, acting like one, or becoming one.

When I was growing up, my dreams were pragmatic—make friends, be awesome, and kick unholy ass.

I blame my dad.

He instilled in me a belief that I could do anything I set out to if I used my brain and heart.

Getting married was never on my vision board.

But today I am *that* person.

It's my wedding day, and I just can't wait to say *I do*. Hell, I've been floating on air since Silvio proposed four months ago, after two mere months of dating.

"Fair warning. You three are going to have to stop me from running across the lawn and into Silvio's arms," I say to my crew as we get ready, my hairstylist working on my updo.

"Ah, so you're going to be one of *those* brides," Emerson quips as she fishes in her makeup bag in the suite at the Legion of Honor, where I'll be doing the aforementioned forty-yard dash into my tall, dark, and handsome groom's arms.

I smile, owning it. "Yup. It's going to be so cheesy, but so romantic, and none of you will be able to stop me. In fact, you'll all melt into puddles of swoon," I say.

Ever so briefly, a memory rushes over me.

A pint of Swoon.

But I push away the imaginary ice cream flavor. It's bad form to think of past men on your wedding day, even for a second. And why would I when my main man might as well have stepped straight out of Central Casting and into the role of my Romeo?

My heart flutters.

I'm getting married.

The girl who never fantasized about dresses or *I dos* is ready to skip to her guy in about an hour.

Hold me back, world.

As my stylist clips the sides of my hair into a silver barrette, I can't stop smiling stupidly at my reflection in the mirror. Karissa surveys my peeps—Jillian is perched on the couch; my sister, Olive, sits on the desk; and Emerson stands next to her, still sorting through a makeup bag. Skyler ran out to refill a water bottle but she should be back soon.

"Say the word, and I'll arm wrestle Katie till she stops waxing on about her groom," Karissa says to my friends.

Jillian taps her chin, deep in thought. "I'm tempted simply because of the arm-wrestling match."

I pinch Karissa's toned biceps. "She'd win. She's got Gal Gadot arms."

"I moonlight as Wonder Woman," Karissa says as she runs a flat iron over one of my blonde curls. My hair has darkened a bit over the years. It was bright blonde when I was younger, golden in my twenties, and now it's heading into a dark blonde palette. Seems fitting—I still feel perky and bold, but stronger, surer of myself, and maybe a touch more vulnerable too. Time has done its thing. So, letting my natural color shine through fits who I've become in my mid-thirties and who I want to keep being—the best me possible.

"But seriously, I am so happy for you I could cry rainbows," Karissa says as she squeezes my shoulder. "You're going to be the most gorgeous bride in all of San Francisco. I swear, Silvio won't know what hit him."

"I don't know what hit *me*." I lean back in the chair, catching Emerson's knowing look as our eyes meet in the mirror.

"What hit you is a smoking-hot Italian artist who's a real-life Romeo," my good friend says. Her smile tells me she's thrilled for me. She has been since he swept me off my feet the night I met him—New Year's Eve.

Jillian straightens her shoulders, tucking strands of silky black hair over her ear. "And who treats you like the goddess you are."

"And who's almost too good to be true," Olive chimes in as she ties a bow around a bouquet of sunflowers. She holds it up for praise. "What do you think? Maybe if the whole numbers thing doesn't work out, I could become a florist."

"Hey! Don't panic the bride on her wedding day," I say, only part joking. "I need my numbers wunderkind."

"I would never abandon Sassy Yoga," she replies and ties the twine in a bow just so. She can't help herself. She has a penchant for crafts. "But if I was to start a floristry side hustle, I would never sell sunflowers. They kind of stink."

"Mom begged me to have them," I say with a shrug. "She said they'd be perfect, and pretty much got down on her hands and knees. It was easier to let her have her way than to argue. I'm not a big flower person, anyway."

"You're a tiger lily," Emerson announces. "That's what you should have."

"Thanks. I'll have tiger lilies at my next wedding," I deadpan.

Emerson crosses the suite, stops in front of Jillian, then swipes the brush down my college bestie's nose. Emerson taught herself classy wedding makeup through YouTube tutorials. No surprise—she loves YouTube.

And I love my friends.

This is my dream come true. A pack of women. Good friends through thick and thin.

"I'm so glad you're all here," I tell them, love and happiness rising to bring a shine to my eyes.

"You say that like we'd be anyplace else," Olive quips, adding a *ta-da* when she finishes another bow.

"Well, you have to be here. You're family," I say to her.

"So's Mom, technically, but I'd say she doesn't *have* to be here." Olive laughs drily.

"C'mon, you know she can't resist a wedding," I tease.

"Who can't?"

I tense everywhere as my mom's voice carries across the suite. Is she a freaking cat? I didn't even hear her enter. But now she saunters in, head held high, clasping a pretty white ribbon and a garment bag, which I presume holds her mother-of-the-bride dress.

I hope she didn't hear me. She'll go full drama llama, tears and all.

"No single *she* in the universe can resist a wedding." Olive jumps in, and I could kiss her for taking that grenade for me. If my mom knew I'd thrown shade on her love of weddings, she'd fling a hand on her chest, fall to the floor in a fit of tears, and demand to know what she'd done wrong.

I can't. Not today.

She hangs the garment bag on the hook on the door. "I love weddings. I just do," Mom says, with a dramatic sigh, and maybe she's why I never imagined my own nuptials growing up. I witnessed too many of hers.

But this is not the day to think about her four failed marriages.

Today I will zoom in on my *one* marriage, and the only wedding I plan to have.

My mom crosses the carpeted floor, her dyed red hair styled in a stunning updo, clearly professionally done. She flicks a hand lightly against a few wisps, drawing attention, silently fishing for compliments.

"You look great," I assure her.

"Thanks. The mother of the bride should look stunning."

Olive rolls her eyes.

"But do you think I should add this white ribbon to my hair?" she asks.

"No. White is for the bride, Mom," Olive answers.

Mom ignores her, then parks her hands on my shoulders and plants a kiss on the top of my head. Karissa snaps her gaze up from the front of my hair. "Careful, there. Don't want to knock a hair out of place. Just let me finish."

Mom pulls away, scoffing. "I didn't mess it up. I just gave her a kiss."

Karissa shoots Mom a sympathetic smile. "Of course you didn't mess it up. But we want the bride's hair to be fabulous."

"Her hair looks perfect," my mom says, bristling, as Karissa silently returns to her work.

The suite goes quiet. Too quiet.

My friends know not to argue with someone who's always right.

But my mother can slice through any silence with her voice. "Anyway, let me know what else I can do as the mother of the bride," she says to the room. Then to me in the mirror, she adds, "Since, apparently, I can't give you away."

Again? We're doing this *again*? "Because no one is giving me away," I say calmly. I'm opting out of some rituals. "Just like I don't have a dowry. Just like we both have engagement rings."

"And I disagree. Your father and I should give you away. Wouldn't that be fair? Aren't you a feminist?" Mom asks, like feminist is the equivalent of a nose-picker.

But I won't take her bait.

"Sometimes I am. Mostly on Wednesdays. On Wednesdays, we smash the patriarchy," I say with a shrug.

Olive snickers.

Jillian reins in a laugh.

Emerson just smiles.

"But it's Saturday," my mother points out, flummoxed.

I sigh. "I know. It's a saying. My point is *this* is what I want." I won't let her win this battle. This is her tenth time trying. "I'm paying for the wedding myself. No one is giving me away. I'm an independent woman. I'm good with this, Mom. The only thing I want that I didn't get is axe-throwing at the reception."

She scoffs at me. "Who would do axe-throwing at her wedding?"

"Who wouldn't? It's crazy fun." I had suggested it to Silvio for the reception, but he politely declined. He also politely declined my suggestion that we have a small wedding by the Pacific Ocean, then do bowling and sushi with our closest friends. But hey, I can't complain about the Legion of Honor and champagne. Or a honeymoon in Dublin, visiting the countryside to take pics, rather than Kauai doing an adventure tour.

"I doubt it's that enjoyable," Mom says about the axe-throwing.

"We'll go do it together sometime, Mom," I offer as an olive branch. I'm in the mood to spread love, not spew snide. "I swear, you'll enjoy it more than giving me away."

"Fine. Don't let me give you away. I'll survive," Mom says as Karissa runs a brush down my bangs, giving them a wispy look. "But I ask you this, darling—are you one hundred percent sure you want to marry Silvio?"

I flinch and hold up a hand to ask Karissa to stop. Then I turn around in the chair, eyeing the redhead who raised me. "Why are you asking this now?"

Olive wheels around from setting the smelly sunflowers on a table. "Yes, Mom. Why?"

My mother squares her shoulders. "It's important to be certain. Isn't that what you two preach in your yoga practice?" She gestures from Olive to me and back.

I answer in a rush. "It's not a religion. We don't preach it.

Also, our brand is yoga that doesn't take itself too seriously." There Mom goes again, winding me up, getting me off-topic. "But why are you asking if I'm certain about Silvio?"

Her question irks me. Earlier this year, I'd asked myself plenty of times if he was the one, but that's normal—it's smart to make sure you're making the right choice. I asked myself over and over if yoga was the right business for me before I launched my company. Natch, I'd do the same for marriage.

My mom scans my crew. "Do your friends think it makes sense to marry him?"

Ugh. Now she's trying to throw me off via my friends?

Jillian cuts in firmly, handling Mom like she handles an out-of-line question from an unruly press gaggle. "We think Silvio is great."

"We were just talking about what a sweetie he is," Emerson adds. "How well he treats Katie."

Skyler strides back into the suite at the tail end of that, water bottle filled and eyes curious.

My mom's lips curve down. "Does he, though? Does he treat you how you deserve to be treated, honey?" She squeezes my shoulder again.

What is going on? Why the frick is my mother trying to dissuade me from getting married an hour before the ceremony?

"I don't understand why you're asking," I say. Maybe my wedding reminds her of her own marital belly flops, the quartet of *I dos* that didn't work out.

With a worried sigh, my mother clasps her hands, her

fingers fidgety. "I'm concerned. That's normal. It seems like it's all happening too quickly. It seems like you might not really know him that well. Or yourself."

What the hell? Just because we had a whirlwind courtship doesn't mean I don't know him well. I met him at a restaurant when our reservations were mixed up, and we dated for two months before he proposed.

Do I know him well?

As well as I need to.

I don't believe you need to spend years with someone before you walk down the aisle.

Sometimes love happens quickly, even if you don't like the same music, food, or wine.

Who cares about that stuff?

"That's not an issue, Mom. I know he gives excellent foot rubs, he loves to snuggle, and he'll probably take at least ten minutes to tie his bow tie even though he's been watching YouTube tutorials for a week. His favorite book is *The Little Prince*, he loses track of time when he works on his murals, but he showers me with kisses when he comes home from his studio. And I feel like I know myself even better too, now that I'm thirty-five. I trust my instincts. I would love it if you would trust me too."

By the end, my throat has tightened like a noose squeezing my neck, and tears sting my eyes but don't fall. I can't believe she's doing this to me on my wedding day. Maybe this is another reason why I never imagined a wedding as a kid—because she'd find a way to ruin it with an ill-timed warning.

But screw it.

I'm not going to let her.

I suck in the threat of tears, swallow them down, and raise my chin. "I love Silvio and he loves me, but I appreciate your concern."

"If you say so," Mom says, letting the words hang in the air like a cloying, passive-aggressive-scented air freshener.

My friends step in like superheroes. Olive grabs my mother's hand and escorts her out of the suite, and Jillian swoops in with a tissue. "Don't let her get to you on your wedding day, or any day ever. She wants to be the center of attention, so she's looking to make it all about her."

I take the tissue and dab my cheek, but I don't think a tear sneaked out. Ha. Take that, Mom.

"Coffee, yoga, and wine, coffee, yoga, and wine," I say, repeating one of my favorite mantras as Olive returns, shutting the door loudly behind her.

"And tonight, there will be wine," Olive declares.

Cheers erupt, and we sing an impromptu homage to wine.

That gets my mother out of my system.

When we're done, Emerson sweeps a tinge more mascara on my lashes, I slide on some lip gloss, and Karissa declares my hair is fabulous. Skyler offers me a sip from the water bottle, but I decline.

"You're ready," Olive says.

I am so damn ready.

I look in the mirror, draw a deep breath, and catalogue

the woman I see. Bold, honest, strong, outgoing. The dress is my best me too. A chiffon A-line, it swishes around my ankles, with cap sleeves showing off my arms. It's simple, white, classy.

We'll exchange our vows at five against the backdrop of the ocean and the Golden Gate Bridge, then we'll head into the art museum for a reception, surrounded by more than seventy Rodins in the galleries.

No axe-throwing, but hey, I like art too, so it's all good.

A deep, fortifying breath lets me put my mother all the way behind me.

Time to go.

My friends and I make our way through the Legion of Honor toward the lawn. But nature calls, and the last thing I want is to think about peeing while I'm saying my vows.

"Let me just pop into the ladies' room," I say to the bridesmaids when I spot the restroom.

Emerson slashes an arm in front of me like a human stop sign. "That one is too close to where the men are getting ready." She turns me by my shoulders and ushers me down the hall the other way.

"We definitely don't want to bump into them. Whatever would we do?" I ask in exaggerated horror. "You superstitious creature."

She shrugs impishly. "I am what I am."

"I'm not worried if I see him before the wedding. I don't believe in all that stuff," I say, as we reach the other restroom.

I stop with my hand on the door because faint voices carry from the end of the hall.

A man and a woman.

Sounding...worried.

They're familiar, but muffled, so I strain to make them out.

"I tried," the woman whispers.

"Of course you did," the man says, gentle, caring.

Ohhh.

That's definitely a voice I know.

I swallow roughly, trying to understand what they're talking about.

Emerson asks me questions with her eyes, and I bring my finger to my lips.

Gathering up the skirt of my dress, I pad as silently as possible to the corner, where I can hear more easily.

"So what now?" the woman whispers.

"There's only one thing to do," he says.

The rustle of clothes. The sound of lips touching lips.

My skin crawls.

The hair on the back of my neck stands on end.

All the breath flees my lungs when I peek around the corner for confirmation.

It's twenty minutes before my wedding, and the man who's supposed to become my husband is kissing another woman.

ACKNOWLEDGMENTS

I owe a huge thank-you to the esteemed sports agent Leigh Steinberg for his insight into the mindset of a young starting quarterback. Mr. Steinberg's depth of knowledge informed Cooper's character, passion, and his dedication to the sport. His information on contracts and the dance of negotiations is unparalleled. Thank you, Mr. Steinberg, for taking my call and sharing so much.

Abiding gratitude to Gale, my amazing hairstylist, who brainstorms stories with me and helps me to look good. You're the inspiration for all of Violet's talent, and thank you for giving your shop name to this story.

Thank you to my husband and my son for their sports knowledge and football fact-checking, and especially to my son for answering every single question about playoff permutations.

On the editorial side, I am fortunate to lean on Lauren Clarke, Kim Bias, Dena Marie, and Jen McCoy for story shaping, and to Virginia, Tiffany, Karen, Marion, and Janice for their keen eyes.

Thank you to KP Simmon for the strategy and support on everything.

As always, I am grateful to many fellow authors for their daily guidance, support, and friendship including Lili Valente, CD Reiss, Laurelin Paige, K. Bromberg, and Marie Force.

Most of all, I am thankful every day for all my readers. You're the reason I write, and I have many more stories to tell!

ABOUT THE AUTHOR

A #1 *New York Times*, #1 *Wall Street Journal*, and #1 Audible bestselling author, Lauren Blakely is known for her contemporary romance style that's cute but spicy. Lauren likes dogs, cake, and show tunes and is the vegetarian at your dinner party.

Website: LaurenBlakely.com
Facebook: LaurenBlakelyBooks
Instagram: @laurenblakelybooks